"I thought you'd be willing to leave with me."

He slowed and shifted to a lower gear. He'd need it to make it to the top of the steep hill where he'd left the sheep. "I wouldn't have come. Not without seeing my animals safe first."

She loosened her grip on his dog and turned to face him. "Don't you get it? There's no *safe* in a fire like this. We don't have a great chance of surviving."

So be it. It was a voice from the darkest corner of his soul. There were plenty of days, after Colby had died, when Aidan had wished for death, too. Maybe that wish had never quite left him. Maybe it was about to come true and maybe that was okay.

Except now he had *her* to worry about. This strong young woman who, misguidedly, had thought he was worth saving. Which changed everything. He couldn't die if it meant taking her with him.

Dear Reader,

If you live in California or any other state prone to long, hot, dry summers, you've probably had some kind of experience with a wildfire. Whether it's breathing smoky air, or driving by a fire, or evacuating, or losing a home, wildfires affect our lives in the western United States.

I'd wanted to write a story about a wildfire for a long while, but could never quite envision what that story would be like. I knew Aidan Bell from the first book in my Heroes of Shelter Creek series, and I wanted him to have his own story. But I couldn't figure out what would bring the love of his life out to his remote ranch in the rugged coast range of Northern California. And then it hit me. A wildfire. Something so realistic that all western ranchers have to plan for and worry about. And what a great opportunity, in a series called Heroes of Shelter Creek, to write about a brave firefighter!

I hope you enjoy Aidan and Jade's story. Please don't hesitate to reach out to me on social media or visit my website at clairemcewen.com. It's always a joy to connect with readers!

Happy reading!

Claire

HEARTWARMING

Rescuing the Rancher

——

Claire McEwen

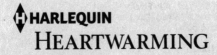

HARLEQUIN
HEARTWARMING

HARLEQUIN®
HEARTWARMING™

ISBN-13: 978-1-335-88986-7

Rescuing the Rancher

This is a work of fiction. Names, characters, places and incidents are either the product of the author's imagination or are used fictitiously. Any resemblance to actual persons, living or dead, businesses, companies, events or locales is entirely coincidental.

This edition published by arrangement with Harlequin Books S.A.

For questions and comments about the quality of this book, please contact us at CustomerService@Harlequin.com.

Harlequin Enterprises ULC
22 Adelaide St. West, 40th Floor
Toronto, Ontario M5H 4E3, Canada
www.Harlequin.com

Printed in U.S.A.

Recycling programs for this product may not exist in your area.

Claire McEwen writes stories about strong heroes and heroines who take big emotional journeys to find their happily-ever-afters. She lives by the ocean in Northern California with her family and a scruffy, mischievous terrier. When she's not writing, Claire enjoys gardening, reading and discovering flea market treasures. She loves to hear from readers! You can find her on most social media and at clairemcewen.com.

Books by Claire McEwen

Harlequin Heartwarming

Heroes of Shelter Creek

Reunited with the Cowboy
After the Rodeo
Her Surprise Cowboy

Visit the Author Profile page
at Harlequin.com for more titles.

To all the California firefighters who work so hard to keep us safe. Thank you.

Acknowledgments

When I felt like I'd taken on an impossible task with this story, my son said, "You'll do it anyway, Mama. You always do," and my husband made me yet another cup of tea. Their unflagging belief in me boosts me up and keeps me going. Sending much gratitude to my wonderful agent Jill Marsal and my amazing editor Johanna Raisanen, who believed in me when I said I wanted to write a story about two lonely people finding love in the middle of a wildfire. And special thanks to friend and dedicated firefighter Britten Miles, who answered my questions about wildfires and firefighting, and supplied me with books and resources. Any mistakes, inaccuracies and embellishments are all my own.

CHAPTER ONE

AIDAN BELL GRASPED at his old, straw cowboy hat, but he was too late. The wind lifted it right off his head and out of his reach. He watched in dismay as it sailed through the barn's wide open doors. He'd just finished hosing off the barn floor and the hat landed in a murky puddle on the uneven cement.

"Darn wind," he muttered and ran to retrieve it, shaking out the battered straw. He'd had this hat for years. Sheila had given it to him when they first bought the ranch. Said it made him a real rancher, and not just a city boy anymore. Though with everything that happened to them after that, maybe drowning by way of manure water was an appropriate ending for the dingy old thing.

He had to go into town later, maybe he could grab a new one at Coast Feed and Supply. Aidan hung the dripping, stinking hat on a nail on the barn wall and went back outside.

Instantly the wind lifted his hair on end with dry, crackling fingers. The Diablo winds only showed up in fall. *Diablo* meant *devil* in Spanish, a fitting name for a wind that sucked in heat from California's Central Valley and blasted it out over the coastal hills. It was like standing too close to an open oven.

Most of the year, Bellweather Ranch came with its own air-conditioning—thick fog from the nearby Pacific that drifted inland at night. But every fall, when the wind shifted and the mercury rose in the thermometer, Aidan realized anew just how much he took nature's AC for granted.

Just thinking about it made him hot. Too hot. The air was pressing in on him, stealing his breath. He grabbed the hose and turned it on himself, gasping as the icy well water sluiced over the back of his neck. Chip, his gray-and-black cattle dog, pulled himself up out of the shady patch he'd been hogging all afternoon. He put his pink tongue out and carefully lapped up some water from the hose. Then he ambled away to flop down in the shade again.

"Yeah, get some rest, buddy." Chip had earned it. This morning they'd moved some of his sheep and cattle to an irrigated field close to the barn. Chip had run like the Diablo wind itself to get the stragglers down the hill and through the gate.

Smiling at the memory, Aidan glanced over at Payday. The big buckskin quarter horse had finished his grain and was nosing at the bucket, turning it upside down, as if that would magically produce more of the special treat. "Pay, here's something else you'll like." He showed Payday the hose, then ran water over the horse's legs and back, washing away the sweat marks from their earlier ride. Payday didn't normally love baths, but today he nuzzled Aidan's shoulder as if to say that he, too, appreciated the chance to cool down. Not that the relief would last long for either of them, in this hair-dryer wind.

Aidan turned the hose off and untied the horse. "You can hang out with your buddies for a few hours. No sense putting any of you in the barn until it cools down a little." The gelding's ears pricked forward, as if he understood. Aidan walked his horse down a grassy lane, past the pond, to the pasture where he'd turned out the rest of the horses this morning. The land here sloped down gently toward the valley below. There was a lean-to shelter that could block the wind and several big oak trees for some deep shade. Aidan opened the gate and led Payday through. Unbuckling the big guy's halter, he gave him an affectionate swat on the rump. "Have fun out there." Aidan watched as Payday's black tail came up, his dark ears pricked forward and he trotted off to join the five other horses that Aidan kept on his ranch.

Six horses were a few more than one man really needed, but Aidan was a sucker for a lost cause. He'd purchased Payday from a breeder, but his other horses were adopted from various rescue groups around the area. He had the acres and the time, so why not?

A glance toward the sun, blazing overhead, told him it was just after noon. He had several hours until dark. Enough time to get cleaned up and into town, to get his errands done before feeding time. Maybe if he was quick, he'd have time to grab a bite to eat at the diner. It would be nice to have a break from his own cooking.

He closed the gate and left Payday's halter on the post, pausing for a moment to take in the view. He'd owned this land for five years now and still couldn't quite believe it was his. His ranch was a series of hills and valleys that rolled west toward the Pacific Ocean. His barn and sheep shed were both on one broad hilltop, and his house was up one hill higher, with a wide-open view for miles. He never got tired of it—hills upon hills, parched to a golden color for most of the year, punctuated by majestic, gnarled live oaks. In the distance, a dark band of redwood forest marked the spot where his land ended and a state park began.

Growing up on his parents' ranch in Wyoming, Aidan's only goal had been to get away. He'd worked hard and earned every dollar of his college scholarship. Out of college he'd thrown his weight behind an internet start-up that had, miraculously, been successful. But ranching must have gotten into his blood, like some kind of chronic disease. He'd missed it. And he'd never felt at home in the city.

Plus, he and Sheila had been tired of their overwhelming work schedules, and Aidan had already made more money than he'd ever imagined. Lured by a dream of living off the land, they'd bought this ranch and Aidan had fallen in love with it all—raising the sheep, the cattle, dealing with repairs and predators, the solitude, and all the ups and downs that came with ranching.

But that same solitude he loved so much had destroyed the person he loved the most. Or at least, that's what Sheila had said when she left for good.

And maybe she was right. Today the dry wind, hissing in Aidan's ears and rattling the dry grass, seemed to magnify the silence, until it filled every space, all around. It was too much, even for him. Aidan returned to the barn to collect Chip. "I'm going to town," he told the dog, who was still lying like a discarded blanket in the shade. And right there, discussing his plans with his dog, was evidence that Aidan needed some human companionship. He knelt down to scratch behind Chip's soft ears. "Come on, good boy, it will be cooler inside."

Aidan jogged up the path toward the house, and Chip panted along beside him. Once inside, Chip made a beeline for his water bowl and then stretched out on the cool tile of the kitchen floor. Aidan jumped in the shower, and within twenty minutes he was back outside at his truck. The wind had slowed a little and the sky looked kind of hazy way off in the east. *Good.* Maybe clouds would form and the weather would shift. Rain in October was rare, but certainly not unheard of. An early storm would cool everything down.

Aidan cranked up the AC, put on a country music playlist and started the truck down the gravel lane that wound down the ridgetop until it met the road. He wasn't much of a drinker, but he might treat himself to a six-pack of beer at the grocery store. It had been a long week. He'd bred his Dorset sheep for fall lambs, so he'd been keeping a close eye on the pregnant ewes confined to his sheep shed all week. Why three of them chose to give birth right at bedtime last night he'd never know, but he hadn't had much sleep as a result.

At the bottom of the drive, Aidan turned right on Mill Creek Road. It wound along through live oak and gangly bay trees that clung to the side of the high ridge that Aidan called home. Then it snaked north for several miles through parched open hills until it reached Willits, the closest town. Humming tunelessly along with Reba, Aidan guided the truck around a hairpin turn. The trees cleared—it was just open hillside here, with a view across the low, grassy hills to the east.

His heart lurched in his chest and he slammed on the brakes. "Oh no." Breath unsteady, he carefully guided the truck into a graveled turnout and cut the engine. Shoving the door open, he jumped out of the cab, shaded his eyes and looked out at the hills, a band of worry tightening across his chest.

That haze he'd seen back at the house hadn't been rain clouds forming. Smoke was billowing up from a distant ridge. A wildfire. It was still far away, but he could almost smell it. A faint charcoal essence rode on the wind, which had picked up again and was rustling the dry shrubs on the slope below.

This was bad. Really bad. The fire was

in the northeast, exactly upwind. It was at least thirty miles away right now, but that wasn't much comfort. Last summer, a wildfire out near Chico had moved so fast it had burned up the space of a football field every single second.

Stay calm. You're prepared for this. He'd written out an evacuation plan for his ranch. Now he just had to put his plan into practice and hope the fire didn't get this far.

Aidan pulled his phone out of his pocket, grateful he and his neighbors had agreed to have a cell tower set up out here on the ridge. He tried Nellie Lovell, his closest neighbor. She was about seventy years old and more stubborn than the mules and llamas she kept on her ranch. *No answer.* He'd have to get over there and warn her in person.

There was no way of telling what would happen. With any luck, fire crews would slow the blaze down, but with the Diablo winds accelerating the flames, it wasn't that likely. Aidan's hands shook as he scrolled through his contacts, his thoughts rushing from fast to frantic. He could lose everything. His livestock could be killed. He had to get his animals off the ranch.

They'd probably open up the fairgrounds in nearby towns for evacuated animals. Aidan lived about equal distance from the towns of Willits and Ukiah. He glanced at the smoke again. The road heading south to Ukiah was wider, a better bet when a lot of folks would be leaving the area.

But he only had one livestock trailer. Nellie only had one, as well. Aidan scrolled through his contacts, finding the number for the livestock hauling company he usually used.

"Marcie," he said to the woman who answered. "It's Aidan Bell. I've got fire coming my way. Can you guys help me out?"

He could hear her answer in her sigh. "Aidan, I'm so sorry. All of our trucks are out there already. And I called around. Every company I can think of has their trucks out picking up animals already."

So much for his evacuation plan. He chewed his lip, willing an idea, any idea, to come into his head. "Can you tell me anything about the blaze? I was coming off my ridge to head into Willits when I spotted it."

"It's a good way off still. If the wind shifts a little more to the south, it might miss you altogether, but I'd try to get your animals out now, just in case. You got any friends you can call?"

Aidan stared at the smoke, racking his brain. He knew most of the ranchers in the area, but they'd all be busy trying to get their own animals to safety. "I'll figure something out. Thanks, Marcie."

"No problem, honey. Just stay safe out there, okay?"

"Will do. Take care."

Aidan hung up and clicked over to his contacts list. Who could help him? His thumb stopped scrolling at the letter *B*. Burton. Maya Burton. The wildlife biologist. He didn't know her too well, but she lived south, closer to Santa Rosa, in the little town of Shelter Creek. Her husband, Caleb, owned a ranch. Maybe she could bring their trailer. Plus, Maya knew pretty much every rancher in the area, so maybe she could get some of them to help out, too.

He called her cell phone, and to his relief, she answered on the second ring. He was lucky she wasn't out in the field somewhere. Quickly, he explained the situation.

"Hang on, Aidan." He could hear her

breath, as if she'd started running. A moment later, she called to Caleb to hitch up the trailer. Relief loosened Aidan's tense muscles and he put a hand on his truck to steady himself.

"Aidan, we're on it. We'll take whatever livestock we can haul back to our ranch," Maya reassured him. "I'll call some of the other local ranchers—I'm sure they'll help, as well. Just get your stock ready. Cattle first, I'd say. If we can't get enough trailers, your sheep will be easier to manage on the ranch."

Aidan tried to find some humor. "Wool is fire-resistant, right?"

"That's what they say," Maya quipped back. "But we'll try to get them out, too, if we can."

"Thanks, Maya." Probably the most heartfelt thanks he'd ever said. She just might be the miracle he needed.

"See you soon. I promise."

Aidan hung up the phone and jumped back in his truck. This was bad, but at least help was on the way. He had more to do than he cared to think about, but first he'd better warn Nellie. Glancing over at the smoke, he was shocked to see how quickly it had thickened and expanded—it looked like a storm looming over the distant horizon. He whipped his truck in a U-turn and drove as fast as he could back up the winding road.

Nellie. She'd stood by him, held him up, in those dark months after his son Colby's death. After Sheila left, throwing blame in her wake.

Aidan had tried to push Nellie away, wanting to be alone in his grief, resenting her determined, quiet care. She hadn't let him scare her off, though. She'd checked on him every day, brought him food when he was too distraught to think about eating. Now she was his best friend, and he had to get her to safety.

Turning up her driveway, Aidan followed the gravel lane, impatient as it wound its way leisurely up a hill. At the top, Aidan passed Nellie's neat farmhouse and kept going toward the barn. That's where his friend would be at this time of day. He honked a few times as he made his way down, in case she was out in the fields or her garden. Nellie appeared in the barn doorway, wiping her hands on the coveralls she wore and straightening the blue bandanna tied over her long, gray hair.

Shoving open the door of his truck, Aidan hurried toward her. Shadow, her border collie, ran to greet him, dancing and barking a wary welcome.

"Aidan! What's with all the honking? Are you okay?"

"Nellie, I've got bad news. There's a fire. It looks like it could be coming our way, across the hills from the northeast."

Nellie's weathered skin paled and she put her hands to her cheeks. "Oh, Aidan, here we go. Our worst nightmare…" Her voice trailed off.

He had to keep them focused. They couldn't give in to fear. "We're going to get as many of your livestock as we can into your trailer. Then you'll drive them south to the fairgrounds in Ukiah or Santa Rosa. I'm sure they'll be taking evacuations by now."

Nellie looked around with wide eyes, as if she couldn't quite take the information in. "But my house. My things."

"We can always get new things, Nellie. Right now we need to save the animals."

That jolted her out of her daze. She loved

her livestock like children. "But what about my llamas? My mules? My sheep?"

Her small flock of sheep was her pride and joy, bred for their lush wool. But Aidan knew her llamas and mules were her babies. "Load the mules and llamas. I'll bring your sheep over to my ranch. I've got friends from Shelter Creek coming with trailers to evacuate. I'll get your sheep out with them."

"It will take too long to move them to your place."

"I'll cut the fence between our properties. Payday, Chip and I can round them up in no time. Don't worry, Nellie. I'll do everything I can to keep them safe. Come on, let's get your trailer hitched."

"Right." Nellie hurried to her truck and Shadow bounded into the seat beside her. She backed the pickup toward the large livestock trailer by her barn. Aidan lowered the hitch for her, linking the safety chains and sliding the pins into place. Nellie turned off the engine and came over to double-check his work. "Okay, let's get the mules. They're in the stalls, thank goodness. And the llamas are near the barn today because the vet was supposed to stop by and check their teeth."

She glanced at the sky, where the blue was losing all its clarity. "I guess he won't be coming by after all."

They ran to the stalls and haltered the two mules, walking them one by one into the trailer and tying them in the front partitioned spaces. Aidan quickly filled a bag of hay for each of them, hoping a snack would keep them calm for the journey.

Meanwhile Nellie had caught one of her llamas, a dark brown, ornery fellow she called Bob. He balked at the trailer ramp, so Aidan scooped grain into a bucket and waved it under Bob's nose, trying to sound cheerful. "Come on, big guy. You know you love this stuff."

Bob backed away, snuffing the air, probably smelling the far-off smoke.

"We don't have time for this," Aidan said.

"Move out of the way," Nellie ordered, and Aidan jumped aside as she smacked Bob on the rump with such force that the startled llama lunged into the trailer. Bob stopped right behind one of the mules and turned to glare at his owner from under his strangely thick lashes. Aidan guided him away from the mule and tied him in. Then he followed

Nellie as she ran for the other two llamas who, thankfully, were far more docile. Once they were secured in the trailer, Nellie and Aidan latched the door behind them.

That was it. The trailer was full. With just five animals. The realization sank Aidan's heart to his boots. There was almost no way he would be able to get all of his animals loaded. He had over a hundred head of sheep now, plus forty head of organic, grass-fed cattle and six horses. Add in Nellie's flock, and even with the help of every rancher in Shelter Creek, it would take a miracle to evacuate them all. But he wouldn't let Nellie know that.

"Let's grab some feed for them." Nellie started toward the barn and Aidan followed, helping her load two bales of hay and a bag of grain, along with some feed buckets. They paused by the truck while Nellie took a last look around.

"Stop by the house and grab your wallet, glasses, computer and prescriptions. Just the essentials, okay?" Aidan glanced at the sky. The air was still only slightly hazy but now there was a definite smoky smell. It was almost pleasant, as if someone nearby had built a campfire. But still, they shouldn't waste a minute. "As soon as you have what you need, start driving."

Tears welled in Nellie's eyes. She reached for Aidan's hand. "Thank you, Aidan. You stay safe. If it gets too bad, set my sheep free. They're tough. They might just find a way to make it."

"Let's hope this is all for nothing. Maybe the fire won't get here at all."

"I'll pray for that." She pulled Aidan in for a hug, and he relished the momentary feel of her, his second mother, in his arms. Then he stepped back and motioned toward her truck. "Now get going."

"I will. But Aidan, don't stay on your ranch too long. You need to get out, too."

"I'll leave soon."

With a last wave, Nellie climbed up into her truck and drove away.

Aidan jogged to his Ford, pulled open the door and slid into the driver's seat. Glancing at his phone, he saw a text from Maya with three welcome words—*On our way.* He started the engine and followed Nellie's truck up the driveway, acutely aware of the dry, brown grass all around. Everything would burn like kindling. He'd given up on praying long ago, but he wished hard that Maya and Caleb, and anyone else from Shelter Creek, would get to his ranch soon.

CHAPTER TWO

SHE'D BEEN GIVEN this job because she was a woman. The fact irritated Jade Carson like a burr in her uniform as she wound her truck up a series of hairpin turns. *Send the girl out to warn the residents, while the big boys fight the fire.* It wasn't the first time this had happened. Jade was pretty sure it wouldn't be the last.

She'd never been in this area, somewhere in the coastal hills, southwest of Willits. Her mission was to evacuate the few people living on this remote ridge, out in Middle-of-Nowhere, California.

Someone local should be doing this chore. Maybe someone from the sheriff's department, or a closer fire station, who knew the roads and didn't have to pull over and glance at the map every few minutes. Though her boss, Mitch, had said that all the deputies and locals were already out warning other residents.

Jade knew better than to pitch a fit when a wildfire the size of this one was coming their way. So she'd answered Mitch with a *Yes, sir* and jumped in the smallest of the trucks they'd brought with them from Shelter Creek—a simple pickup truck they'd used to haul their personal luggage. She'd pitch her fit with Mitch later on, once the fire was out. For now, she had to let go of her resentment and focus on saving lives.

Slowing for yet another tight turn, Jade could see that she was nearing the top of the ridge. To the north and east of her, the fire was eating away at the dry hills like a ravenous beast. Smoke boiled into the sky, and though Jade was too far away to see any flames, she knew it wouldn't be long before she would be able to. She had to hurry, had to get these people out fast.

Turning left, she rattled up the first driveway, a narrow gravel lane that wound up a hill. Eventually it led to an old, neatly kept ranch house. Leaving her truck running, she jumped out and ran for the door, pounding hard and shouting, "Fire! Evacuate, now!"

The silence around her was thick with cicadas buzzing in the bushes and the hot wind whispering smoky threats. "Hello?" she yelled. "Fire! You need to get out!"

After jogging to the truck, Jade gunned it down the lane, farther into the ranch. Hopping out again, she dashed for the barn and found it empty, too. Maybe they'd already left. There was no truck, nor the expected trailer, so that was a good sign.

Back at the house, Jade ran in a circle around it, banging on windows and the back door in case someone was inside. Satisfied she'd done all she could, she taped an evacuation notice to the front door, then drove back to the main road. There were more trees here, and she drove through the shade of oaks and bays until she saw a sign for Bellweather Ranch.

Turning up the neatly graded, gravel driveway, Jade quickly veered to the side, as close to the bank as she could, to make room for a big pickup pulling a trailer toward her. To her surprise, several more trucks with trailers followed, and she could see the backs of cattle that had been loaded inside. It looked like this ranch was evacuating, but she'd better speak with the residents to make sure.

After the last of the trucks had gone by with a friendly wave from the driver, Jade started up the driveway again. No one answered at the old clapboard farmhouse, so Jade drove on down the lane toward the barn she could see farther down the hill.

Two big pickup trucks with trailers attached were parked in front of the barn. A pretty beige-colored horse, saddled and bridled, was tied to a smaller trailer. Three people stood nearby, in front of the barn doors, and as Jade parked and got out of the truck, the sound of their argument drifted toward her.

"Aidan, don't do this." A small woman, her long brown ponytail whipping in the wind, was looking up at a blond giant of a man. "It's not time to be a hero. You've got to get out. Turn the sheep loose and leave."

Suddenly Jade recognized the woman. It was Maya Burton, a biologist who lived in Shelter Creek.

"I promised Nellie I'd save her flock." The man Maya had called Aidan was well over six feet of stubborn energy. He was gesturing with one big hand toward the hills above his barn. As Jade drew closer she could see the obstinate set of his jaw. "I need to get her sheep down here."

Jade quickened her pace toward the group. The afternoon was starting to feel a little too much like evening, the sun dimming almost imperceptibly with smoke. "Excuse me," she called out.

All three of them seemed startled as they turned to look at her, as if they hadn't noticed her until now. The protesting moos from the cattle loaded in the two big trailers must have drowned out the sound of her approach. Jade recognized the other man standing there all dark and brooding. It was Caleb Dunne, Maya's husband.

"Jade!" Maya's smile was soft with gratitude. "I'm so glad you're here. Please tell my friend Aidan that it's time to leave."

"Hey, Caleb." Jade returned Caleb's nod, then turned her attention to the tall rancher. "I'm Jade Carson with State Fire. We've issued mandatory evacuation orders for this area. A wildfire is heading this way and you all need to get out now."

"See?" Maya looked at Aidan, her palms open in front of her in a pleading gesture.

"Maya, I'll be fine." The big rancher ran a hand through his thick hair, already tousled by the endless wind. "Thanks to you, and Caleb, and your friends, we're getting the cattle out. But I have to try to save the sheep. Mine and Nellie's."

Caleb, who'd been silent until now, intervened. "I know it sounds callous, but sheep can be replaced. Insurance will cover your losses." Caleb was a tough-looking, dark-haired guy with black tattoos on his arms, but there was compassion in his deep voice. "Don't lose your life for a bunch of sheep."

Aidan nodded once at his words. "I'll leave. I promise. But I have an irrigated pasture here. The ground is already wet and, if I leave the sprinklers on, I can create a refuge from the fire and give the sheep a chance. I should at least provide that."

Convincing idiots to do the right thing was the hardest part of Jade's job, but she had to try. "Sir, the fire is approaching rapidly. All three of you need to leave *right now*. Please get in your vehicles and evacuate the premises immediately."

Maya and Caleb looked at each other. They seemed to have an entire conversation in one glance. Tears glinted in Maya's eyes, but she shrugged and Caleb slapped the stubborn rancher on the shoulder. "Jade's right. We're heading out. I hope you do the same."

Maya reached up and gave Aidan a hug. "Stay safe and get out of here. I know this is a terrible choice, but you have to get out alive, okay? Leave now and let the sheep find their own way."

"I'll be fine." Aidan stepped back, out of her embrace. "Thank you for bringing everyone up here. For saving my cattle, and the other horses."

Maya looked out over the fields behind the barn. "I just wish we could have brought enough trailers for the sheep."

"You did all you could, and I'm grateful," Aidan said.

Caleb pulled Maya in for a hug and kiss. "Stay right behind me. We'll take it slow and steady off this ridge, okay? Use the lowest gear and try not to ride the brakes too hard."

"Got it." Maya raised her keys in a salute

to Jade. "Good luck, Jade. Please be careful, okay? You need to evacuate, too."

"Believe me, I'll be right behind you," Jade assured her. "Stay together on the road. If one of you runs into mechanical problems, let the animals out of that trailer, take the other vehicle and get out. You hear me?"

"Yes, ma'am." Caleb glanced at Aidan one more time. "You need to get out of here fast."

Aidan walked over to where the horse was tied and unhooked the animal's lead rope. "Payday *is* fast." He led the horse toward the door of the pickup and opened it. A cattle dog with gray-and-black mottled fur bounded down with an excited bark. "And Chip here is faster. I'll be tailgating you down the highway before you know it."

Caleb nodded and Maya gave a half-hearted wave and they climbed into their trucks. Jade watched as Caleb's truck and trailer started up the driveway and Maya's followed. At least they, and the cattle they hauled, would be safe.

She turned to the cowboy, who was tightening the cinch on his horse's saddle. It was a beautiful animal, a big dun-colored horse with a black mane and tail. The dog, Chip, sat alert and eager, near his master. The injustice of it sparked her anger. He had a chance to save this dog, this horse and himself if he left now.

"Why are you doing this? You need to load your trailer and get out."

He glanced over his shoulder, looking a little startled, as if he'd forgotten she was there. "Nellie. My neighbor. She's a good person. Always been there for me. I promised her I'd save her sheep. I'd like to save my own, as well."

"You're not going to be able to save them *or* yourself if this fire comes through here." Her words were harsh, but she wasn't worried about diplomacy now. This could be life-and-death, and he was choosing the latter.

Aidan put a booted foot in the stirrup and swung up on his horse, settling himself easily in the saddle. He reined in the horse when it started walking. "I brought these animals onto this ranch, so it's my job to see them safe. I have a plan and I'll see it through before I leave."

"You may not be able to leave if you don't go now."

He shrugged and a strangely bleak expression tightened his features. "Maybe I'm not meant to."

What was that about? "You have choices. Make the right one and get out of here."

"I don't see *you* going."

Jade glared at him in exasperation. "Trust me. I'll be back with my crew as soon as I warn the other residents on this road. I've been told there's just one other property. Is that true?"

"Yeah, that's right. Just a mile or so past mine, on the right side of the road."

She couldn't afford to stay any longer. More delay meant danger and no way was she going to be burned like a piece of forgotten toast because this fool cowboy seemed to think sheep were more important than staying alive.

"Thanks for driving out here to warn me. My name's Aidan. Aidan Bell. My family has a ranch in Wyoming, just south of Cody."

Jade nodded, surprised by the tightness in her throat. He was telling her whom to notify if he didn't make it. Letting her know that he understood the danger he was in.

Would she be the last person to see him
alive? She had to swallow her emotion before she could speak. "No one is going to be
able to get in here to rescue you after this.
Do you understand? Violating mandatory
evacuation orders means you are on your
own. We will not be able to help you, even
if you call 911."

He nodded once. "I understand. Thanks
for the warning. And good luck out there."
He whistled to his dog, spun the horse on
its hindquarters and took off at a gallop up
the lane toward the house. Jade watched as
he turned right off the lane and cut uphill,
across the straw-colored grassy slope at an
angle, the sheepdog loping easily behind.
Poor horse. Poor dog. Poor sheep. Poor man.
They'd need a miracle to survive this, and
Jade sure hoped they got one.

But she couldn't stay and worry. She had
another family to reach and then she had
to drive back to the staging area and get to
work fighting this fire. Jogging back to her
truck, she glanced at the cowboy one more
time. He was making his way across the
hilltop now, and then he was out of sight.
"Good luck," Jade called into the quiet. She

climbed inside and gunned the engine up the hill toward the house.

THE NEXT RESIDENCE was only a couple miles up the road. As Jade turned left out of Aidan's driveway, she had to peer through dingy air. The smoke was thickening. Jade radioed her boss to inform him that one ranch was empty and one dumb rancher wouldn't evacuate yet and might not make it as a result. Mitch's answer came in loud and clear. "The fire is picking up speed. Get to that last property and then get out."

Jade set the radio back in its holder with a shaking hand. Pressing on the accelerator, she cut corners on the turns, relieved when she spotted the mailbox for the last residence on this remote road. Her tires screeched on the pavement as she took the corner. Her hopes crashed when she saw an SUV in the driveway. These people were still home. How could they have missed the smoke?

She left her engine running and jogged to the front door of the low, modern house. Not a ranch full of livestock, thankfully, but someone's country retreat. Hammering on the door, she called out, "Fire department. Open up! This is an emergency."

Footsteps pounded up close on the other side of the door and a tall, thin man wrenched it open, looking pale and harried. "We're trying to get out. We're just packing now."

God save us from people and their possessions. Jade refrained from rolling her eyes and kept her voice stern. "There's no more time to pack, sir. The fire is headed this way. You're under mandatory evacuation orders. Leave now."

The man turned away from Jade, toward the interior of the house, and called, "Honey? Are you ready to go?"

A dark-haired woman came around the corner, a diaper bag over her shoulder. She stopped in her tracks when she saw Jade. "Oh hello."

Jade figured it was time to skip the formalities. "You need to leave. Get your kids, any prescription medicines, your wallets and your car keys and leave. If you have wool blankets, put them in the car. Do not pack any more possessions than that."

"Oh no." The woman's hand fluttered near

her heart. "We didn't realize it was so serious."

This wasn't going to be a knock-and-run situation. These people were panicking. "How many children do you have, ma'am?"

"Um…three."

Jade pointed to the diaper bag. "One of them is a baby?"

The man nodded and Jade put a firm hand on his shoulder. "Go get the baby and put it in the car seat. Load up the kids, too. Do not waste time getting anything else except your medicines, wallet and those blankets. Go!"

Both parents seemed to break out of their panicked daze. They ran off into the house, calling for their kids.

Walking into their kitchen, Jade opened their cupboards until she found three water bottles. She filled them and brought them out to the driveway, where the couple was loading their children into the SUV. The man pointed to a pile of blankets. "What do I do with these?"

"Put them on the floor of the front passenger seat."

The man took the blankets and got behind the wheel of the SUV. Jade handed him the water bottles. "It's always good to have some water. Stay hydrated no matter what. You should be fine, but if, by some small chance, you get trapped in fire, get everyone down low on the floor of the car under the blankets."

His eyes widened, as if he finally grasped the seriousness of their situation. "Okay. Will do."

"The highway is still open, as far as I know. Head south."

The man nodded and started the engine.

The woman was buckling a young boy and girl into their seatbelts in the back seat. The baby, dressed in pink pajamas, was already safely in her car seat. Sensing the tension, the kids were starting to cry. "It's okay, sweeties," the mother said, reaching out to give the children hugs.

Jade reached for the woman's arm and gently pulled her out of the car. "Focus on safety over comfort," she said sternly. "You have to get on the road."

The woman gave Jade's hand a fervent squeeze. "Thank you."

"Of course." Jade helped her into the front seat. "Now, stay calm. You'll be fine. Just drive south and don't stop for any reason. Do you understand?"

"Mommy!" The little girl's voice wailed from the backseat. "Elliott!"

The woman put a palm to her forehead. "Oh no. The cat! He's probably under one of the beds." She moved to get out of the car.

"No." Jade put a hand out to stop her. "The smoke is getting worse. Leave now."

"We can't leave our cat." The woman seemed like she was about to push past Jade to get out of the car, so Jade gently shut the door. "I'll get the cat," she told the woman through the open window.

The woman put her hands together in a prayerful plea. "You'll save him? He's a black-and-white cat. A little skittish."

"I'll do everything I can." What was wrong with these people? Did they have no sense of the danger they were in? Jade leaned down to meet the worried gaze of the man in the driver's seat. "Time to go," she said, and he nodded. "I work with State Fire, Shelter Creek office. Contact me there about the cat."

"Thank you," he said, and the woman repeated his words, reaching out the window to touch Jade's arm as the SUV pulled away.

Jade watched them until they'd turned onto the road, then ran to her truck to radio Mitch and tell him the last family was leaving. But when she tried the radio, all she got was static.

Not wanting to think about what that might mean, she ran back into the house and down the hall, shoving open bedroom doors and peeking in closets and under beds. In the master bedroom, she flopped down on her belly, lifted the velvet bed skirt and spotted Elliott, his white-tuxedo chest and paws giving him away as he cowered in the shadows of the far corner. She'd been through this before and knew what to do. Before Elliott could react, Jade propelled herself under the bed, straight toward the startled cat. She got him by the scruff in the same moment his claws slashed her bare arm—a bad day to choose a short-sleeved uniform—but she didn't let go.

Wiggling backward, she kept her fingers clamped on the yowling, squirming, clawing cat. As soon as they were out from under the bed, she reached for a white bathrobe left draped on a chair and wrapped Elliott up so he couldn't attack her anymore. Running out of the house with the bundled-up cat, she climbed into the truck and set him on the passenger-side floor, where he promptly went still, peering out of the robe with wide green eyes.

"It may not seem like it, but hopefully, I'm saving your life."

Elliott shrunk back into his robe as if he understood the danger.

As Jade screeched out of the driveway, she tried the radio again. Mitch was there, his voice coming in fragments through the static.

"Carson, where have you been? Return to the staging area. Take—" his voice muffled as if he was speaking to someone else "—take Hart's Point Road to Circle Bluff. Do you hear me? That way is still open."

That way is still open. Which meant that other ways were closed. Jade swallowed hard. "On my way, Mitch."

She floored it up the driveway, screeching around the corner onto the road. A few minutes later, a familiar driveway flashed by and Jade slowed, pulling over to the side of

the road on instinct, even though there was
no one but her on this godforsaken ridge. No
one but her and that rancher, Aidan.

Stopping the truck on the gravel verge,
she put it in park and drew a shaky breath.
She'd already warned him. She'd done her
job. If he was fool enough to try to survive
this fire, that was his problem.

The thing was, Aidan might be dumb as
dirt for refusing to evacuate, but he seemed
like a good guy. He clearly felt a real responsibility to the animals in his care. He
had friends in Shelter Creek, her hometown.
Maya and Caleb had come to help him, had
begged him to drive with them to safety.

But he'd refused. So she was under no obligation to go back for him.

Except, she was here to save lives, not
abandon them. He had no way of knowing
that the fire had picked up speed. He could
leave with her now, and they'd drive out together. Surely he'd come with her once he
realized that the situation was dire.

She glanced down at the cat. "Sorry. Elliott, you were rescued by the world's big-
gest fool." Shoving the truck in Reverse,
Jade backed up the road to the cowboy's

driveway, turned in and careened up the deserted lane. She didn't even bother to stop by the house. He'd be at the barn for sure. Driving down the hill, she spotted his truck and trailer still parked outside and her heart sank. She'd hoped he'd have left already. But of course he hadn't. He must have some kind of superhero complex or something.

"You stay there, okay?" The cat was still in the robe, staring at her with a dazed expression. All of her crazy driving had probably scared it into some kind of terrified trance. Jumping out of her truck, Jade slammed the door behind her and ran into the barn. "Aidan?"

The silence was eerie, as if the whole world was preparing for the destruction coming its way. "Aidan, are you here?"

Jogging past empty stalls, she exited the far doors and saw the irrigated land he'd mentioned earlier, a few acres of bright green oasis in the dry grass. A small group of sheep grazed peacefully in the center. "Aidan?" A dozen black sheep faces popped up to regard her, but there was no other answer.

She couldn't stick around any longer. Racing back through the barn to her truck, she grabbed an evacuation notice and a felt pen she kept in her gear bag. She scrawled *Get out! Fire near!* She stuck the notice onto a rusty nail protruding from the barn door.

Back in her truck, she flew up the drive and out to the road, her heart thudding in her chest. This had been a bad choice. She hadn't managed to rescue him, and she'd endangered herself.

Her wheels screeched and Elliott yowled as she took a turn too fast. Jade bit her lip as she pumped the brakes. She had to put that rancher out of her mind. He'd made his choice, and now she had to focus on getting herself out of here as fast as possible. "Sorry, buddy," she told the cat. "I'm trying to keep us from getting crispy-fried." It was gross firefighter humor, but it made her feel tough to say it aloud.

Jade navigated a few more twists and turns. The trees cleared and through the thick air she could see east, across the hills. The flames were visible now, though still far beyond the valley below, devouring the distant hills with flickering, orange teeth. Through the brown air, she could see a thick wall of smoke above the flames. The wind was gusting hard, jostling her truck like it wanted to push her right off the road.

Jade's hands felt numb as they gripped the steering wheel, as if all the blood in them had retreated to fuel her machine-gun heartbeat. She'd been in fires many times, but always with water, equipment and a plan.

Around the next corner, Jade glanced down toward the valley and spotted a road running north like a thin, gray snake. It had to be the one Mitch had told her to take, but to get to it she'd have to make it down this ridge and then drive toward the flames. A race against time as the dry devil wind urged the fire her way.

She had to stay calm. Had to somehow still the trembling in her jaw. She was a firefighter. She'd fought wildfires for years now. Why was she so frightened? Jade forced herself to ease off the gas, then carefully braked into the next turn. She knew the answer. Because she was alone out here. No camaraderie to lift her spirits, no team to prove herself to. Just her and someone else's cat, racing for their lives.

A deer leaped across the road in front of

her truck and Jade slammed on the brakes, gasping as the animal scrambled up the steep bank above her in a panic to get to safety. Elliott gave a strangled moan, like he'd gone from scared to sick.

"It's okay, buddy. Things are just getting a little hectic around here. We can handle it, though." At least she hoped they could.

Jade focused on the margins of the road, slowing as a few rabbits bounded across. No more deer, though. Farther down the ridge, the road plunged into trees again—oaks, bays and buckeyes tangled together and blocked her view of the fire. Once she emerged from these woods, she'd be at the bottom of the ridge and the road would straighten out. She'd gun it toward the fire, then hang a left and she'd be all set.

The branches above her truck had been swaying in the wind, but now they began to thrash more wildly, as if a storm was coming in. Maybe the wind was picking up, or maybe it was the approaching fire itself, stirring up the air with its heat, making its own weather. Chewing her lower lip to keep her focus, Jade stayed in the center of the two-lane road, cutting corners, grateful as the road flattened. She was off the ridge, and in moments she'd be in the open.

But now the wind was even more chaotic, knocking small branches and twigs into the road and onto her truck. A loud crash had Jade slamming on the brakes in a move so instinctive, she was already skidding, already spinning, already stopping, before she'd even registered the danger. A huge branch lay across the road in front of her, still attached to the old oak it belonged to by a few thick, torn splinters.

For a moment everything was silent except for Jade's harsh breathing. Even Elliott had nothing to say—in fact his eyes were half-closed now. Jade didn't blame him. This was bad. Really bad. If she had the luxury, she'd try to shut it out, too.

Jade got out and ran to survey the situation. The branch was immense, and there was no way around it. She had a chain saw, but even if she had time to cut through it, she'd have to wrap chain around each piece and drag them out of the way with her winch. The fire was too close. She didn't have time.

Fear, raw and jagged, cut through the

last of her composure. This was it. She was trapped on this ridge. She buried her face in her hands, tears slicking her palms. For an instant, she thought of her parents. Her dad. Her older brothers. All firefighters and cops. Tough as nails. She could almost hear them. *Get it together, J.* They'd never forgive her if she just fell apart and panicked. She'd never forgive herself.

She might be trapped but she was a firefighter, from a family of firefighters. So she'd fight.

Running for the truck, Jade jumped inside and tried the radio again, not surprised when all she heard was static. She turned the truck around and drove back up the ridge, accelerating into each curve. Elliott yowled in protest. "Hey, kitty," Jade said through clenched teeth. "We're going to be just fine." *Ha. Not likely.* She'd been a fool to check on Aidan again and lose so much time. He'd been a fool, too, for trying to save those sheep. But who knew? If two fools joined forces and got real, real lucky, they just might survive this fire.

CHAPTER THREE

AIDAN WAS LOADING the dog crates into the back of his truck when he heard wheels on the gravel drive. He stared in dismay at the small red pickup truck emerging from the smoky brown haze that had filled the air. He recognized the figure behind the wheel. It was Jade, the bossy firefighter from earlier. She'd already stopped by a second time, or someone had, to leave him a note on the barn. Why wasn't she off fighting the fire by now?

She stopped so quickly on the gravel, she almost skidded her truck into his. Jumping out, she jogged a couple steps toward him, wisps of black hair escaping her ponytail as the hot, dry wind tugged it loose. "Fire's coming this way fast."

"I figured," he told her. "I saw the note. Did you leave it for me?"

She nodded.

Irritation flared. She'd put herself in danger by coming back here for him. He didn't need her hanging around making this situation worse. "Why are you still here? You need to stop trying to save people and get out of this area."

"Saving people is my job. But I'm trapped." She shrugged as if it was no big deal but he saw the worry in her eyes. "So are you. Part of an oak tree fell across the road."

Trapped. He'd known he was in trouble when he saw the note she'd left on the barn wall, but he'd been holding out hope that he could get his sheep in one place, get the sprinklers set up around them and still get out. Without that hope, the adrenaline that had fueled him seeped away, leaving a grim resolve. He'd do everything he could to save his animals and himself, but there were no guarantees now.

He could deal with that, for himself. But this firefighter… She might be annoying in her persistence, but she was obviously very dedicated to her job. She didn't deserve this.

An awful thought struck. "That family up the road. Mallory and Phil Jones. They have a few kids. Did they get out okay?"

She nodded. "I think so. They left before me and I didn't see them on the road. That oak must have fallen after they drove by."

That was some relief. At least there were no kids stuck out here. And thank God Nellie had left. But that meant it was just him and this firefighter, and a wildfire heading this way. "Why didn't you drive out with them?"

"I was trying to find their cat, Elliott." She waved her hand toward her truck. "He's in the cab. Scared stiff, poor guy. I don't blame him. Do you have any kind of crate I could use for him? I need to get him out of the truck before he gets too hot in there."

"Yeah, I have some I use for the barn cats." He turned to go get one from the storage room in the barn, and she followed him.

"Won't you need them?"

"I imagine my cats are long gone by now. They're half feral and most likely knew to run from the smell of smoke." They weren't pets, but he enjoyed them, talked to them as they lazed in the sun and watched him work. They were a tough, wily bunch. Hopefully they'd find a way to survive the fire.

"I'm not sure how much time we have

to get ready," Jade said, hefting the plastic travel crate he handed her. "A couple hours if we're very lucky. It's probably going to start with some spot fires. If we work on putting those out, we have a chance to stay in control of the situation."

Possible outcomes if they didn't stay in control crowded Aidan's mind and they weren't pretty. It was probably best not to think too far ahead. "Let's just focus on the task at hand. We'll get Elliott set and then I need to move the rest of my sheep."

Back outside, he followed Jade to her truck. She tossed orders over her shoulder. "We'll put the crate on the driver's seat. If you stand right behind it, Elliott can't go up and over. I'll go around to the passenger side and shoo him your way."

She was making this awfully complicated. "Can't you just reach into the truck and pick him up?"

Jade turned and handed him the crate, then held up her forearms, covered in red scratches. "He doesn't like me much."

"Ah. I see." He couldn't totally blame Elliott for lashing out, though. Jade *was* a little intense. Aidan opened the driver's side door and shoved the crate onto the seat. Elliott was sitting on the passenger-side floor on what looked like a bathrobe, his mouth slightly open. The poor cat was really stressed. "Hey, big guy, why don't you get in this crate and we'll get you some water."

Elliott answered with a plaintive meow and shifted farther back in his corner under the glove compartment.

"Come on, kitty. You're okay." Aidan tried what he hoped was a cat-friendly voice, but the black-and-white beast was immune to his charms, hunkering down as if he could make himself smaller.

"We don't have time for this." Jade opened the passenger door and reached for Elliott. With a yowl, Elliott flew out of her grasp, scrambled across the seats, launched from the crate and landed on Aidan's chest.

"What the— Ow!" Aidan wrapped his hands around Elliott's shoulders and tried to pull the cat out to arm's length, but its claws were embedded in his skin. The cat clenched its paws and dug in deeper. Aidan felt his eyes bulge out. "Help me get him off of me!"

"Hang on." Jade came around the truck and carefully picked Elliott's claws out of

Aidan's chest. Her fingers were small and delicate, reminding him that, for all of her tough attitude, she was tiny compared to him. She was on his land, so she was his responsibility now. A responsibility he didn't want. He stepped back, out of her reach, and the last of Elliott's claws loosened their hold.

If she noticed his abrupt retreat, she didn't let on. Just said, "That's bound to sting," and took Elliott from him. Aidan put the crate on the ground so she could shove the squirming, terrified cat inside.

Aidan rubbed his scratched chest with his T-shirt, pretty sure he was mopping up blood. "I always figured rescuing cats was the easy part of a firefighter's job."

"It is." She picked up the crate and started for the barn. "Can I put him in here for now?"

"Yep. I'll get him some water." It was an excuse to get some space, to rub the smarting scratches on his chest, to wrap his mind around this impossible situation. Fire approaching. No way out. He wished Jade had gotten off the ridge in time. He was sure he had a better chance of survival with her at his side, but he didn't want her here.

She'd come back to warn him again, and that choice meant she might die here. He didn't want another death on his hands.

Tension aching across his shoulders, he found the water bowl he'd left outside for his barn cats and brought it into the barn. Jade was kneeling, talking to Elliott, and the tenderness in her voice surprised him. "We're going to do everything we can to save you, big guy," she was saying as Aidan walked up. "We'll get you back to your family and they'll spoil you rotten for the rest of your lives."

"Lives?" Aidan asked. He knelt down, opened the crate and set the water inside. "All nine of them?"

"Well, I figure after this, he'll have eight left. That's still pretty good."

"I don't know. If this fire gets here, it may count for a few. It's getting pretty smoky." He closed the crate, not wanting to think about Elliott and how many of his lives were at stake. Not wanting Jade to be nice and kind to cats. He'd been trying for so long not to care about anything. He didn't want to care about her.

He went to a far stall, where he'd left Chip

resting on some clean straw. The dog sprang up eagerly at the sight of him, and Aidan let him out. He ran for Jade, but stopped and sat at a quiet command from Aidan.

"He's well trained." She held out her hand and Chip looked at Aidan, waiting for permission. Aidan nodded, and the dog ran to Jade and sniffed her hand. Then he ran to the crate to snuffle at Elliott, who let out an outraged hiss.

"Leave it," Aidan said, and Chip returned to his side, following along as Aidan led the way quickly out of the barn.

"The fire is definitely coming this way," Jade told him. "I could see it from the ridge. We need to make a plan if we want to survive this."

Aidan went to his truck. "I have a plan. I'm going to bring in the rest of my sheep." He opened the passenger door. "Get in. We can talk on the way."

Her hands were on her hips and her tone was sharper now. "The fire is almost to the valley. Once it crosses, it will race up this ridge. We don't have time to chase any more sheep. You need to listen to me."

"Trust me. You're coming in loud and

clear." He gave up waiting for her and went to the driver's side. Chip jumped into the cab, and Aidan followed.

Jade had no choice but to come with them if she wanted to keep arguing. Jerking open the door of his truck, she muttered something about *men* and *idiots* while she fastened her seat belt. She put a hand to the dashboard to stabilize herself as he accelerated a little too quickly.

"Why'd you come back and leave that note, anyway?" He couldn't get it out of his head. That choice had gotten her into this mess. "You'd already told me to leave. You didn't owe me anything more."

"I made an oath, a while back, that I'd try to save lives."

He hated the obligation settling on his shoulders. "I don't need you to save mine."

"That's too bad. You're stuck with me now."

He gunned the engine up the rutted track and all three of them bounced a few inches above the bench seat.

She glared at him as she grabbed Chip and steadied him. "Be careful."

"Just trying to hurry. Last I heard, there's a fire heading this way."

"If you'd taken my first evacuation order seriously, neither of us would be here right now."

Guilt turned to anger and rose hot in his veins. He sure hadn't asked for her to stay. "You stayed for a cat. And then you decided to stop by my ranch a second time. Those were *your* bad choices."

She was still hanging on to Chip, though which of them needed steadying, Aidan wasn't sure. "I thought you'd be willing to leave with me."

He slowed and shifted to a lower gear. He'd need it to make it to the top of the steep hill where he'd left the sheep. "I wouldn't have come. Not without seeing my animals safe first."

She loosened her grip on Chip and turned to face him. "Don't you get it? There's no *safe* in a fire like this. We don't have a great chance of surviving."

So be it. It was a voice from the darkest corner of his soul. There were plenty of days, after Colby had died, when Aidan had wished for death, too. Maybe that wish had never quite left him. Maybe it was about to come true, and maybe that was okay.

Except now he had *her* to worry about. This strong young woman who, misguidedly, thought he was worth saving. Which changed everything. He couldn't die if it meant taking her with him. He didn't try to hide his frustration, just glared. "You always give up this easy?"

"No!" His words must have stung her pride, like he'd meant them to. "I've fought fires for years. I'm not giving up, I'm just telling you the statistics."

"Statistics aren't predictions."

"I hope you're right," she muttered, slumping back in her seat and looking out the window.

Aidan took a deep breath and focused on a bend in the dirt road. For all his tough talk, fear was smoldering in the spaces between each breath. Give it a second of oxygen, and it could flare up and destroy his ability to reason. What if he couldn't save her?

No. No getting dramatic. She'd been losing her nerve just now. All the more reason he couldn't lose his. He'd prepared for fire season, sort of. He'd plowed a firebreak around the edge of his property. He had water—extra spigots he'd run to various parts of his ranch to make sure there were water sources within easy reach. His preparations weren't perfect, but he could do this. Especially now that he had help. Ornery and opinionated help, but help nonetheless.

"Why don't we start over," she said. "Like we've never met. I'm Jade."

They really had gotten off on the wrong foot. "I'm Aidan."

"From just south of Cody, Wyoming, right? You told me that so I could notify your next of kin, I assume?"

When he'd said it, he'd figured it was just a precaution. "Guess you won't be able to do that now, will you?"

"Not if we don't survive. Aidan, I'm serious. I'll need you to listen to me, so we can make it through this."

"Funny, I was just thinking the same thing." They'd reached the top of the ridge and Aidan could see his Anatolian shepherds, Thor and Odin, circling the flock, restless and worried. They could smell the smoke and maybe even hear the sound of the approaching fire. He cut the engine and set the brake. "Stay here, okay?" He got out of the truck and went around to the back to open the tailgate and pull down the ramp.

Jade ignored his request, opened her door and stepped out. "Seriously, Aidan, you need to—"

"Wait!" But it was too late. Chip jumped out of the cab, eager to work. Thor and Odin immediately spotted him and their ears went down and back. They were huge beige dogs with black faces and strong bodies. The two of them could easily rip a cattle dog like Chip to pieces. And they might, if they felt he was a threat to their flock.

"Get the dog back in the car!" Aidan yelled at Jade. Startled, she reached for Chip but he was already gone, creeping quickly toward the flock, ready to herd them toward the truck. It was his and Aidan's usual routine, except they'd missed a key step. Normally Aidan put the guard dogs in their crates in the back of the truck first.

Thor and Odin, already on the alert from the smoke, decided Chip was the threat they'd been worried about. They hurtled toward him, barking and snarling.

"No!" Aidan raced for Chip, trying to

come between him and the guard dogs. He
scooped the squirming cattle dog into his
arms when Thor and Odin were just a few
yards away. "Stop!" he yelled at the shepherds.

The big dogs slowed, but they were still
agitated, growling as they circled Aidan and
Chip.

"Thor, down!" Aidan tried the more obe-
dient dog first, and it worked. The shepherd
stopped in his tracks and shook, as if switching himself out of protective mode. Odin
kept barking, but his attention was veering
toward something else. Out of the corner of
his eye, Aidan saw Jade approaching cautiously. *Oh no.* Weren't firefighters supposed
to have more sense? "Jade, don't! Go back
to the truck. These are guard dogs. They
don't know you."

She retreated, walking backward, eyeing
Odin cautiously. Thor seemed to have refo-
cused on the smoke, and was trotting back
to the flock to make sure his charges were
still safe.

"Odin. Enough."

Reluctantly, the big dog stopped growling. Aidan pointed toward the sheep. "Go!"

Odin turned and retreated to the flock, his tail down. He glanced back at Aidan a couple times with an expression so grumpy that, in a different situation, Aidan might have laughed.

But with the smoke getting thicker and the wind still whipping the grass around his legs, he didn't feel like laughing. Still carrying Chip, he strode toward the truck where Jade was waiting. He set Chip inside the cab and shut the door. "You have to listen to me out here," he bit out as he turned to face Jade. "I told you to stay in the truck. There was a reason for that."

She had the grace to nod. "I had no idea they'd attack poor Chip."

"Their entire life is protecting this flock from coyotes and mountain lions. When Chip starts herding, nipping at the sheep's heels to get them moving, they see him as a predator." He shook his head, fear manifesting as disgust. "And coming close to them like that... They could have attacked you, too."

Her chin set, ready for battle. "I thought they were going to bite you. I figured I could help."

She was small, maybe five foot five to his six-three. How had she been planning to help him, exactly? "You're no help if you get bit by one of my dogs. Lose the hero complex."

"Me? You're the one who's risking his life to save all these animals. You're like Snow White."

It was so ridiculous it surprised a laugh out of him. "I'm pretty sure Snow White was a girl. Plus, she didn't save animals. She sang to them."

She shrugged. "Sang. Saved. Whatever."

"You're just trying to distract me from the fact that you're lousy at following directions."

Her slight smile allowed a glimpse of her white teeth. "I could say the same for you."

"You're probably right." There was no time to say more, though he was actually enjoying their exchange. Strange that he could enjoy anything at a time like this. Or maybe, with such danger so close, there was never a better time to savor each minute. "I have to get the dogs. Promise to stay in the truck with Chip this time?"

She nodded silently, and Aidan grabbed

leashes from the back of the truck and jogged back to the sheep. "Thor, Odin, come," he commanded. Reluctantly, the shepherds broke away from their sheep buddies and shambled toward him. Grateful that he'd come out here to practice with them on occasion, Aidan slipped the leashes around the dogs' necks and walked them to the truck. Aidan pulled a dog treat from his pocket and used it to convince Thor up the ramp and into his crate. He did the same for Odin, then picked the ramp up and slid it alongside their crates. Closing the tailgate, he walked to the cab and opened the driver's side door. "Okay, Chip." The cattle dog jumped out, ready to get to work.

"What do you want me to do?" Jade scrubbed her hands across her eyes. "Ugh. This smoke is already getting to me."

"Yeah, it's not good." That was an understatement. Aidan's mouth tasted like bad barbecue. His throat felt scratchy when he inhaled. "I want you to drive the truck real slowly down the hill, to that green field behind the barn. I'll ride in back, and Chip is going to bring up the rear with the sheep."

She slid across the bench seat toward him. "Okay, let's do it." She reached for the key.

"You want to pump the gas once or twice. It pulls to the right. The brake is—"

She held out a hand to stop him. "I've driven a few trucks before. I think I'm okay."

Right. She was a firefighter and probably used to driving vehicles a lot more complicated than his truck. But man, she was prickly.

Jade fastened her seat belt, then glanced up at him. "How were you going to get these sheep moved without me here?"

"Two trips. One to pick up the dogs, one on horseback with Chip." He might not want her here, but he was grateful he didn't have to make those two trips. If Jade was right, the fire would be here soon. He shut the door of the cab. "If I need you to stop, I'll bang on the roof. Try to take it slow so we can stay with the sheep."

She was a good driver. She kept it in low gear to spare the brakes and found the best route down the rutted track, navigating around potholes and ditches so he didn't get bounced around too much. Aidan stood in the truck bed, between the cab and the dog crates, shouting commands to Chip. The dog was a streak of gray across the grass, racing back and forth behind the flock, making sure no animal strayed or was left behind. Under the dog's expert direction, three dozen sheep flowed down the track like dirty white water, bleating their disgust with the move, but cooperating nonetheless. These were his spring-lambing crew, so many of them were pregnant, but they still made good time back to the ranch.

The air, though. Yuck. It was turning to a foul soup. Aidan pulled his bandanna out of his back pocket and tied it over his mouth and nose. The fire wasn't visible yet but he could almost feel it, rumbling over the low hills and valleys toward the ridge, destroying everything in its path. Nellie's ranch would go up first, and he tried not to think about the lifetime's worth of treasured heirlooms and memories she was likely to lose.

She was safe. That's what mattered.

And now he had to find a way to keep Jade safe. And keep his animals safe. People had done it. He'd read it in the news. People had stayed during wildfires, fought for their land and survived.

Of course, others had stayed, and hadn't.

They made it down the hill, and the pasture was in sight. Jade parked a short distance from the gate and got out just as Aidan jumped down from the back.

She pointed toward his bandanna. "Pull it up a little higher so it's really covering your nose." She reached forward as if to help him.

"I don't need you fussing at me." He backed away, adjusting it himself, not wanting her touch. She was already getting under his skin with her humor, her quick willingness to admit a mistake and, yeah, even her bossy attitude. He didn't want her anywhere close to him. Hadn't let anyone close to him, except Nellie, in so long.

She shrugged, but he saw the flash of hurt in her eyes. "Didn't mean to invade your space."

He'd been rude. But keeping his distance would help him focus on the tasks at hand, so he didn't offer an apology. "Will you open that gate, all the way?"

When she had it open, Aidan jogged through and toward the sheep already in the pasture. It was getting crowded in here, with all of Nellie's sheep and the ones he'd moved here earlier in the day. He waved his arms, shouted and drove the sheep farther from the gate. The last thing he needed was any of them running out while the others were coming in.

And here came the new flock, ears perking up at the fresh grass and the other sheep. Some stopped to eat right away, blocking the path of those behind, but Chip took care of it, rushing at their heels, hustling them forward until all the sheep were in.

"Good boy," Aidan told him as Chip ran to him, panting through a doggy grin. "Very good boy." He ruffled the dog's soft ears, and he and Chip left the pasture.

Jade closed the gate behind them. "Chip seems pretty good at his job."

"Couldn't run this ranch without him." Aidan opened the cab door and Chip jumped inside. "Last step," he told Jade. "We need to let Thor and Odin back in with the sheep. It will help keep them calm."

She smiled faintly. "And I sit in the cab with Chip. Lesson learned."

"Thanks." He waited until she was safely inside. Chip seemed to like her. The dog snuggled right up under her chin with a blissful expression when she rubbed his ears.

Aidan let the shepherds out of their crates and guided them into the pasture. Thor and Odin took their duties seriously, stopping to mark their territory near the gate before wandering off to investigate the new pasture. Normally Aidan would watch them carefully if he were combining flocks together like this, making sure that the dogs treated the unfamiliar sheep well. But there wasn't time now. He shut the gate and climbed back in the truck.

"Let's get these dog crates back in the barn. That way we'll have room in the truck if we need to move any equipment around." He started the engine and headed for the barn.

Jade drummed her fingers restlessly on her knee. "Any other animals we need to save? Or can we start saving ourselves?"

He might hate that she was here, hate that he felt helpless to ensure her survival, but if he was going to be stuck out here with anyone, a firefighter was probably the best possible person. "I've got some new lambs and their mamas, and a few very pregnant ewes down in my sheep shed. That's the other barn, lower down on the property. I've got to move them up here. Then that's it for the animals."

She shaded her eyes, squinting at the shed. "That building has a metal roof?"

"Yup. Both my barns do. And the sheep shed has metal walls, as well."

"Good call. Close it up tight and it might make it through the fire."

Aidan pointed through the windshield to his main barn. "And this one?"

She shrugged. "It's hard to say. If we spray off the walls and the ground around it really well, there's a chance. It looks like it's in good shape. No cracks between the planks on the siding, so that will help keep the embers from getting stuck in there and igniting."

It was a relief to hear. "I'd be grateful if we could save it. It's the heart and soul of the ranch."

Her smile softened her features and made her look a lot less tough. "I wonder if your sheep know how lucky they are?"

"What do you mean?"

"You didn't leave them. Most people would."

"Everyone's different." He glanced over at her. "Don't make me seem like some kind of sheep-saving hero. I'm just a rancher who doesn't want to lose his investment." And a rancher whose hold on life had frayed. Without Colby, danger didn't seem quite so dangerous anymore.

"Call it what you want—you could have opened the gates, let the sheep free and drove on out of here." Jade said. She shook her head like she still couldn't fathom his level of stupidity. "You should have."

Aidan shook his head. "I like my sheep, but they aren't that smart. I've heard of animals running back into a burning barn, simply because that's the place they've always considered safe—" he couldn't resist a jab at her "—and let's not forget that you stayed back for a cat who may have scarred your arms for life."

"Touché." She ran her hand down Chip's back and the cattle dog flopped onto the seat with a sigh of bliss. "Guess we're both a couple of softies when it comes to animals."

"I won't tell anyone if you won't." Aidan guided the truck along the side of the barn toward the front. "Is there any way to get news of the fire?"

"My radio was down before. I can try again, but I'll probably just get static."

Aidan turned the corner and slammed on the brakes. "I don't think you'll need the radio." He leaned forward and pointed up the hill. The sky to the north of them was a solid wall of smoke. "Looks like the fire is getting pretty close."

Jade craned her neck to see what he did. Aidan saw her go into command-mode— straightening her shoulders, tipping her chin up like she was all set to give the fire a piece of her mind. "Time to get busy. Let's round up some supplies and start saving your ranch."

CHAPTER FOUR

JADE EYED THE wall of smoke looming in the north. Saving Aidan's ranch might be too lofty a goal. If they could save themselves, the dogs, the cat and the sheep, they'd be lucky. Jade went to her truck, parked in front of the barn. She opened the door and reached for the radio. If she could contact Mitch, maybe she could get some more information about the fire. Only static greeted her. Maybe she'd have better luck with her cell phone. She pulled it from her pocket and pressed the button to bring the screen to life. No bars. There had to be something wrong. Maybe a tower had gone down somewhere. Maybe there was just too much fire and smoke and wind between here and the rest of the world.

She set a piece of her hope down with her phone. Some part of her had been hanging on to the chance that they might get through.

That Mitch might know a way out, or send in a helicopter or something. But the reality was, he didn't even know where she was right now.

Suddenly the world grew, as if some lens in Jade's mind was zooming out and out until she was just a tiny speck in a vast landscape, a minute particle of life, possibly soon-to-be ash.

No. She shook her head, shut the truck door and glanced around, trying to ground herself. Nothing had changed. The air was still smoky, the barn still stood and Aidan was looking at her like she might just be a little crazy.

Jade swallowed down the fear that rose in her throat. Fear didn't matter. The only thing that mattered right now was what, out of all the possible things they could do right now, would give them the best chance for survival. Make a list. Itemize. Prioritize. "I didn't see a firebreak when I drove in."

"I've cut breaks." Aidan pointed up the lane that led back toward his house and, eventually, the road. "There's one that crosses the driveway and runs along the perimeter fence."

That was good news, but why hadn't she noticed it driving in? "When did you last work on it?"

"Late spring."

Jade looked up at him in shock. "That's not good enough. You have to keep going over it all summer long. It's probably overgrown. We'll have to go over it right now."

He shot her a dubious look. "I don't think we have time. I still have to get the lambs."

"We'd better make time. It's our most important defense. If we're lucky, it could steer the main fire around the property instead of through it."

Aidan glanced at the sheep, grazing in the green field. "I want to set up irrigation around them, as well."

"They've got sprinklers in their pasture. If we don't have time to wet the area around them, they'll huddle under those." What was his problem? This was about them *all* surviving, not just the sheep. Sprinklers might not be enough if the fire went right over them, if it seared their lungs and made it impossible to breathe. She tried to pacify him. "We might still have time to set up extra sprinklers, even if the fire is getting close. A good firebreak will slow it down. It's a clear choice."

He was silent for a moment, and Jade bit her lip to keep from yelling at him. The guy was acting like he had all the time in the world when really they had almost none. She tried to put all the authority of six years of firefighting into her voice. "Aidan, listen to me. I know what I'm talking about."

Aidan looked over at the pasture, and Jade followed his gaze. She could see the big shepherds circling the sheep, keeping them close together, probably still concerned about their new surroundings. The sheep seemed oblivious to the fire approaching. Their heads were down, their entire focus on the rich, green grass of this one irrigated pasture. Finally, Aidan glanced down at her and gave a quick nod. "Okay."

Jade tried to hide her relief. "Let's get your lambs. Then we'll deal with the fire-break."

"I'll get the trailer hitched up. We can use it to move them to the pasture." He jogged toward his truck.

Jade glanced around anxiously, tak-ing stock. The air had taken on a distinct brown tinge, and she could taste smoke in her mouth. Her eyes were watering, and her nose was starting to run. She went to her truck and grabbed a handful of tissues from the box there and shoved them in her pocket. She searched her duffel bag for a mask. Usually she had a couple of spare N95s, but there was nothing. This day was definitely not going her way. She tried the radio again as she watched Aidan pull the truck up in front of the trailer and back it toward the hitch. Still static, no matter which channel she used. Okay, then.

Aidan had the trailer hitched up and was waving her over, so she shut the door and went to join him and Chip in the cab. The sheepdog nosed her cheek and made her smile. She stroked his thick, rough coat, and he flopped down and put his head in her lap.

"You're going to spoil him," Aidan said.

"He deserves it. He's a hard worker," Jade said, rubbing the dog's soft ears.

"He is." Aidan turned the truck down a grassy lane that went past the barn and through a field. Jade noticed a pond on their left. A place of refuge if things got ugly.

They continued along a sloping hillside,

with fenced pastures on either side of them. "This is where I had my horses and cattle until earlier today. I'm so grateful for folks in your town who came up to evacuate them to Shelter Creek."

Pride for her town swelled in Jade's heart. "That's Shelter Creek for you. People really step up for each other." The mention of horses made her think of the beautiful one Aidan had been riding earlier. "What will you do with the one horse you kept here?"

"Payday? I'll have to put him out with all the sheep. He has pretty good sense. Hopefully he'll stay there with them."

Jade hoped Aidan was right. She'd seen plenty of horses get spooked in fires. But maybe if they had all the sprinklers going on that pasture, he'd feel the water on his back and know he'd be okay.

They pulled up in front of the second barn.

"Welcome to my sheep shed—" Aidan raised his hand in a flourish "—one of the best places on the ranch."

Jade knew he was referring to the lambs born here, but she agreed with him for a different reason. The building had been built on a concrete pad. It had gravel spread all around it for yards. Nothing was growing near it at all. And, even better, it had a metal roof and metal walls. "This is a firefighter's vision of perfection," she told him as she opened her door and got out. "Well done."

"It's pretty new." Aidan led the way to the big doors at one end. "I had it built after a few really bad fire seasons. Guess we'll see how well it holds up."

"Do you store your hay and bedding inside the building?"

"Yup."

"Even better." Jade watched as he slid the door open. A strong smell of sheep permeated her senses as she stepped inside, despite the ceiling fans circulating the air. It was cool inside the shed, a nice break from the heat.

"This is going to be a little tricky," Aidan told her. "I don't think the pregnant ewes will be a problem, but the ones with brand-new lambs aren't going to want to move house right now."

"You could consider leaving them here," Jade pointed out. "But the concern would be extreme heat. With water on them, they may do better with the temperature during the fire." She knew by saying this she was counting on a best-case scenario. Hopefully she could slow the fire, or redirect it around the property. But if a firestorm rolled right over them, all bets were off.

Aidan had stopped by a small, fenced-in corral. Jade stopped, too. Inside, lying down, were an ewe and two tiny lambs, all curled up together. At the sight of them, one of the lambs stood in an awkward, rocking-horse motion and tottered a few steps away from them. It was beyond cute, with fuzzy ears sticking out on either side of its small brown face. Its mouth opened to produce a miniature bleating sound. "Look at its knobby knees." Jade glanced up at Aidan. "How can it be so sweet?"

He looked down at her with paternal pride in his eyes, and for a moment Jade forgot the fire and danger and took in the sight of Aidan looking almost happy. Without his scowl he was quite handsome. *Where had that thought come from?* Jade returned her focus to the lamb, and the adorable way it wobbled back to its mama and collapsed into the straw.

"Will it get too cold under the sprinklers?"

"With a fire coming through?" Aidan shook his head. "They're born with wool coats, you know. A lot of ranchers let their ewes give birth out in the pasture and the lambs start life out there, rain or shine. I use this shed because I have a lot of mountain lions and coyotes in this area. I need to make sure my lambs have a fighting chance."

Jade stood. "Speaking of fighting chances, we need to get these guys loaded and moved. Tell me what to do."

Aidan pointed to some bales of straw stacked near the entrance to the barn. "Can you break off some pieces of that and scatter straw all over the floor of the trailer? Make it a few inches thick so these little ones have some cushioning for the ride."

Jade nodded and went to get the straw.

Twenty minutes later, the trailer was full. Six pregnant ewes complained bitterly. Three mamas, with five lambs, lay in the straw bed Jade had made. Jade had carried three newborn lambs in her arms and fallen in love with each one. If a wildfire hadn't been imminent, she would have wanted to sit in the straw and cuddle them for hours.

Instead, Jade, Aidan and Chip were back in the truck, pulling up next to the irrigated pasture. "Are you worried about Thor and Odin and these tiny lambs?" Through the truck window, Jade watched the big dogs warily. Chip whined and shoved his nose toward her cracked window, though how he could smell anything but smoke, Jade had no idea.

"Not at all," Aidan answered. "If anything it will just make them even more protective, so we'll have to be extra careful to keep Chip away from them." Aidan stopped by the gate. "Will you drive? And stay in here with Chip? I'll get these lambs and mamas settled."

"Of course." Jade held Chip's leather collar while Aidan climbed out of the cab, and then slid to the driver's side. When Aidan opened the gate, she drove the truck and trailer into the pasture, then waited while Aidan got the sheep and lambs out. The mama ewes quickly took their babies away from the rest of the flock, keeping a distance even as they started to crop the grass. Thor and Odin came over to give them and the new lambs a few sniffs, but quickly seemed to lose interest.

"All good?" Jade asked after Aidan had closed the gate and climbed back into the driver's seat of the truck.

"All good," he said. "Except I want to get those extra sprinklers set up around here."

"*After* the firebreak," Jade reminded him.

He started them along the lane back to the main barn. "It's hard, listening to you," he grumbled.

"You'll get used to it," she assured him.

He rolled his eyes. "Maybe. So you like the lambs, huh?"

"How could anyone not?" Jade leaned an elbow on the door and rested her head on her hand. "I never really understood why anyone would want to live way out in a place like this, and work so hard, every single day. But holding those lambs, maybe, just maybe, I can understand it a bit more."

"Glad I could open your mind just a little."

Jade glanced at him, trying to figure out if he was being grumpy or sarcastic, then gave up. He was hard to read. Guarded, as if he were determined to keep everyone a safe distance away.

What was she doing? She had a fire to fight. She couldn't waste a scrap of mental energy trying to psychoanalyze this guy. When Aidan parked the truck at the back of the barn, Jade jumped out and ran to unhitch the trailer.

Aidan stored a lot of his equipment in a carport that was built against the back of the barn. Like the main barn, it had a metal roof. The ground back here was covered in thick gravel that, Jade noted, could also act as a firebreak on this side of the building. That was good news, as Aidan had made it clear he wanted to save this barn.

Aidan didn't waste any time. He went to a green tractor and climbed into the driver's seat, gesturing for Jade to come closer. "Guide me backward and help me get the box blade on."

He started backing toward a low rectangular box with some spikes pointing down toward the ground. Jade ran to where she could see the hitch. "To the left," she shouted over the noisy engine. "*Your* left."

He backed up, looking over his shoulder, squinting at the blade to make sure he was on target. He must have done this many times before, because he got the angle right the first time, stopping just a few inches short of the hitch.

"Just a little more," Jade called. "And stop!"

Aidan jumped down, shoving his shaggy blond hair back so it stuck up in the growing breeze. He fastened the blade with the clamp and bolts, his hands a combination of bones, sinew and scars that testified to a life of manual labor.

"We'll need tools," he said. "There's a door in the barn, on the right as you enter. It's a tool closet. Grab anything you can think of to clear the ground."

"Isn't the tractor supposed to do that?"

The grimace on his face spoke regret and worry. "The ground is so dry this time of year. Folks call the soil summer cement. We'd do better with a real bulldozer and a stronger blade, but this tractor is all we have. We're going to have to make it work."

"We don't have much time to chip away at the ground with hand tools," Jade told him, trying to keep her voice steady when she was feeling less and less so. Without a crew of firefighters, their abilities were limited.

"Then we'd better get started."

He had a point. Jade had a Pulaski, a specialized firefighting axe, in the truck. But, as far as she knew, that was it. The truck she'd brought was just a regular pickup. It wasn't stocked for fighting fires. She ran toward the barn and found the door he mentioned. Flinging it open, she saw that, thankfully, the room was well organized, each tool hanging on a hook or leaning neatly against a wall. She grabbed every digging tool she could and staggered out of the barn. Aidan met her there and took the tools, loading them onto the floor of the tractor. Jade ran for the truck and grabbed her Pulaski. The familiar weight brought some comfort. "Let's go," she called as she jogged back to the tractor.

Aidan ran for the driver's side and Jade climbed into the passenger seat. The engine roared as he accelerated up the driveway, but, over the sound, Jade could hear Chip's muffled barking. They must have left him in the cab of the truck.

"Stop!" Jade put a hand to Aidan's arm. "You can't leave Chip in the truck."

Aidan stopped the tractor. "Now you're going to tell me how to handle my dog?"

"Yes. Let's let him run. You'll have to lock him up later, once the embers start coming down."

He glared at her but put on the brake. "Go on, then, go get him."

She couldn't resist poking at him a little. "Because you know I'm right."

"I didn't say that." But something tugged at the corner of his mouth, a quirk that might possibly be related to a smile.

Jade ran back to the truck and let Chip out. The cattle dog did a happy dance of gratitude and followed her back to the tractor, shooting Aidan what looked like a reproachful glance before running off into the grass to sniff at something.

Aidan accelerated, and Jade held on tight to the edge of her seat as they bumped up the driveway, with Chip running joyfully alongside. If the dog was worried about the fire, it was eclipsed by his happiness at running free and being included in this adventure.

They drove past Aidan's old farmhouse,

until they came to an open gate where the field around Aidan's house started to give way to trees. Jade hadn't even noticed it driving in, but now she could see that there was a barbed wire perimeter fence here, and the ground on this side of it had a lot less grass than everywhere else. On the far side of the fence was a little more open meadow, but that quickly gave way to a tangle of oaks and shrub. Her stomach twisted. That was a feast for a wildfire. It could fuel the fire into an inferno right before it hit the ranch.

Deep breaths. In...and out. She couldn't control that. All she could do was check out the firebreak. Which she could immediately see wasn't nearly wide enough. "This is only ten feet across. Out here it should be twenty to thirty."

Aidan turned the tractor onto the plowed break and stopped. He pointed ahead of them. "Couldn't do it. The slope is too steep up ahead. I didn't want to roll the tractor."

Jade stood in her seat and shaded her eyes. Sure enough, the hill angled down sharply toward the west about thirty yards ahead of them. Okay, not ideal. *Think, Jade, think.*

"Let's try to widen the break right here

near your driveway as much as possible,"
she said. "The goal isn't to save all of your
grazing land at this point. Just the ranch
buildings and the sheep." *And us.* She tossed
the tools down off the tractor and jumped
after them, landing on the uneven soil of the
overgrown firebreak. Chip came to greet
her, wagging his stub tail in happiness. Jade
stroked his soft, pointy ears and considered
what to do next. "Drive the entire break and
scrape it clean. While you do that, I'll try to
widen this area a little."

Aidan really did smile slightly then, just
a hint of humor deepening the lines of his
craggy face. "Yes, boss."

It was a strange moment for smiling but
his expression, or maybe Chip's comforting
ears, settled her racing heart. "Glad we're
clear on who's in charge." Grabbing her Pulaski, she headed for the edge of the plowed
lane. The ground was so dry that she could
see cracks in the soil. This wasn't going to
be easy.

Jade watched as Aidan and the tractor
bumped on down the firebreak, the lowered
box blade scraping errant weeds and grass behind them. Chip zigzagged after him, sniff-

ing at the dirt the tractor churned up. Aidan was certainly a prickly, grumpy guy, but at least he was a hard worker. That was all she could ask for right now. His possibly-a-smile and perhaps-a-sense-of-humor were unexpected surprises. If they showed up again, they would certainly make this fight a little easier.

She shifted her grip on her Pulaski and went to the spot where the firebreak met the driveway. She raised her arms and brought the sharpest end of the blade down hard about six inches from the edge of the firebreak. It barely made a dent in the soil. "Summer cement is right," she muttered, and tried again, just a few inches from the edge of the break this time. The blade bit in and she hauled it toward herself, breaking up dirt as she went. Taking a step to the right, she repeated the motion again, then again and again. Sweat started down her face, mixing with the dust stirred up from the soil. The wind was blowing stronger, but it was hot, sooty and brought no relief.

Glancing up twenty minutes later, Jade surveyed her progress, and her heart sank toward her dusty boots. She'd come maybe ten yards and widened the break by about a foot, and her arms ached from chipping away at the rock-hard soil. She glanced north, at the black smoke blotting out the sky there. Now she knew how an ant felt, trying to move a breadcrumb by itself. So much effort, for so little reward.

Aidan was coming back her way with the tractor and she walked to meet him, dragging her Pulaski dejectedly behind her. He stopped, waiting for her to approach. Chip ran to greet her, shoving his cool nose into her free hand. "This is taking too long," she told Aidan, heaving herself up to sit beside him again. "How about we scrape the existing firebreak as far as we can and move on to plan B?"

"Sounds good." His voice was neutral but she could see the way his brows drew down. He looked worried. "What's plan B?"

"I don't know yet. But I'll come up with it soon. And you were right. Your soil is cement."

"Next year, when the ground is still wet, I'll make the break wider wherever I can." Aidan revved the engine and steered the tractor a little to the right, making sure to scrape the area that Jade had tried to conquer with her pickax.

"And maintain it," Jade added automatically. *Next year.* It was impossible to look that far ahead. If Jade looked ahead more than ten minutes, panic threaded through her veins.

Aidan shrugged with what might be remorse. "Lesson learned. I should have taken this more seriously."

It was nice to know he could admit when he'd been wrong. Maybe the stubborn rancher wasn't quite as stubborn as he seemed. "We have other options. Do you have a hose that could reach up here?"

"I think we could run one from the house," he said.

If things got bad, they could set a backfire on the other side of the firebreak to deprive the main fire of fuel. But despair whispered in her ear. Setting a backfire and keeping it under control was usually a team effort. There were only two of them. But they had no choice. They had to keep trying. Hopefully trying would be enough to get them through.

AIDAN GLANCED AT Jade as he dragged the box blade along the firebreak, taking down the thistles and wild fennel that had seeded itself in the churned-up soil over the summer. She was right. He should have maintained this. They were losing precious time scraping it now. But if it could stop the flames, or at least divert some of them, it would be worth it.

He knew they were in trouble. Jade was pretty calm, acting like they had plenty of time, but the fire was getting closer. The day was dimming, not just because it was late afternoon, but because the source of the smoke was closing in on them.

Aidan steered the tractor along the rutted firebreak, lowering the box blade as the track sloped down. Why had he let this get so overgrown? Ever since Jade pointed it out, Aidan had been wondering if he was neglectful, or maybe just suicidal. A clear firebreak was everybody's first priority out here. Wildfire wasn't just a possibility. A rancher could expect to have to face it at some point. Between the drought, the longer, dryer summers and the warmer winters, fire was the new normal.

Was it possible he just didn't care anymore? He cared for his animals. He wanted them to not only survive, but thrive. And the last few years he'd been pretty interested in experimenting with new ways to manage wildlife out here—mountain lions, coyotes, even the occasional bear. He'd found ways for his livestock to coexist with these predators and still keep them at bay. He'd even gotten a grant to help fund his work, and now he was a demonstration ranch. Other ranchers visited to learn from his methods. That's how he'd gotten to know Maya and Caleb. But when was the last time he'd repaired anything on his house? And why hadn't he tended to the firebreak?

And now here, with this firefighter, her confident manner and her dark eyes that looked right into him as if she wanted to know what made him tick, he was embarrassed.

"How long have you been out here on this ranch?" She was looking out over the property as she spoke. They had a good view from here.

Too long. Not long enough. It was his refuge, his heartland and the source of so much grief. "About nine years now," he finally answered.

"You must really like it out here."

"Yep." Why was she making small talk now? Seems like they should save their breath for breathing, the smoke was getting so thick.

"And you live all alone out here?"

"What is this, some kind of interview for Firefighter Monthly?" The moment he said it, he knew it was rude. She was stuck out here for better or worse, trying to help. But he didn't want to justify his life. He didn't want to explain his choices, or why he was all alone. Not to her, not to anyone.

"I wasn't trying to pry," she said. "I was just curious."

"Well, don't be." Aidan wasn't sure if he was more disgusted with her or himself. But somehow he couldn't stop his harsh words. "Not everyone wants to share all the details of their life. I know that's hard for people to understand. Everyone nowadays is always oversharing, putting their lunch up on social media. Why would I care what someone else ate for lunch?"

She turned to gape at him. "Are you ninety? You sound like a crotchety old man."

He was. Inside at least. Thirty-five years old, going on a hundred. "We don't need to explain our lives to each other. We just need to fight this fire."

"Right." She blew out a breath like she was trying to keep her patience. "Fine. Let's talk about your power source. What do you use out here? Are you off the grid?"

"I use solar." Aidan stopped the tractor, cursing the fire and the crushing feeling of hopelessness that threatened to paralyze him. "We've got to turn around here. It's too steep for the tractor up ahead."

Jade glanced behind them at the wall of smoke, and Aidan followed her gaze to where it was towering in the sky now. In the west they still had light, but the setting sun, obscured by smoke, was an eerie, orange orb, hovering at the horizon. The hills that made up the rest of his western view were sepia-tinted and blurred, as if Aidan was seeing them in an old photo. They were running out of time. He turned his attention to turning the tractor around. It wasn't easy to do on this narrow part of the hill.

"You have batteries right? To store your solar power? Where are they?"

She was still full of questions, but at least they weren't personal this time. "I'll show you the batteries when we get back to the house."

"They power the pumps on your wells?"

"I've got separate solar panels for the pumps."

"And you've cleared the area around them, right?"

He had. Back in spring. Just like this firebreak, he'd let everything go. Where had his mind been? He'd lost Colby over two years ago. But lately it had caught up with him. He'd thrown himself into his work during those first terrible months, as if staying busy could make the pain go away. But this summer he'd stopped working as hard. There'd been more days than he could count where he'd found himself leaning on a fence, the weight of grief heavy on his back, staring into space instead of getting his chores done.

Jade's sigh was audible. "I take it from your silence that you haven't maintained defensible space around the panels for your pump?"

There was fear within her sarcasm. Aidan could hear it. He cranked the tractor around, and after an awkward five-point turn got them heading back on the now-cleared fire-break. "I've got a weed trimmer. It will work for those areas."

"And how are you for hoses?"

"I've got a fair number. Backpack pumps, too." He glanced her way, sure that would earn him back a little respect.

It worked. She was looking less tense. She moved a hand in his direction, with her knuckles curled under.

Aidan eyed her hand. "What's that for?"

"You've never done a fist bump?"

"It's been a while." He took a hand off the wheel long enough to bump knuckles. "I guess that means you're happy about the backpack pumps?"

"They can make a big difference when we get spot fires."

He noted the word *when*. There were no *ifs* here.

They drove in silence for a moment, Jade staring at the approaching smoke as if lost in thought. Aidan turned down the main drive-way, calling Chip to make sure the dog followed. Chip emerged from behind some coyote brush, looking annoyed at being interrupted. He'd probably been chasing a rabbit. But he was a good dog to the core, and obediently trotted alongside the tractor as they made their way down the driveway and back toward the barn.

Jade's questions started again. "Where is your propane tank?"

Aidan pointed it out as they drove past his house. It was out back of the house on a concrete pad, the regulation distance from the building.

"If that thing blows it's going to take the back of the house with it."

She didn't inspire confidence in a guy, that's for sure. "I followed all the rules for where to site it," he told her.

"The rules are bad," she said. "Most people put them farther away from structures now."

"I guess they don't give you much training on people skills at your job?" There he went. Rude again. Her confidence, her know-it-all attitude brought it out in him. Or maybe he was getting defensive because she clearly thought he was a fool. Not that he even cared what she thought. He'd given up on worrying about other peoples' opinions a long time ago. So why was he reacting so much to hers?

Maybe because she's right, an unwelcome voice from deep inside muttered. He had neglected a lot of things lately. He'd been barely getting by, let alone keeping up on changes to propane tank regulations.

"Please tell me your solar batteries are protected from the fire."

"They're in that shed over there." He pointed to his shed, set up next to a large array of solar panels, angled to catch the sunlight. As soon as he did he realized his mistake. The panels and battery shed were downhill from them, about halfway between the house and barn, sitting on a poured concrete pad. But in the past few years, he'd let grass and bushes grow up all around them.

"You've got to be kidding me," Jade groaned. "Stop the tractor." When he did, she jumped down with her firefighter's ax and a pair of long-handled garden clippers she'd brought from his barn. "We're wasting valuable time here, Aidan." She yanked her gloves out of her belt and pulled them on. "We've got to go clear that brush." She stormed off, disgust visible in her rigid posture, traitorous Chip bouncing alongside her.

Aidan parked the tractor, which would never make it down the brushy slope, and grabbed his gloves and tools, as well. He followed her, and they hacked the bushes in silence, chopping down coyote brush and ripping out blackberry brambles, throwing it all in a big pile. Jade worked in a controlled hurricane of motion, whacking at the base of the brush, obliterating grass. She might be critical and annoying, but she was tough, no one could argue with that.

She pointed northwest, down the slope. "Haul this stuff about twenty yards that way. If it flares up, at least it will blow away from the house and the barn. Assuming the wind doesn't change."

Aidan did as he was told, and after about twenty minutes they had a few yards around the battery shed and solar panels reduced to shorn stubble.

Jade grabbed a huge armload of brush and carried it to the pile Aidan had made. "Where's the closest hose? Let's wet this area down."

"It's by the pasture with the sheep," Aidan told her. "Follow me."

They made their way back to the driveway and Aidan drove the tractor to the carport. As he shut off the engine Jade jumped down and pulled the tools off the tractor, leaning them against the barn wall. "I have a feeling we'll need these again."

Aidan read her meaning loud and clear. She was expecting a lot more problems, all because he'd neglected his chores lately.

He hadn't wanted her here. Didn't want to feel like, because of his negligence, her life was in greater danger. But he also knew that while Jade might be tough to take, she definitely knew what she was doing. Annoyed and defensive as he was, he should count himself lucky to have her here with him. Only it was hard to do when she was right so very often.

CHAPTER FIVE

JADE AIMED THE hose at the shorn ground around Aidan's battery shed. This wasn't good. They'd cleared about a ten-foot circle surrounding the shed and panels, but it wasn't really enough, and they didn't have time to do more. If the bushes beyond the cleared area went up quickly, the flames could get so high they'd still damage the panels. And Aidan had explained that these panels powered most of the ranch, including the pump for the well near the house. The well they'd be using to defend the upper half of the ranch from the flames. How could Aidan be so irresponsible to live all the way out here in these dry hills and not be more prepared for a wildfire?

At least he'd mowed the grass around that upper well pretty recently, since it was so close to his house. There was one thing to be thankful for. That pump should make it through the fire as long as the batteries did.

Thank goodness the battery shed had a metal roof and noncombustible shingles on the walls. Aidan had told her he had lithium-ion batteries inside, which were supposed to be nonflammable. Maybe she'd been too hard on him for not being more prepared. He'd certainly taken precautions to keep his power source going. But not *every* precaution. Without this power that upper well wouldn't work. Without water on the upper end of the ranch, the fire would rage through the rest of the property at its hottest. And their chances for survival would plummet.

The bushes behind her shook and shivered in the wind, which was gusting now, lifting her hair, shoving at her legs, blowing dust and debris into her face. The smoke in the sky had changed from a thick haze on the horizon to clouds piled upon clouds, towering over the ranch. Pretty soon they'd get ash falling, and maybe even some embers. She needed to ask if Aidan had an extra bandanna she could tie around her face. Then maybe she could avoid breathing the worst of it.

Jade started as the water from the hose sputtered, then trickled, then stopped. She turned toward the pasture, where the spigot was, and squinted through the smoky air. "Aidan? Turn the water back on!" There was no answer, just the rushing sounds of the buffeting wind. And another noise, so distant it would be out of earshot if she didn't know what to listen for. A faint roar, a low rumble. It was the fire, probably starting to make its way up the ridge.

Jade dropped the hose and ran for the spigot, checking as she went to see if there were any kinks in the hose that were blocking the flow of the water. Nope. No such luck.

Aidan had said he was going to start setting up more irrigation around the pasture where the sheep were, to create an extra barrier of water between the livestock and the fire. Jade shaded her eyes, as if it would help her see through the brown, soupy air, and called again. "Aidan?"

At the faucet, Jade knelt and unscrewed the hose. Then she turned the faucet handle. Nothing. She turned it off. Turned it on again. Nothing. "Oh no," she breathed. Was it the water pump batteries? Had they damaged them somehow when they were clearing the area around the battery shed? But that made no sense. This faucet was connected to a different pump.

Looking up, she saw Aidan's tall form emerging from the smoke. "I was putting Chip in a stall in the barn, so he won't go mess with Thor and Odin. What's going on?"

"There's no water."

"What?" He tried the faucet himself. "You've got to be kidding me."

"Do you think it's the power? Or the pump?" Jade glanced at the darkening horizon. "We really need to get the water running." Her heart was speeding, tripping, like a wild thing in her chest. They had to have water. Now.

"Let's try the pump first." He started for the barn, and Jade ran to follow him. They jogged past the entrance to the barn and stopped the base of the hill on the other side. Aidan led her to a small cinderblock building and Jade saw, to her relief, that it, too, had a metal roof.

"This is the well house." Aidan pointed

to the solar panels next to it. "And its power source."

"Where's the battery?"

"Inside. Conduit runs underground to connect them. I hope that's not the problem. We don't have time to dig."

Jade crossed her fingers, hoping the same thing. "Once we get the water going, we should spray around these panels. You don't want them damaged. Where's your weed trimmer?"

"In with the tools in the barn. We can take care of that in a minute. Let's find out what's going on." Aidan pulled open the door to the small building. Inside was a mostly empty room with a pressure tank in one corner and a series of batteries in the other.

"There's a spring way down deep below here. I even get enough water to feed the pond through a pipe that runs around the edge of the barn. And I pump water up this hill, so as it comes down it gives me water pressure for this part of the ranch." He knelt by the pump. "This smoke is making everything so dark. Hit that switch by the door."

Jade flipped the light switch and a single bare bulb came on.

"Well, at least we've got power." Aidan looked visibly relieved. "It's got to be something with the pump." He got down on all fours to look more closely at the machinery.

"Here." Jade pulled out the flashlight she always wore on her belt and angled it to give him more light.

Aidan glanced up at her with an almost-admiring look. "You're useful to have around on a day like this."

That was probably as close to a compliment he'd ever give her. Jade peered over his shoulder, trying to discern the various components of the pump. "We'll see. This is a complication we didn't need."

Aidan flipped a switch on the pump. Nothing happened. He sat back on his heels and stared thoughtfully at the faulty system.

Jade tried to stay calm and wait for him to figure it out, but she could almost feel the fire breathing down their necks, and here they were without water. If they couldn't wet things down, everything around them would burn all at once and the air temperature might rise to a level they couldn't survive. She pulled in a shaky breath and let it out. *Don't think about that.* She forced herself to focus on the pump.

"Let me borrow that flashlight," Aidan finally said. She handed it to him, and he used the handle to rap sharply on a tube below the switch. There was a whirring sound as the pump came on.

"You fixed it." Jade's knees were shaky with relief. "Thank goodness."

"Not really," Aidan said. "There's got to be a problem with the wiring in the switch. It's likely to turn back off again at any time if we don't figure out what's wrong." He handed her back the flashlight. "See that breaker on the wall? Cut the power."

"You're going to fix it *now*?" Jade regretted the panic that sharpened her voice. She needed to stay calm to keep him calm. Except that he was *too* calm. As if he didn't even care that a wildfire was coming their way.

The glance he gave her was edged in sarcasm. "You want to run out of water in the middle of this fight?"

Of course she didn't. Jade tried to stand patiently while Aidan unscrewed the cover on the switch with a screwdriver he pulled out of his pocket. Carefully, he extracted two wires and started poking at the metal contacts in the switch with the end of the screwdriver.

Jade gaped at him. This couldn't be the solution. "What are you doing?"

"The contacts are corroded. The switch needs to be replaced, but we don't have time for that now. Normally I'd use a nail file to get the corrosion off, but this will have to do." He chipped at the switch some more, scraping the tip of the screwdriver back and forth on the tiny metal plates like he had all the time in the world.

Their fate was dependent on *this*? Scraping corrosion off a damaged switch? Jade's frustration boiled over. "Why are so many things on this ranch in disrepair? Isn't maintaining your pump kind of crucial when you're living out in these drought-ridden hills?"

Aidan didn't look up but she saw his shoulders rise and his back stiffen. "I guess I've had a lot on my mind lately."

"I'm sorry. It's none of my business. It's just, being a firefighter, we're *always* working on our equipment. It's part of our way of life—making sure parts are replaced before they get too old, testing everything to make sure it's in top condition. We can't show up at a fire and have things go wrong. People are relying on us."

Aidan squinted at the switch. Apparently he wasn't satisfied, because he began scraping with the screwdriver again. "Well, that's where we're different. There's just me out here. No one else relies on me."

"Your animals do. Your sheep, your dogs, all those cattle I saw getting trucked out of here earlier today."

He snapped the wires back into the contacts. "That should do it." He put the cover on the switch and began screwing it in. Only then did he speak. "Is part of your duty as a firefighter to criticize the folks you're trying to save? Because it seems like you should save your oxygen for other things. Like breathing."

Jade froze, stunned. He was rude, but he was right. She shouldn't be giving him such a hard time. It was her own fear that had her nagging at him. Yes, he should have been more prepared. But she knew better than to antagonize someone who she'd have to rely on to survive. And there was no point in lecturing. He'd made his choices, and she had to live with that. *Size up the incident. Evaluate conditions. Develop a plan.* There was nothing in her firefighting manuals that mentioned berating the victim. But something about this man got under her skin and made her forget how to behave.

Aidan flipped the switch, and the pump purred to life. "Looks like we're set. Why don't you finish watering down the battery shed, and I'll cut the weeds around the solar panel here? Then we can get the extra irrigation set up around the pasture, so the livestock have a better chance at surviving this thing."

Jade glanced around, suddenly overwhelmed by how much they had to do in so little time. Out the door, she could see that the afternoon had become evening. Or was that the smoke? She glanced at her watch. It was only five o'clock. The sun set around six thirty in the fall, so this was smoke, getting thicker now that the fire was closing in. "How long will the irrigation take? You have to think about what you want to save, Aidan."

He led the way out the door of the well house, and Jade shut it behind her. "Let's get the animals set first. Then we'll see what else we can salvage."

Outside, flecks of ash wafted down on them like tiny flakes of desolate snow. "Let's hurry," Jade said. "We don't have a lot of time left."

At the barn, they parted ways. Jade jogged to where she'd left the hose, got the water running and climbed the slope to the battery shed to spray it all down some more. When she was sure the ground was soaked, she dragged the hose back down to the pasture.

Aidan caught up to her at the barn, weed trimmer in hand. "The weeds are gone and I watered all around the panels," he said. "Assuming the switch holds up, that lower well should be okay."

"And after the fire—" Jade began.

He held up a hand to stop her. "I'll replace the switches, check them more often, etcetera, etcetera."

"You know, your local fire department offers inspections for free." Jade followed him behind the barn to the graveled carport area where they'd parked the tractor. "Once you get everything set up after the fire, you could have someone out here just to check that you're prepared for the next one."

"As long as they don't send you."

"What's that supposed to mean?" Jade put her hands to her hips, but Aidan didn't notice her indignation. He'd knelt down and was busy hitching a small trailer to an ATV.

"Just that I think I've already had an earful of your opinions on my choices."

"Safety precautions shouldn't be choices," Jade countered. "They're no-brainers. Just plain common sense, so you're prepared for situations like this."

Aidan straightened, and only then did Jade see that he was laughing at her. "See what I mean? Would you want to have you following you around, criticizing you while you tried to do your job?"

She didn't know if she wanted to laugh or if she was furious. "So I take my job seriously. So what?" Her dad had been the Shelter Creek fire chief for years. Her brothers had followed in his footsteps in one way or another, and Jade had, too. Only she'd learned early on that she had to work about ten times harder to get the credit and admiration that her brothers received so easily. If that made her pushy, or earnest, or whatever it was about her that Aidan was dismissing here, well so be it.

Only it stung a little.

"Never mind." Maybe he sensed her confusion, because he cut her some slack. "You know what you're doing, so that's something." Aidan pointed to a pile of hose, attached to curious round black disks with sprinkler heads inside. "Irrigation," he said. "Let's load it up."

"Lift from beneath?" When he nodded, Jade crouched down and got her hands under the coiled mass. Aidan crouched on the other side. "On three," she said, and counted off. Staggering under the surprising weight of the tubing, Jade managed to hold up her end and help him dump it into the cart.

"One more." They got the next pile loaded on top of the first, so the cart was heaped with hose. Aidan jumped on the ATV. "Hop on," he commanded, and Jade swung her leg over the seat behind him. There were handles by her legs and she gripped them tight. Aidan guided the ATV carefully out of the carport, and they bumped along toward the pasture. The air was thick in Jade's lungs, sticky on her skin, scratchy in her throat.

"This is like living inside a barbecue," Aidan said.

"Yup. And our job is to keep from getting roasted."

Aidan glanced over his shoulder at her. "Ew."

"Firefighter humor. Sorry." This irrigation better not take too long. They hadn't even gotten the most basic firefighting supplies together. They hadn't made a plan, let alone the backup plans they would need if things went really wrong.

But looking at the pasture, Jade could see that Aidan was actually right about this. If they could get these extra sprinklers around the fence line, it would create a buffer zone between the animals and the flames. Without it, the huge flock of sheep would all have to huddle beneath the sprinklers in the center, and they might not all be protected. Or worse, they might panic, with the fire so close.

Not that the sheep seemed worried now. They were still eating peacefully. The dogs were getting more restless, though. Thor and

Odin were pacing the outskirts of the flock, tuned to the distant roaring of the fire.

Aidan parked the ATV and hopped off. Jade followed. "Okay, here's the deal," he said. "I'm going to attach one end of this hose to the wagon and start driving. I need you to make sure it doesn't tangle as it unwinds. It's tricky because the sprinkler heads can get caught on the hose if you're not careful."

"Got it."

They lifted the pile of hose out, and Aidan tied the end of the hose to a bar at the back of the ATV's wagon. "I'm going to go slow. If it gets really tangled up, yell for me to stop." He jumped on the ATV and started driving away, the hose following him.

Each disk was attached to the hose several yards apart. The black plastic buffer was like a small tire around each sprinkler head, keeping them from getting ruined as they bumped along the ground. Jade shook out a piece of hose that had looped around one of the sprinklers, but the system unfurled without further mishap. It was obvious what she had to do next. She ran along the hose, which now lay on the outside of the pasture fence, and flipped the sprinkler heads over if they'd been turned upside down.

Aidan untied the hose from the ATV and drove back to where they'd started. Jade jogged to meet him.

"Now we'll pull this other hose in the opposite direction," he said. "Then the pasture will be surrounded by sprinklers."

Jade glanced north again, grateful that she didn't see any flames. "We have to hurry."

It only took a few minutes to get the other line of sprinklers in place. Aidan used a double nozzle to connect both hoses to a spigot near the pasture gate, and turned it on. The irrigation system hissed to life and fountains of misty water rose around the fence line.

Jade's heart leapt at the sight. "We did it!" She raised her hand for a high five and, after a moment's hesitation, Aidan slapped her palm with his. But there was no more time to celebrate.

"I think this is the best we can do for the sheep," he said. "I just need to get Payday out of the barn and put him out here, too, and then we'll be set." He shot her a worried glance. "How much time do you think we have left?"

"It's hard to say." Jade lifted her fingers to assess the wind speed. "The, wind seems to be dying down a little. We might have an hour. Maybe a little more? But you never know. Fire can run, which means part of it might make its way down a gully or a dip in the land. If that happens, it could show up here at any moment."

"Let's go, then." Aidan got back on the ATV, and Jade climbed on behind. They drove quickly back to the barn, now that they didn't have to worry about the teetering pile of irrigation line.

"I'll get Payday," Aidan said. "He might not appreciate being in with the sheep but he'll hopefully stay there where he's safe."

"There's only so much you can do, Aidan. Remember that, if things get out of hand around here."

He didn't answer. Just jumped off the ATV and led the way into the barn.

"I'll check on Elliott," Jade said. "I wish I could let the poor cat out of his crate to go to the bathroom and move around, but if I do he'll probably run away."

"Move him to the tack room." Aidan pointed to a door at the far end of the barn.

"He can move around in there. There's no way out." He pointed to a couple metal bowls by the wall. "Give him one of those. There's food in them for the barn cats. Pile some straw in a corner. Maybe he'll use it for a litter box."

He disappeared into a stall. Jade went to a bale of straw near the first stall and broke off a chunk for Elliott. The tack room was quiet, smelling of leather and horse. Saddles were stacked on wooden racks and bridles hung from the walls. She found a corner and piled the straw there. When she went to get the cat, Aidan was leading the beautiful tan horse Jade had seen him riding earlier today through the barn. He was talking to his four-legged buddy, and Jade overheard his words.

"Payday, my friend, you're going to stay with the sheep. I know they're a lot smaller than you, so be respectful."

Jade smiled at this unexpected display of silliness. This was a side of himself that the grumpy rancher would never show if he knew she was there. Payday was restless, jogging beside Aidan, but the horse seemed to quiet as the tall cowboy continued to speak with him. Then they left the barn and disappeared out into the smoky evening.

Jade set the food bowl inside the tack room and went to get poor Elliott. Inside the tack room, the terrified cat cowered in the back of the carrier when Jade opened the little metal door. She took out his water bowl and set it on the floor. "Hey, buddy. Want to come out to eat and drink?" Elliott just stared at her, his big, green eyes unblinking.

"Jade," Aidan called from outside the tack room door. "Ready to go up to the house?"

"Coming," she called back. "Good luck, Elliott," she told the cat. "I'll try to come back and check on you. And I'll get you out of here if the barn is in danger of catching fire. I promise."

When she exited the tack room, Aidan was looking at her with an amused expression, crinkling unfamiliar lines around his eyes. "Did you have a good talk with Elliott?"

She couldn't help but smile. Busted chatting with a cat. "It was lovely, thank you. Did you have a nice conversation with Payday?"

"You heard that?"

"Your secret is out. You're sweet with your horse."

He shook his head. "Just trying to calm him down, that's all."

"Yes, I'm sure that's all it was," Jade teased. This would have almost been fun, except when they left the barn Jade could hear the fire more clearly. It was a rumbling roar that couldn't be missed now.

Aidan turned to her with alarm in his eyes. "Is that sound what I think it is?"

"It's the fire," Jade said. "When it gets here it will be really, really loud."

It only took a moment for Aidan's expression to fall back into its usual calm appearance. "Not looking forward to that," he said, and motioned toward the ATV. "Ladies first."

Jade rolled her eyes. "So chivalrous."

He must have enjoyed her sarcasm because he smiled for a brief instant. "You've got ash all over your hair," he said. "You're going gray."

She automatically ran her fingers through her hair and realized how gritty it was. "Yuck." She peered more closely at him. "It doesn't show up as much on your blond, but yeah, you're gray, as well."

"Nothing like a deadly fire to cause premature aging."

Jade stared at him in disbelief. "Did you just make an actual joke?"

He smiled then, and it softened his harsh features, turning him suddenly and shockingly handsome. He got on the ATV, sat down in front of her and started up the engine. "We better get going. We don't have much time."

CHAPTER SIX

THERE WERE THINGS in life too big to fathom. The night they'd told Aidan that Colby was dead, Aidan's mind had gone blank. There were no synapses, nerves or levels of consciousness equipped to handle that information. Instead, he had just kept repeating *it can't be true*, while a nameless social worker sat with him in a sterile office, holding his hands.

He felt a little like that now. The smoke was piling up on the horizon, as if the wildfire was preparing for an all-out assault on his land. His house, usually a pale yellow, had taken on the same brownish-gray hue as the rest of the world. Destruction was imminent, yet all he could do was peer through the haze feeling somewhat bewildered. *It can't be true.* But it was.

He hadn't wanted Jade here. Had loathed the idea of having to try to look after someone else, when he knew in all likelihood, he'd fail. But the truth was, her knowledge, combined with her ruthless concentration and determination, was the thing keeping them going. She pushed them into taking one step, and then another. Steps that would hopefully keep them, and his animals, alive. He watched as she climbed nimbly off the ATV, rubbed her hands on the pants of her navy blue uniform and calmly assessed the turn-of-the-century farmhouse he called home.

When she looked back at him, he saw compassion in her eyes. "We don't know what's going to happen to your house, Aidan. Why don't you go inside and gather up anything you want to save and let's bring it down to the barn?" Her tone conveyed understanding, while still being matter-of-fact. He wondered if firefighters and cops sat around the office, practicing how to talk like that. She didn't wait for him to answer. "I'm going to start hosing things down."

Aidan watched her as she walked over to the hose coiled at the side of the house. She seemed so calm, while he was standing here juggling existential questions. What to save?

He had no idea. Nothing, maybe? What was there to save, really, in the wreckage of his past? He glanced around the yard, and his gaze strayed toward the back of the house. There was one thing he cared about.

He walked quickly around the back and grabbed the hose that was by the back door, pulling it over to the small garden he'd created there. It was full of every cheerful-looking flower he'd found at the nursery in Willits, a patch of rainbow in the summer-brown landscape of his ranch. Aidan turned the water on and began spraying down the small, rectangular patch of flowers.

It had been Colby's sandbox. After his son's death, he hadn't been able to look at it every day. He'd gone out with a sledge-hammer to knock the cute, corrugated-metal walls into pieces. But just before he'd struck it, he'd realized that this was his memorial. A place he could have on this big, wide ranch that would be all about his beloved son. He'd added soil and flowers, and no way was he going to let it burn now.

He contemplated the riot of color while he watered. Somehow he'd managed to keep flowers alive in this bed for a few seasons now. Almost longer than he'd managed to keep his son alive. He closed his eyes while guilt clogged his lungs, pinched his throat, clawed at his skin. He let it wreak its havoc, let it shred his very soul. He deserved this pain and worse.

When he finally opened his eyes, the flowers were flooded, sitting in muddy pools, their beautiful heads bowed under the weight of the water he'd poured over them. Aidan turned the hose on the mowed brown stubble that was his poor excuse for a lawn, and started wetting the ground that surrounded the flower bed.

"What are you doing?"

Aidan turned to see Jade jogging toward him.

"Aidan, stop. We don't have time for flowers. We need that water to save your house!"

"Don't tell me what to save." It came out in a low growl from some painful pit deep inside him. Just moments ago, he'd been glad she was here to take charge. Now he wished she'd be quiet.

She grew still, and a wary look stole over her face. "The fire is really close. You need to get in the house and find your computer, keys, family photos, financial documents, especially insurance. Please tell me you have those things packed in a go bag?"

She was right, but this was Colby's place. He hadn't been able to save his son. He was going to save this garden. He moved quickly, but kept his focus on his task, spraying down the ground.

Jade walked right up to him and put a hand over his, on the hose. Her palm was warm, small and soothing. She looked up at him, and Aidan saw that the ash was falling thicker now, gray flecks spiraling in the air between them like dirty tears. "I'll wet this down for you," she told him. "I promise. Just go inside and gather your things. We're almost out of time here."

The panic in his chest calmed. He knew she'd keep her promise. He slid his hand out from under hers, reluctant to leave the warmth and comfort of her touch. "Thanks, Jade."

"Of course. And while you're inside, Aidan? Grab any wool blankets you have. Or cotton. Something that will hold water."

She said it casually, but he heard her meaning. They might need those blankets to smother fire, to cover themselves, to try to stay alive if the fire passed over. He nodded. "Will do."

When he pushed open the back door and stepped into the kitchen, it was oddly serene. The sound of the wind and the distant roar of the fire were muffled here. The clock on the wall ticked into the silence. He stood for a moment, wanting to pretend that all was well. That he could sit down, have a cup of coffee and read a book, just like he might on a regular day. But that wasn't reality. All this, his kitchen, his books and coffee maker, would likely be gone by the end of the night.

They should have water. He went to the cupboard to the right of the sink, pulled out the four bottles he had there and filled them. Then he grabbed a canvas shopping bag hanging from the pantry doorknob and put them inside. Opening the pantry he grabbed granola bars, trail mix, the snacks he usually grabbed on a busy day, but now they'd likely be his and Jade's meals for the next while. There were a couple of apples in a bowl on the counter, so he added those to the bag, as well.

He left the bag by the front door, since that was closer to where they'd parked the ATV. He opened the hall closet and pulled out his two heaviest jackets, one for him and one for Jade. It was hard to imagine needing them when fire was bearing down on them, but they might come in handy later on. *If there is a later on.*

Jade would be happy about one thing. He had a go bag in here. A backpack filled with copies of all his most important documents. He ran with it into the small room off the living room that he used as an office and added his laptop, the cord, his phone and a charger. What else did he need? He reached into the desk drawer and found a file at the bottom labeled Colby. It had his son's birth certificate, his medical records, his death certificate. If Aidan didn't have those, who would know that his sweet little boy had ever even lived?

Aidan's stomach twisted in a grief too strong for tears and, for a moment, he almost doubled over with the pain. *No.* If it was just him here, he could fall to his knees with the weight of it. He could curl up on the floor and let the fire take him. But Jade was here because she'd tried to save him. Chip was down in the barn, mad as heck to be locked in the horse stall. Odin and Thor were out there, and the sheep and Payday. Colby had been the most loving boy, and he'd never want Aidan to turn his back on anyone or anything.

Aidan pushed his shoulders straight and zipped up the backpack. He went to his bedroom and pulled a duffel bag from the closet. He threw in jeans, his other pair of boots, socks, underwear, sweaters. He pulled his sleeping bag off the top shelf. In the bathroom, he grabbed his toothbrush, toothpaste, razor and the first aid kit he kept in the lower drawer of the cabinet under the sink. He found a couple old wool blankets in the linen cupboard. It was almost like he was heading out on a camping trip, except he'd most likely be camping on his own land, unless the house survived.

He stacked his possessions by the front door and went to face the thing he'd been dreading most. Pushing open the door just down the hall from his bedroom, he stepped inside Colby's old room. It was pretty much as it had been the night his boy had died. The twin bed with the cute cowboy quilt. Letters spelling Colby's name in white on the pale blue wall. A mobile of horses dancing near the ceiling. Colby's teddy bear, named LaLa as the little boy was learning to speak, was tucked in to the bed. Aidan picked up the bear, hugged it tight and closed his eyes.

There was still part of Colby in this room. His beautiful son had lain here at night, breathed this air, played with the toys now stacked neatly in the bookshelf. Colby had held this bear tight every night for months and months. Sometimes Aidan came in and stood just like this, trying to absorb whatever part of his son was still left, even if just a few molecules or memories. How could he walk away now, when there was a good chance it would burn? And yet, part of him wanted it all gone, up in flames. A Viking funeral fit for his brave boy who'd fought so hard.

"Aidan?"

Jade's voice in the hall startled him out of his thoughts.

She appeared in the doorway. "I loaded your stuff in the ATV, but we… Oh." Jade stepped into the room. Her eyes widened, as she took in the walls, the bed, the toys. "What—"

"I don't want to talk about it." His words came out in a snarl.

She took a step back into the hallway and held up both her hands, palms out, as if to calm him. "Okay. I respect that." She studied him, and the bear, for a long moment. "Aidan, as a first responder, I have to ask you, are there any other people on this ranch? We need to keep absolutely *everyone* safe."

He gaped at her, trying to catch her meaning. And then he realized. Seeing this room, she was wondering if he was some kind of terrible parent, or kidnapper, or something equally horrible. Shock woke him from his stupor of grief. "Of course not!" But, through his defenses, he realized that she had to ask. Lord knows what sick situations she might have seen in her work. His outrage cooled a little.

She was still watching him warily. "This is a child's room."

"It *was* a child's room."

He could see understanding dawn and spread pallor over her skin. "All right," she said quietly. "I'm so sorry to hear that. I didn't mean to interrupt. I was getting worried about you. And wondering if you have an extra bandanna I can use to cover my face. The ash is getting so thick out there."

"Top drawer of the dresser in the master bedroom." He wasn't ready to walk out of this room with her. "I just need a minute."

"Okay. I'm going to keep hosing down the house. You should leave as soon as possible to drive your belongings down to the barn." Her eyes shifted to the bear. "We're going to try to save this house, but there are no guarantees. Bring anything important with you." She disappeared out the doorway.

Aidan heard the creak of his bedroom door and the bump of her opening and closing the dresser. He listened as she went down the hall, out the front door and closed it with a thud behind her.

Only then did he go to the bed and kneel down, putting his hand on Colby's pillow. He smoothed the flannel pillowcase, as he used to smooth his son's hair back from his eyes. Clutching LaLa tight, Aidan allowed a few tears to fall, felt them sliding down his cheeks like the rain they desperately needed right now. "I love you so much, son," he whispered to the silence.

With LaLa in his arms, he walked out of his house and shut the door behind him. When he looked up, he saw a distant orange glow between the trees to the north and the black sky above.

"It's go time, Aidan." Jade was standing in his front yard, arms raised, water from the hose aimed at his roof. She'd tied his blue bandanna around her mouth and nose. "Take that stuff to the barn and come right back. I'm going to need you."

She'd changed her plans. Aidan figured that orange glow had something to do with it. "Is there still time to hose down the barn?"

Jade shook her head. "I'm going to try to buy us some time up on this end of the property, so hopefully we can do that later on." She pointed to the ATV and the trailer she'd heaped with his belongings. "Drive back up here in my truck. The keys are inside. And throw all the shovels, pickaxes, extra hose, backpack pumps, anything you can think of that might be useful in there, too."

He nodded absently, still caught in the

emotion he'd felt in Colby's room. Thankfully, Jade didn't say anything more. Just took the hose and started dragging it across the yard and up the driveway, toward the entrance to his property. She clearly had a plan, and he'd best follow it.

He squeezed one hand into a fist, digging his nails into his palm, using new pain to replace the old. He needed to clear his head if he was going to help Jade save his ranch. Forcing his leaden limbs to get moving, Aidan ran for the ATV. He tucked LaLa into his duffel of clothes, and climbed aboard. As he turned the vehicle around, he glanced at the sky again. It seemed to be glaring right back at him with venomous orange eyes. "You've taken a lot from me," he yelled, as if the fire were disease, loss, grief and guilt sucked into one roiling, choking mass. "You're not going to take my animals. And you won't hurt Jade. I won't let you."

Then he gunned the engine and headed for the barn.

JADE HAULED THE hose as far up the driveway as it would go, and then ran back to collect the hose they'd used to water the flowers.

She coiled it quickly and ran back up the driveway. What she'd seen just now wouldn't leave her mind. Aidan standing in that little boy's room, clutching a teddy bear. Aidan in his front yard, looking lost, still holding that bear. She didn't know the story but, still, it broke her heart. "It *was* a child's room." His voice had shattered when he said it.

All the more reason to save the poor guy now. It seemed he'd already had too much tragedy in his life. Her job was to minimize the damage this fire would do. She needed to put aside all her ideas about what might have happened to Aidan and his family. That wasn't her business. Saving this ranch, and the forlorn rancher who owned it, was.

She was screwing the two hoses together when Aidan drove up in her truck. He got out and knelt down next to her. "I can finish that."

"I've got it." Her voice came out sharper than maybe it should have. He looked startled but she didn't explain. Couldn't explain the protective instinct she felt for him now. She gave one last twist to knit the hose ends together and then stood. "You should put your bandanna back on," she told him. "It won't do much but it can help protect your lungs a little."

She brushed past him, went to the truck and climbed up into the bed. Opening the tool case, she pulled out the drip torch, noting that the canister was full. Good. There were a few extra flares in the box, too, so she shoved them into her belt. Then she grabbed the shovel and pickax Aidan had brought, and handed them to him. He eyed the drip torch in her hand. "I'm not sure I want to know what you're going to do with that."

Jade set it down next to her. "Probably not."

He'd tied the bandanna on and he looked like a tall, dusty, tired bandit. His gaze flicked to the sky behind her. The orange glow was brighter, the fire was closer. Ash was all around them, and the air felt warmer.

"Things are going to get ugly soon, aren't they?"

Jade looked back at Aidan and tried to read the expression in his eyes. They were blue, red-rimmed from smoke, but gave away nothing else but the same deep weariness she'd sensed since they met. "It is. But listen to me. If we work together, communicate constantly and don't get separated, we can do this. Okay?"

He nodded. "Just tell me what you need."

"Will you go turn the water on for this hose? I'm going to haul it farther up the road."

He turned and jogged back to the house. Jade picked up the drip torch with her free hand, and hauled the hose up the driveway until she was at the firebreak they'd tried to widen earlier. Again, she wished the plowed area was wider, but it would have to do. She felt the hose jerk as the water pressure arrived and she compressed the nozzle, spraying the firebreak, wetting down the scraped earth and the grass on the near side of it.

Her progress was achingly slow. She needed more hoses, a crew of firefighters. A small voice in her head whispered that this was futile. She stamped it out like an ember. She couldn't let thoughts like that have airtime or they'd grow just like the fire.

Aidan emerged from the thick air like a gray ghost. Visibility was going down by the minute. "What's the plan?"

The fire was getting louder, a steady, distant roar. Jade had to raise her voice to be head above the sound. "We're going to set a fire on the far side of this firebreak."

Aidan stopped in his tracks. "You're going to light my ranch on fire? I thought that's what we're trying to prevent."

"It is." Jade pointed to the grass and bushes that covered the ground between the firebreak and the trees. "If we can burn this before the fire gets here, we deprive it of fuel. Then it might burn off to the sides, and spare the buildings on your ranch."

"The wind, though. How will we keep the flames from blowing back onto us?"

"Water. Plus I'm hoping the wind will die as night falls."

He gaped at her. "You're *hoping*?"

Hope was all she had. "It's worth the risk. Setting a backfire can buy us extra time."

It was a gamble. But it was all they had. Jade waited, giving him time to think. After a moment he held out his hand. "Okay then."

Jade handed him the hose and tried to sound more confident than she felt. "Spray the firebreak as far as you can on either side of the driveway."

He hesitated. "Are you sure about this?"

She wasn't sure about anything. "Do you hear that noise? That's the fire bearing down on us like a truck with no brakes. Think of a backfire as one of those runaway-truck ramps you see on steep freeways. It's not an ideal solution, but it just might slow it down."

Aidan nodded. Her analogy seemed to have worked, because he walked a few steps away and started spraying an area of the firebreak she hadn't gotten to yet.

Heart thudding hard against her sternum, Jade crossed the firebreak and headed a few yards past the perimeter fence, putting Aidan's ranch behind her. Then she pulled a flare from her belt. Carefully, she tugged off the cap, yanked the tab and hit the flare on the strike plate. With a hiss, it ignited. Using all the desperate energy she had, she chucked the flare as hard as she could toward the fire. It landed somewhere in the distant brush near where the first oak trees rose up.

Good, but not good enough.

"No offense, but I think I might have a stronger arm." Aidan had dragged the hose up behind her. He must have forgiven her for lighting his ranch on fire, because a slight smile tugged at his mouth when she raised her brows at him.

"Really?" The teasing helped calm her nerves a little. "You know you're talking to the captain of the Shelter Creek Hot Shots softball team. And pull your bandanna up."

He ignored her, of course. "How does that compare with college baseball?"

She took the hose and handed him a flare. "Let's find out. Just aim right into the trees, as far as you can off to the right a little." She understood the grimace on his face. "I know. They're beautiful, but they're going to burn anyway. This way they'll burn to save your ranch."

He nodded and pulled the cap off the flare. He hesitated for a moment, squinting into the smoke-shrouded landscape in front of them.

"Those pines over there look stressed from drought." Jade pointed to the scraggly stand. "They're like kindling. I'd aim there."

Aidan lit the flare, brought his arm back and his leg up like a pitcher, and sent the flare flying into the pines. A direct hit. He glanced at her, a vaguely disappointed expression on his face. "It's not working."

"It will. Just be patient." She pointed to where she'd thrown hers. A thin column of smoke was rising. "Mine's just getting started now. She handed him her third and last flare. "Try this one, off to the left a bit."

He grinned suddenly, surprisingly, his teeth white in his ash-dusted face. "Aha. So you're admitting I throw a little better than you?"

"I'm admitting that you're a whole lot taller than me. You have more leverage."

He laughed a little wildly and chucked the flare so it arced off to the left, sailing an impossible distance before it landed somewhere behind a thicket of scrubby oak. "Leverage. That's what it is, huh? I was thinking maybe it was talent?"

Jade had to laugh, too. It was a relief to have this cocky sportsman in front of her instead of the broken man she'd found in the house a while ago. "Okay, so if you ever move to Shelter Creek, I *might* let you on my softball team."

He peered through the smoky air. "What do we do now?"

"Hope they all catch. And you're going to move back a little and keep hosing down everything within reach on the ranch side of the firebreak. I'm going to take this drip torch and go light some more fires. The faster we get this area burning, the better."

"What happens if the main fire gets here before all this stuff burns down?"

"We'll have a really big fire on our hands." Jade put a hand on his arm. "Don't stress, okay? Let's just take this a step at a time."

"I'm not stressed," he muttered.

"Right." She couldn't help smiling at his grumpy, macho streak. Maybe after being caught in such a vulnerable moment in the house, he was trying to put his protective shell back on. But it was too late. She'd seen through the cracks in his crusty facade. And, as much as she hated to think that he might have lost a child, she could see now that this tough, independent rancher was actually a vulnerable person underneath. It certainly made her understand why he didn't want to let anybody else in. If he carried that kind of pain inside, it must be easier to keep all emotions at bay.

Nothing like a fire to keep things real,

her boss, Mitch, always said. She sent a silent plea to him, her mentor, that she was doing the right thing. Then she walked up the driveway, toward the fires they'd set. The flares were a start, but she needed to help things along.

Several yards past the boundary fence of the property, she turned off to the right and headed into the woods. Scrubby oaks, stunted from drought and heat, survived here surrounded by brambles and brush. Jade pushed her way through prickly leaves and thorny blackberry tendrils that grabbed at her pant legs. She kept going until she was pretty sure she was farther away from the driveway than Aidan's barn was. Only then did she hold her drip torch to some tangled stems of shriveled bracken. It only took a moment for the flaming fuel to set it alight.

Jade quickly retraced her steps back to the driveway, setting fires as she went. Strangely, there was something satisfying about the sizzle of ignition and the first small flames that leaped to life. Maybe all firefighters were part pyromaniac. Maybe you had to be fascinated by fire to spend your life trying to understand it, and risking your safety to stop it.

She crossed the gravel driveway and plunged into the wood on the other side. Holding her drip torch up, she jogged through the woods, dodging brambles, ducking under tree branches. She needed to get far enough away from Aidan's house, his propane tank and his irrigated pasture full of sheep. Once she was pretty sure she had the distance she needed, she peeked through the trees, trying to make sure she hadn't gone beyond Aidan's firebreak. The churned up ground was visible through the branches and the wire fence, so she ducked back into the woods and started setting things alight. She had plenty of help. The flares they'd thrown out earlier were bright blazes now, sending out embers to start new fires that climbed the oaks and claimed the shrubs.

A small cottontail rabbit raced by her and Jade whispered an apology. Though maybe she was saving its life by getting it out of here before the main fire arrived.

Jade jogged back to the driveway, starting fires along the way but making sure she stayed ahead of the flames. When she reached the driveway she made a dash back to Aidan, arriving just as he threw down the hose and started toward her.

He grabbed her by the upper arms and pulled her against him for a brief instant. "I thought I was going to lose you in there. It's really starting to burn."

Jade's skin felt hot as she pulled away, though it could be from her dash out of the flames. "Welcome to the world of firefighting. There's always some excitement happening somewhere." She took the hose from him to cover her confusion over the oddly sweet comfort she'd felt in his arms.

She pulled the hose off to the left of the driveway and trained the spray on the grass at the edge of the firebreak. "With the wind direction, I suspect this is where the fire might jump, if it's going to jump anywhere. Let's really soak it." Watching the flames leap and grow on the other side of the boundary fence, her heart picked up speed. "Did you grab those backpack pumps? Why don't you go fill them up? We might get some embers coming over soon. We have to be ready to put out any spot fires."

"Okay. I'll take the truck and be back as soon as possible. Stay safe."

"You, too." He turned to go but she called him back. "Aidan? Keep your eyes open. The main fire might seem like it's far away but it could show up almost anywhere, at any time."

He nodded and got into the truck. When he drove down the driveway, the truck disappeared almost instantly into the thick, sludgy air.

Jade listened to the hiss and crackle of the nearby flames, and the growl of the wildfire rumbling her way. Everything was taking on a surreal quality—the darkening sky, the thick, smoky air, this ranch where a lonely man had been hiding out with a heart full of pain.

Was it possible that she'd ended up here for a reason? Because even without the threat of fire, Aidan seemed like a guy in need of a rescue.

CHAPTER SEVEN

AIDAN HEAVED THE full backpack pumps back into the truck bed. He'd filled them at the faucet behind his house, which had given him one last chance to say goodbye to Colby's garden. Now, driving back up the driveway to where Jade had set the backfire, he felt like he was driving toward hell. In the ten minutes it had taken to fill the pumps, the fire they'd set had grown into a twenty-foot wall of flame, devouring everything on the other side of the firebreak. It was almost dark out now, an eerie dusk where the silhouettes of trees stood out stark and black against the vivid orange flames just before they were consumed.

The unreal quality of it was disconcerting. This was still his ranch. There, through the darkening haze, was his house, and the spot on the front porch where Chip loved to sleep in the morning sun. There was the firepit he'd built back when fire had been a comforting, fun thing to have around. But the smoke blurred all the outlines and changed all the colors. Everything seemed like a troubled dream where familiar things looked inexplicably different and were no longer his to keep.

Aidan's pulse thrummed with the uncertainty of it all, but when he pulled the truck up next to Jade, she looked as calm as if she were watering her garden on a Sunday afternoon. Details had disappeared with the glare of the fire behind her. She was a black form, a shadow puppet. "Glad you could make it," she called. "The party's just getting started around here."

He got it. She was trying to keep him at ease in a terrifying situation. So he'd try to do the same for her. "I don't remember getting my invitation to this particular party." He had to shout over all the noise. Crackling, hissing, snapping and always that roar from the main wildfire, even louder than before.

Her bandanna hid most of her face, but he could see relief in her eyes. After his near meltdown in Colby's room, she was probably glad he was holding it together. "I

think this party has mandatory attendance."
She came closer to eye what he'd brought
in the truck. "Why don't you put on one of
those pumps and take a walk along the firebreak? Make sure there are no embers getting started on this side."

Aidan went around to the truck bed and
wrestled the pump away from the tools
stacked next to it. It was basically a big
sack filled with water that he could wear
on his back. He staggered a little as he got
the straps situated. Five gallons of water
was an awkward load. He arranged the hose
and took the nozzle in hand. "Maybe bring
a pickax, too," Jade called. "If you have a
chance to put embers out with dirt, go for
it. That way you'll conserve the water in
your pump."

His pump was on his back, he had the
pickax, but it was hard to walk away from
her. Aidan knew Jade didn't need his protec-
tion. She was far more competent in this fire
than he was. But she was a petite woman
and she looked even smaller against the towering flames. He didn't want her hurt on his
land. On his watch.

But that was his ego talking. She was the

one saving the day here. If she hadn't shown up, there'd be no backfire and, thus, no way to send the fire around his ranch. It would just be him, hosing things down and waiting for the full strength of the fire to crash over him.

Despite the heat, a chill ran over his skin at the thought. He'd always assumed he could handle everything on his own. It was easy to see how wrong he'd been.

Strange that ever since Colby died he'd thought he wanted to die, too. Some days he'd even thought up ways to make it happen. But faced with it now, his whole self reared up with a resounding *no*. Not because he was looking forward to some bright future. More because Jade's life was at stake. And innocent animals' lives were at stake. Or maybe it was just that his competitive streak had kicked in and he wouldn't let this fire win.

The flames across the firebreak were alive and hungry, jumping quickly from bush to tree, gobbling up grass, belching flames ten, twenty, even thirty feet in the air. It was tempting to aim the hose on them, just to feel like he was in some kind of control, but thanks to Jade he knew better. They wanted that area to burn, so he had to let it be and focus on this near side of the firebreak. Aidan stomped through the dry grass alongside the plowed strip of land, looking for sparks, smoke, any hint that the fire had jumped the break. Nothing. That was good news.

The wind was picking up, and it was different now. Not the steady blowing that had brought the fire closer to them all day, but disorganized gusts that twisted and turned. It sent sparks shooting up in the air. The wind caught an ember and flung it over Aidan's head. He turned, trying to see where it landed, but there were bushes behind him, it was almost dark. He should grab one of the headlamps he'd thrown into Jade's truck. He usually wore them when he had to go out at night and check on the livestock. They'd come in handy now.

He started toward the truck, but then he saw it. The tiny flame sputtering where he'd last seen that ember. His heart jolted. This was it. His first spot fire. Even though it was barely more than a single flame, his pulse pounded in his temples. He needed to stay calm. There'd be a lot more of these before the night was over.

Aidan walked quickly toward the flame. It caught onto the grass around it, doubling in size almost immediately. Now it was the size of a campfire. Now it was double that. He opened the valve on his pump and sprayed until it sizzled out. Then he stomped on where it had ignited to be sure it was gone. Steam rose up, infused with charcoal, making his eyes water even more.

"Aidan, *behind you!*"

He turned at the sound of Jade's voice, and there was another flame fluttering to life where another ember had landed. He flipped on the nozzle of his pump and doused it. Something bright landed just to the right of him. Instantly the dry grass flared up. He was going to run out of water soon if he wasn't careful. He shouldered his pickax and brought it down hard, breaking the soil up around the flames, and tossed the dirt on to smother them. Hack and toss, hack and toss. Sweat slicked his forehead, but finally he had the fire out.

He glanced around. The gusts of wind seemed to have quieted, at least for a moment. It was a deceptive lull, the crouch of a big cat before it leaped on its prey. He jogged to where Jade was using her ax to bury another flame closer to the driveway.

"What's the plan?" He hated that he needed reassurance. That he was totally out of his comfort zone right here on his own ranch.

Jade threw more dirt onto the fire and stomped on it with her boot. "Out, damned spot."

He gaped at her. "You're quoting Shakespeare? Now?"

She gestured at the wall of flame twenty yards away from them. "Is there a better time?"

There she went again, using her offbeat humor to keep things calm. "To answer your question, the plan is to hold this line for as long as we can, to keep the backfire where we want it. Keep chasing after any embers. But pretty soon the real fire is going to catch up. Do you feel the difference in the wind? A big fire makes its own weather."

He wanted to know more. "And when it gets here…"

Her mouth thinned into a frown. "I think

at that point we should cede our ground. Get down to the house and focus on saving that. Remember, our goal was to slow the fire and send the brunt of it around us. After that, we just try to save what we can and survive. We're never going to stop it entirely."

He'd known it. He'd expected her to say it. But it echoed in his ears and shot adrenaline through his body. This was it. And he could be upset and worried, or he could put one foot in front of the other and fight like hell.

He knew a little bit about that. He'd been trudging forward in a fog as thick as this smoke for years now.

He turned away in time to see an ember sail past him. He followed it and slammed it with the flat end of his ax before it could catch. When he turned around, there were flames between him and Jade. She had her back turned, putting out a different flare-up. "Jade, watch out!"

She turned to look and ran backward with the hose. She trained it on the new flames and he did the same with his pump. But it was Jade who put out the flames, calmly moving the hose back and forth between one spot fire and another, steam rising and blending with the smoke.

Farther along the firebreak, a bush flared. Aidan stumbled over the plowed earth and used his pump to put it out. Moments later, another bush caught, then a swath of grass behind it. The smoke and the night turned the world black, except where the orange glow from the flames lit it up. In this whack-a-mole world, Aidan ran from one fire to the next, throwing dirt, dumping water, switching out his pump at the truck and dashing back toward the firebreak to stop another ember from becoming something more.

Adrenaline made his breathing uneven and he worked to slow it, to steady himself so he wasn't gulping in the thick smoke. He glanced at Jade but she was yards away, digging up dirt to stop yet another patch of flame.

Across the firebreak the flames still roared. Shouldn't they die down soon? So when the main fire hit, there'd be nothing but ash in front of it? Aidan looked again. Maybe the flames did seem a little smaller. Or maybe that was his wishful thinking. Or lack of oxygen in all this smoke.

Aidan's pump was out of water again. He had one pack left. He dashed for the truck, switched backpacks and started back, only to see the grass flare up to the left of the driveway, between the firebreak and his house. "Jade, bring the hose!"

She didn't hear him as she continued to put out a spot fire that raced a few feet ahead of her through the grass. Maybe she couldn't hear him because the fire was suddenly a whole lot louder, roaring in Aidan's ears like a furious giant. The sky brightened behind the firebreak, flashing orange and red. The main fire was almost here, but it wasn't the only thing turning the evening into day. There were flames visible on the ridge to the right. The ridge that separated his ranch from Nellie's. Regret stabbed him as he realized her ranch was likely destroyed already. Her buildings and pastures were the fuel that had those flames rising and falling, shimmering and flickering.

Like Jade had said, the fire could come from any direction. Now it was coming at them from two sides.

Aidan froze. He hadn't imagined this. He felt cornered. Trapped.

Jade must have seen the new fire, too, because she came running and shoved the hose into his hand. "Bring this back to your house. Start spraying everything down. I'll get the truck." Then she was gone, running to collect their tools. As he wrestled the hose along the bumpy driveway, she loaded the pickup and jumped in, revving the engine as she turned around.

Aidan stumbled down the driveway with the backpack pump flopping awkwardly on his back. The hose coil trailed behind him, a giant snake at his heels. Once in his yard, he headed for the side of the house closest to the fire. Maybe the flames up on Nellie's ridge would stay on the northeast path that the wind had been taking all day. If that happened, they could miss the house. They might even miss his barn.

Or they might run right down the side of the hill and take everything he owned with them.

Aidan turned the hose on the house, wishing he had a real fire hose instead of this measly garden hose. Jade pulled the truck into the driveway and jumped out. She ran for the place where they'd joined the two hoses together before, and started twisting. It only took a moment for Aidan to realize what she was doing. He ran to help, arriving just in time to get sprayed with water as she separated the two hoses.

"Oof." The water was cold on his chest, paralyzing his lungs and causing the fabric of his T-shirt to cling.

"Just trying to cool you off a little." Jade's smile was brief and grim. "Take your hose and find another faucet. That way we can both try to save this place. Once it gets bad, we'll retreat down to the barn and spray that."

"It's not bad now?" Flames meandered toward them through the grass and bushes, as more embers sailed in and ignited the dry hillside above his house.

"It's not perfect, that's for sure."

His harsh laugh surprised them both. "You have a talent for understatement." He turned away and ran toward the other corner of the house, and the faucet there, the hose trailing behind him.

Once his hose was hooked up, Aidan sprayed water over the walls and roof, conscious of the growing fire at the top of his property. It was hard to say if Jade's backfire had helped or not. Hopefully it would slow the coming fire, but by jumping the firebreak like this, it was putting a lot of pressure on them. Still, if this hillside burned now, maybe it would help slow the main blaze when it came.

"Make sure you spray the ground all around the house, too," Jade yelled. The smoke was so thick, she was barely visible in the murky, black air. Aidan kept spraying, alternating between the roof, the side and the back of the house, and the ground around. The fire on the hillside, their backfire gone astray, was getting closer, the flames almost as tall as he was as they found more fuel to consume. Aidan watched with uneasiness churning in his stomach. They were playing a game of chicken here. How long until Jade gave up?

Suddenly she emerged from the thick smoke, just a few yards away. "We need to go," she told him. "It's too close!"

This was it. They had to cede ground to the fire just like she'd said. Aidan looked up at his house, an angular shadow looming over them, backlit by the eerie orange glow.

His feet felt rooted to the ground. This had been his home for so long now.

"Aidan, there's not much time." Jade took the hose from his hands. "I'm going to shut this off now. We've got to take the hoses with us. Mine is already in the truck.

He followed her to the faucet and waited while she turned off the water and unscrewed the hose. Looking up at his beautiful old farmhouse with its wide plank siding, the carved porch railing, the gabled windows on the second story, he felt tears come and swallowed hard. This home had stood here since the early 1900s. It had seen families raised, joy, love and, lately, so much pain. Aidan closed his eyes, envisioning Colby's room one last time. The blue walls he'd painted with such care, his son's bed, the toys, the books. The ache in his heart threatened to split open his chest as he wished Godspeed to whatever energy or love was still there.

Jade's gentle touch on his arm brought him back. "We have to go," she reminded him. Her voice was quiet, but he could hear the urgency behind it.

He nodded. She was right. They had to

focus on the barn now. On saving the animals. Still, it was hard to walk away, knowing that despite their efforts his house might soon be ashes.

"Aidan." Jade's voice held an edge of command now. "We need to move."

The glow behind the house was rising, the wildfire lighting up the night with its horrific power. He knew in his heart the house couldn't possibly survive it. Maybe they wouldn't either. The thought brought no fear for himself. At least, then, he could be with his son.

But Jade wasn't part of that mourning. Jade was caught up in this mess because she'd driven back here one more time, to try to save his sorry skin. He couldn't let her suffer for that choice. "If it burns, it burns," he said aloud, more in defiance of the approaching fire than to Jade. "Let's go."

He squared his shoulders and followed Jade's shadowy form as she ran along the side of the house and back to the truck.

CHAPTER EIGHT

JADE GUIDED HER truck through the smoky darkness and tried to plot her next move. She'd been studying for her fire captain's exam, had gone through scenario after scenario in her textbooks, but her lessons had never taught her what to do when stranded on a burning ranch with a confusing, cranky and probably grieving rancher who was now going to lose pretty much everything he hadn't lost already.

The main thing at this point was simply to stay alive, but she really wanted to save his barn. She'd lost hope of saving the house. The fire was going to come at it too strong. She should have set her backfire sooner, though honestly, even if she had, she didn't know if she would have been able to keep it from jumping the firebreak. They'd needed more than just the two of them to keep it under control.

If they got really lucky, maybe the fire would pass over the house. They'd wetted it down so well. But it was an old building, the wood weathered and dry inside. Plus, there were too many places for embers to lodge and start burning. Spaces between the boards on the siding, between the porch floorboards, between the decorative shingles over the front door.

But sometimes in fires there were miracles. The one house that ended up unscathed, when the rest of the block burned. The people and animals who managed to survive. Hopefully they'd get a miracle or two here tonight.

At least the barn might not require a miracle to make it through. It had a metal roof and a lot of defensible space since Aidan had put gravel all around it. Bless him and his desire to keep things less muddy in the winter. As long as the pump held up and they could wet the building down, Jade was pretty confident they could save it. Unless the fire came down the hill behind the well house.

Jade glanced out her side window. "Up there on the ridge, where it's burning now, that's where you rode off to get the sheep today, right?"

He grimaced. "Yup. It's my friend Nellie's ranch."

Jade remembered the quaint outbuildings and the sweet farmhouse she'd circled, banging on the windows, trying to see if anyone was home. "I drove out there to evacuate her, but she was already gone. The place was deserted."

"I got her out as soon as I saw the fire. I was going to go into town today, but when I got to the part of the road that overlooks the valley I could see the smoke. So I went to Nellie's and helped load up her llamas and mules."

Jade navigated the truck carefully around behind the barn. There wasn't room under the carport, but she parked right up close to it, hoping the barn would shelter the vehicle from the flames. Aidan's truck was there, too. "And then you risked your own life to go get her sheep."

He glared at her, his inner grump on display. "Don't paint me as some kind of hero. Nellie has been really good to me. Like a mom. I wasn't going to let her sheep die up there. That's all."

When he got all huffy like this, she couldn't resist poking at him. "So you saved her, and saved her sheep, but you don't want anyone to notice it?"

In the dim glow from the light above the carport, she could see that he'd pressed his lips into a thin line she was starting to recognize. He did that when he was trying not to smile. "Yeah," he said. "Something like that."

"Okay, then. Now that we have that straight, let's water down the barn. And let's pay special attention to the side that faces Nellie's property. I think we're going to have fire running down that slope."

They got out of the truck and got the tools from the back. "Let's lean these on the wall just inside the barn," Jade said. "That way we know where they are and we can grab them easily if we need them."

"Want me to refill the backpack pumps?"

"Absolutely. We can put those near the entrance of the barn, too." She held up the hoses they'd brought from the house. "Where should I attach these?"

"I've already got a hose on the west side of the barn. It's where I wash the horses. And there's another here." Aidan turned on one of the headlamps he'd brought and shined it on a faucet at the side of the carport. "So let's bring these hoses to the front of the barn. There are faucets on both front corners."

"I know I've been critical of some of your ranching habits," Jade told him. "But you have great plumbing on this property."

He burst out laughing, a rich sound in the bleak night. "No one has ever told me that before."

"Glad I could be the first."

They walked side by side to the front of the barn. Jade hugged the coils of hose and Aidan carried their pickaxes and shovels. Jade hated to sour the mood, but she needed to make sure they had their plans in place. "Our goal right now is to get the barn, and everything around it, as wet as possible. But if the fire comes racing down that hill too fast or too high, we have to have a backup plan. I think at that point we should get in the pasture with the sheep."

She could see Aidan frown in the dim

glare of the headlamp he carried. "Thor and Odin are going to be riled up. They might not be hospitable to you or Chip. And definitely not Elliott."

"We can drive a truck in there if we need to, and the animals and I can stay in the cab. You've got sprinklers on in there. It's our safest bet, I think."

He nodded. "So that's plan B?"

"Yes."

"Do firefighters always make this many plans? Or is that just you?"

She smiled nervously, noting the fiery wall growing at that top of the ranch. It looked like the main fire had caught up with their backfire. She squinted, trying to see if it was going to veer around the ranch, or jump right over the fire line and come straight at them. "We make lots of plans. Especially nowadays when fires are burning hotter than ever. We can't predict what's going to happen. So we try to have a plan for every situation."

"Is there a plan C?"

"The pond."

He glanced at her in alarm. "We get in the water. With Chip and the cat."

"Yup."

He was silent for a moment, as if taking it in. "Okay, then."

They'd reached the front of the barn and Aidan went inside to put the tools down. He must have flipped a switch, because a floodlight in front of the barn came on. It was sheer relief to have it. The sky was fully dark now, which made the orange flames heading their way even more terrifying.

With the light on, it was easier to find the faucets Aidan had mentioned, at the front corners of the barn. As soon as Jade got the hoses attached, she went to the east side of the structure, near the steep hillside. She sprayed the barn wall, starting with the eaves and working her way down. Three deer came bounding down the hill and ran right past her, through the pool of light in front of the barn, their hooves clattering on the gravel.

Aidan came out from behind the barn with the backpack pumps and stopped abruptly when the deer ran right in front of him. They disappeared into the darkness beyond the barn, and Jade said a little prayer for them. It was hard to think about all the animals that would be affected by this fire.

She moved along the front of the barn, soaking the wood. "Aidan," she called. "Can you close the barn doors? I need to spray them off."

He set the pumps down and went to close the doors. Jade kept the hose moving, trying to soak every inch of the wood. Up the driveway, clouds of red and orange flames suddenly billowed into the air. It took a moment for Jade to realize what caused the flare up. Aidan's house was burning.

Words failed her. She looked over at him, horrified. He'd seen it, too. He'd stopped filling the pumps and was standing, staring, letting the water from his hose run onto the ground. This was awful, but they needed those pumps filled.

"Aidan." She dragged her hose over to where he stood, continuing to spray off the barn while she spoke to him. "You have to let it go. We have to keep our focus on fighting this fire right here at the barn. You want to save it, don't you?"

It took a moment, but eventually her words seemed to reach him. He nodded once and picked up the hose again. When he knelt to fill the pump, he turned his back to her.

Jade pulled her hose around to the far side of the barn, to give Aidan some space. Her heart was breaking for him, but she was more resolved than ever to save this barn, no matter what.

AIDAN SPRAYED DOWN the western wall of his barn and watched the ravenous flames devour his house. Sparks exploded, fire billowed and it was hard to know if the tears on his face were sorrow for what he was losing, or relief that his house, with so much grief inside it, was well and truly gone. He was grateful that Jade was giving him space. He didn't need her witnessing the barrage of emotions washing through him.

In a weird way, he was grateful they had a long night of firefighting in front of them. The task he was doing now, and the ones ahead, were the things keeping him sane. Without the structure they provided, he wasn't sure what he'd do. Was it possible for someone to feel much all at once?

A sudden loud hissing sound jolted him out of his thoughts, and he stumbled a few paces back when he saw a huge spire of flame shoot up in a column near his burning house. He'd never seen or heard anything like it before, but he was pretty sure he knew what it was.

Jade ran around the corner. "The propane tank is venting," she gasped when she stumbled to a stop beside him. "That's a good thing. It should keep it from exploding."

She was sweet to come check on him, and to make sure he wasn't too scared, but her concern humiliated Aidan enough to make him tamp down his emotions. "One thing to be grateful for, I guess. Do you think the barn is wet enough?"

"It better be." She pointed up into the sky, and Aidan looked. It would have been beautiful if it weren't so dangerous. Embers were swirling toward them on a chaotic wind wrought by the oncoming fire. Just then, grass at the edge of the gravel area around the barn caught fire.

"Go," Jade commanded, and Aidan ran with his hose, spraying the flames into oblivion. When he looked up, Jade was shouldering a backpack pump. She staggered a little as she shifted the weight on her shoulders.

He rushed toward her. "That's heavy. Are you okay?"

If looks could be lethal, hers would kill in seconds. "I'm *fine*. I fight fires a lot, remember?"

Amazing how he managed to wedge his foot into his mouth even as his ranch was incinerating. "Sorry." She seemed so tiny to him. If that pump was awkward for his six-foot-three frame, it seemed impossible that she could manage it at five-foot-something.

But clearly she could, because with one last stern look she said, "We need to be ready for anything. I'm going to try to defend the side of the barn closest to the hillside and the well, and back by the carport. You're in charge of the front here and the west side. But yell if you need me, okay?"

"Likewise." She turned to go but he wasn't ready. He didn't want to part with her so angry and him such a fool. "Jade, hang on." She turned to look at him, eyebrows raised in a question. "Just now, I was dumb. You're the toughest firefighter I've ever met."

She smiled. He could see it in her eyes. "Don't tell me how many you've actually met. Let me just enjoy the compliment." Then she turned away, walked to the barn and pulled open the big door.

Aidan watched her go inside and come back out with the ax she called her Pulaski. "You look ready for anything," he called.

"You better believe it," she yelled back. "Get yourself some tools, just in case."

"Yes, ma'am."

"That's boss to you," she tossed back, and jogged around the corner of the barn, out of sight.

His world was burning, but Aidan smiled as he watched her go. Then he took her advice, found a pickax and shovel, and heaved a backpack pump on. He tightened his bandanna around his nose and mouth and tried not to think about the state of his lungs. He'd been breathing in ash and smoke for hours now. As the fire got closer the air felt warmer. Aidan knew warm might turn to hot before the night was through, but he pushed that thought aside. They'd survive. They had to.

Another ember lit the grass, but he put it

out easily with his hose. As the fire raced toward him alongside the driveway, it sent more and more firebrands flying his way. Flames started up to his right, then to his left and now there was fire right behind him.

"Jade!" He wasn't holding ground here. He bellowed her name one more time and she came running, hose in hand, stopping to put out a fire over by where he usually parked his truck. This was all so surreal. His house was a tower of roaring flames, and now his other landmarks were catching fire. The hitching post by the water trough looked like a torch until Jade sluiced it with her hose. The spot alongside the driveway where the deer sometimes slept, leaving the grass flat in the mornings, went up. It was beyond the reach of his hose, so Aidan used his pickax and covered it with dirt, then added a little water from his backpack pump for good measure.

Just then, another sound penetrated his ears, somewhere between the oncoming jet-engine roar of the fire, the venting propane tank and his own blood pounding in his veins. Barking. *Oh no. Chip.*

Aidan turned in time to see his dog run

out of the barn and stop, searching the smoky air for his master. Chip must have been spooked by the fire and climbed right over the stall door. Aidan had only closed the lower half. Panic washed over Aidan's skin like an icy wave. He'd lost too much today. He couldn't lose Chip, too.

"Chip, sit!" His command only succeeded in giving the dog a destination to run to. Chip came barreling for him, stubby tail wagging, then let out a yelp. He must have stepped on an ember in the gravel. The dog veered off into the darkness, terrified.

"Chip, come!" Aidan dropped the hose and fumbled for his headlamp, shining it in the direction Chip had run. The smoke was too thick, the particles beamed the light right back at him. "Chip, come on!"

Jade appeared at his side. She grabbed the hose. "Don't let this melt, we need it."

Aidan turned to her, frantic. "I've lost Chip."

"I heard. Try to calm down, okay? Panic is not our friend right now. Take slow shallow breaths."

Aidan tried to slow his breathing. Chip was smart. He wouldn't run right into fire.

"How about you walk a little ways in the direction he went, but don't go too far away from the barn." Jade's words were slow and measured, like she was talking to a child. "We don't want to get so far apart that we won't be able to help each other if anything goes wrong. Chip got startled, but he might double back to you if he hears your voice. Try to sound normal."

They both looked at each other then, and burst out laughing. Except their laughter had an edge of hysteria to it.

"Normal?" Jade giggled and waved her hand at the sparks falling around them. "Sure, this is totally normal. Come on, Aidan, act normal." Then her gaze shifted to a spot behind him. "Fire." And she was gone, running toward flames that were igniting near the trough and spraying them down with water.

Aidan returned his pickax to the barn, then stepped into the dark smoke that was oozing over his ranch. He shuffled forward blindly, his headlamp almost useless. Chip had run in the direction of the sheep pasture, which was good because they had sprinklers there, but bad because the guard dogs wouldn't welcome him. "Chip," he called softly into the smoke and darkness. "Chip, come on, buddy."

He wandered around for what seemed like forever, but was probably only five or ten minutes. He put out a few spot fires with his backpack pump, kept calling for Chip and tried to keep up hope when despair crept in. Finally, he turned around and circled the barn. It broke his heart to give up on Chip, but he had to get back and help Jade. And there, in the carport, was Chip, perched in the driver's seat of the ATV.

"You've got to be kidding me." He walked slowly to his dog, not wanting to scare him off again. On any other day, he'd be laughing right now. Chip was sitting upright, looking like he was ready to start up the vehicle and drive away. Except they were in a fire, and Chip was holding one paw up, looking terrified and miserable.

"Hey, buddy," Aidan said softly, holding out his knuckles for Chip to sniff. "You had me pretty worried there."

Chip nuzzled his hand, and Aidan pet his soft head, then carefully scooped the dog up. "We're in a bit of an emergency here, buddy.

I'm going to hose off your paws, and then I have to put you back in that stall. I can keep you safe as long as you stay there. I promise." He carried Chip to the hose and ran water over the dog's paws for a couple minutes. Chip whimpered but stayed still. When Aidan turned off the water and aimed his headlamp directly at Chip's paws, he could see that the front paw pads were pink and raw. "Ouch."

He should keep the water on for longer, but there was no time. Aidan scooped up his dog again, and carried him around the side of the barn. Jade was there trying to put out two different spot fires at once. Flames were streaking down from the house now, far more purposeful than they had been, running in an orange river along both sides of the driveway.

Aidan ran into the barn with Chip. He carefully set the injured dog down in the straw on the floor of the stall. This time he closed the upper half of the double door, as well. "I'll be back for you. I promise," Aidan told Chip through the door. "Trust me."

Then he ran out of the barn to help Jade keep the fire at bay.

CHAPTER NINE

THERE WAS A lot more fire when Aidan emerged from the barn, He grabbed his pickax and immediately ran to put out a few embers flaring up on the west side of the building. Just a few dry weeds that had caught a spark.

Jade was a black silhouette in the smoke, hosing the flames along the driveway. Aidan jogged to meet her. "How are you doing?"

She squinted at him over her bandanna. "Just dandy. Did you find Chip?"

"He was sitting on the ATV, looking like he wanted to drive on out of here."

Her eyes crinkled in a tired smile. "I don't blame him. Is he hurt?"

"I think his paw pads are burnt. I hosed them off and shut him in the stall. He can't escape now."

"Poor guy. You'll need to get him to the vet as soon as you can."

"I can't stand that he's in pain, but he'll have to hang in there until tomorrow." A horrible thought struck him. "This will be done by tomorrow, right?"

"At the rate it's burning? I think we just have to make it through the next few hours and it'll be past us."

A few hours. Hours that would determine if they lived or died. "You have any advice for me?"

"Well, your house is gone and your dog is hurt, but try to keep it in perspective. Your barn is okay, right? And your livestock are as safe as they can be, all surrounded by sprinklers. It's the best scenario we can hope for at this point."

He liked her practical way of looking at things. How she could point out the positive without sugarcoating the negative. Aidan pointed to the flames spreading out on either side of the driveway. "Are you worried about that?"

"Sure." Jade nodded. "But I'm also hungry. And thirsty. What do you have to eat?"

Aidan gaped at her. "Are you joking?"

"Absolutely not. We need to keep our energy up and get hydrated, because this fire is going to try to suck the life right out of us. If we've eaten and had some water, we have a much better chance of survival if we end up in a bad situation."

"You don't call this situation that we're in bad?"

She quirked her lips in her go-to sarcastic smile. "It's not great, but we're not dead yet, either. Go grab us a couple of those granola bars and a water bottle, okay?"

It went against all his instincts, but Aidan ran back to the barn and rummaged in the items he'd brought from the house until he found the food bag. He stuffed granola bars in his pocket, tucked water bottles under his arm and ran back to Jade. "Here you go."

"Awesome." With a relieved sigh, she took the water bottle he offered, pulled her bandanna down and drank. Aidan started on the other bottle and realized she was right. He was thirsty. Beyond thirsty. He drank until the bottle was nearly empty.

When he finished, Jade gave him the thumbs-up. "Adrenaline is tricky. It makes you forget hunger and thirst because it's a chemical designed for immediate survival. But we'll be in this mess for a while, so we've got to make sure we're taking care of ourselves." She ripped the wrapper off a granola bar and took a huge bite. "Delish," she cooed, patting her stomach like she was indulging in the finest meal.

"Very funny," Aidan told her, but he opened his own bar and finished it off in a couple of bites.

"Humor helps," Jade said. "But now that we've feasted, I'm going back over to the other side of the barn. There's so much dry grass over there, it's just a matter of minutes before it ignites."

"What do you want me to do?"

"Stay here and keep soaking these flames around the driveway. Try to keep them back, away from the barn. When the fire on the hillside gets a little closer, come help me out."

How she sounded so matter-of-fact when they were in the middle of an inferno, he'd never know. The heat was getting to him, sweat sliding down his back. He pulled his bandanna back up to try to block the thick smoke.

"Shallow breaths," Jade reminded him. "If you get dizzy, get back to the barn before you fall over."

"That's reassuring," he muttered, but she'd already jogged off, a blurry figure in the smoke. Aidan watched her go, idly spraying the ground in front of him. Then something caught his eye.

The barn. He'd left the door wide open and there was a faint orange light flickering. He was running before he'd told his feet to run, pointing the hose ahead of him. He lunged through the door to see confirmation of what he already knew. He was an idiot. An ember had sailed through the open door and landed on the bale of straw near the entrance. Flames were rising from the bale, crackling and reaching for something else to burn.

"No!" He turned his hose on the straw, spraying water not just at the bale but at anything close to it, spraying until he was sure that the last spark was out. If he'd had adrenaline before, it had tripled now, coursing through his body like an overdose of electricity, leaving his hands shaking, his ears ringing. He staggered back out of the barn and shut the doors behind him. That was a close call.

JADE WATCHED THE flames work their way down the hillside from Nellie's ranch and hoped she'd soaked the grass at the foot of the hill enough to slow it. There wasn't much wind right now, and the fire seemed to be moving at a more leisurely pace. It was so dark, and the smoke was so thick, she wasn't quite sure what was happening right now. It was hard to know if the main wildfire had even hit them yet, or if all this fire on the ranch was her backfire gone wild.

Not that it mattered too much at this point. She just had to keep the base of the hill near the barn wet enough that the fire went right on by. Grass burned quickly, and fire was an opportunist. If all went according to plan, the flames would follow the dry grass and bypass the wet ground. Then the flames wouldn't get close enough to the barn to cause any damage.

Aidan was several yards away, hosing down another portion of the hill. From his spot he could still defend the front of the barn, as well, so occasionally he'd disappear around the corner, presumably to put out a spot fire.

Jade turned her hose on the barn wall

again. She'd been going back and forth between the barn and the hillside like an indecisive sprinkler. Every time she watered one, she worried that the other needed more water.

The fire was loud, hissing, crackling and roaring, but another sound caught her attention. A squeaking noise coming from behind the barn. She listened intently, trying to determine what it was.

"Aidan!" He didn't hear her call so she made her way closer to him, spraying water as she went. "Aidan, I'm going around the back of the barn."

"Okay." He was spraying down a few embers and he glanced over his shoulder. "Be safe."

Jade pulled the hose with her around the side of the barn. The fire on the hillside was closer now, but, as planned, the flames were staying several yards uphill from the barn. *Phew.* Then she heard it. There was that squeaking noise again. It sounded like it was coming from somewhere high up over her head.

Jade pulled her flashlight off her belt and pointed the light at the carport roof. The smoke was too thick to see much, but she was sure she saw a flash of green eyes. "Who is up there?" The green eyes caught the light again. "Are you a kitten?" A second pair of eyes appeared in the harsh beam of the flashlight.

"Two of you? Oh wow." Jade set the hose down, letting the water run in the soil beyond the carport, and beamed her flashlight around the parked vehicles. An aluminum ladder hung from the barn wall and she ran to it, pulled it off and carried it to the edge of the carport. Carefully, she leaned it against the roof. After a few shakes to make sure it felt steady, she climbed up the rungs.

They were kittens. Jade could see them now, huddled together where the carport roof met the barn wall. What was it with her and cats? First Elliott, and now these two. They stared at her with twin sets of alarmed round eyes. "Here, kitty," she called quietly. "Come on, kitty." Nothing happened. "Oh come on, do not play hard to get, you guys."

Finally, after what seemed like ages but was probably a minute, one kitten, dark with a few white spots, made its way cautiously over to her, nuzzled her outstretched hand

and began purring. She pet it a few times, then took it gently by the scruff of the neck and held it to her chest. "I'll be back," she told the other one, and descended the ladder.

She found Aidan on the west side of the barn, hosing down the open grassy area between the barn and the pasture. "I've found someone who might belong to you." She directed her flashlight so it highlighted the kitten under her arm. "He's very sweet."

He squinted. "A kitten? Where did you find it?"

"On your carport roof. With another one who's still up there. Do you have another carrier?"

"In the last stall in the barn, yeah." He held out a hand and touched the kitten gently on the head with one sooty finger. "Maybe one of the barn cats had a litter? You didn't see a full-grown cat anywhere near?"

"Nope. Maybe the mama ran off because of the fire." She couldn't spend much more time on this. The propane tank near the house was venting again, such a chilling sound. *It's good news*, she reminded herself. *It won't explode if it vents.* "I'm going to get the crate and then try to catch the other one."

"You and your cats." Aidan shook his head.

"It's the way of the firefighter." She was relieved that he was keeping his head. Things were getting unsteady around them: the wind, that had seemed to calm before, was starting to gust again. The main wildfire must be here, or maybe the weather was changing. Something was stirring the air, and that wasn't good in a fire like this.

Jade ran to the barn with the kitten in her arm and pulled the door open. "Oh my gosh." There was a blackened straw bale to the left, soaked in water. It was hard to know whether to laugh or cry. They'd almost burnt this place from the inside out. But there was no time to wonder how it had happened. Hurrying to the last stall, Jade found a plastic carrier and put the protesting kitten inside. "Sorry buddy, I know this is no fun." She picked up the box with its mewing inhabitant, and jogged awkwardly out of the barn, closing the barn door carefully behind them.

Back at the carport, Jade set the carrier down carefully and climbed back up the ladder. "Are you here, buddy?"

An answering squeak told her that the kitten was still huddled against the roof. "Can you come here? Come on, kitty. Come on."

The kitten didn't budge.

The carport roof was made of corrugated metal. Jade put her hands on it and pressed. Would it hold her weight? Carefully, she climbed higher on the ladder, and then lay down on the roof, praying it would hold. Extending her hand, she called the kitten again. This time it crept forward and sniffed her extended fingers. "Okay, that's good. Now come just a little closer and…gotcha!" Jade caught the loose skin of the kitten's neck and started backward, pushing herself toward the ladder with one hand, holding the squirming, protesting kitty with the other.

"Jade, are you okay up there? You need anything?"

Aidan. For once she didn't mind that he was asking if she needed help. Truthfully, she did. "Can I hand you this kitten?" She scooted back a little more and got her feet over the edge of the roof, trying to catch sight of the ladder over her shoulder.

"Hang on." She heard Aidan's boots on the ladder, and then his hands were on her ankles, guiding her toward the rungs. "Keep scooting back," he said "Let your legs dangle." His big hands on her calves guided her feet until she could feel the rungs. "Okay, now, carefully stand up."

"Easier said than done with a kitten in one hand." But she managed to stand, and with his guidance step down one rung, then another. When she was well-balanced, he climbed all the way down and came around to stand at the side of the ladder. "Hand the kitten to me."

"Gladly." Unlike its fairly mellow sibling, this one was a twisting, turning dervish who didn't appreciate Jade's risky rescue. She lowered the kitten into Aidan's waiting hands and watched as he put it carefully in the crate. Satisfied that the kitties were safe, Jade started down the ladder. Just then, a sharp gust of wind hit suddenly, so strong it pushed her and the ladder back. Jade jumped away from the tilting ladder, sending it crashing to the left of her as she went right, landing hard on her side in the dirt just a couple feet away from the cat carrier.

"Jade." Aidan was by her side in an instant. "Can you get up?"

Her elbow stung and her ribs ached. Jade gingerly sat up, Aidan supporting her back gently. "I think I'm okay."

The wind was getting wild. Jade looked up and saw embers spinning overhead. "The fire is changing. We need to see what's happening."

"Can you stand?" He cradled her against him, his warmth and solid bulk offering a comfort she couldn't take right now. They were in danger. She could feel it in the gathering energy in the sky. Chaos waiting to break loose.

"Of course." Jade went to stand and sat back down hard, pain shooting through her left ankle. "In a moment."

"You're hurt." Aidan said. "Is it a break?"

Jade carefully wiggled her toes inside her boots. "I think it's a sprain. Come on. Pull me up. We need to get moving."

"If you're sure."

"Pull me up!" All this time she'd been trying to cover her fears with humor. But the sky above his head was glowing orange. "We have to get out of here."

He glanced up at the sky, gripped her wrist and hauled her to her feet. Jade put her foot down to try to take a step and winced at the pain. Aidan put an arm across her back to support her. "I'm fine," she protested.

He made a sound that was almost a groan. "Jade. You're not fine. Can you please accept some help? Just this once?"

She slipped out from under his arm and hopped a few steps. "I've got this."

He shook his head and went to get the kittens. "You don't. And you're slowing us down."

Her ankle was throbbing, the pain jolting up her leg every time she hopped. And the fire was closing in. "Fine," she relented. "I could use a hand."

He was by her side in an instant, his big arm around her back once again. She put her arms around his waist and used him to support her weight as they made their way to the truck.

"Take me to the driver's side," she told him.

"You should let me drive. You're hurt."

"I'll be fine," Jade bit out, wincing as she jostled her injured ankle. "It's an automatic."

He opened the door and helped her get behind the steering wheel. He set the crate with the kittens on the passenger seat next to her. Everything around them was taking on a spooky orange glow. Jade swallowed down her dread. "Aidan, It's time for plan B."

He nodded. "Into the pasture with the truck?"

"Yes. This fire is about to blow up. We have to get under those sprinklers."

"Tell me what to do."

"Run to the barn and get Elliott and Chip into crates. Grab those wool blankets we brought from the house. I'll drive to the door of the barn and meet you."

"Got it." He took off at a run around the corner of the barn.

Jade started the engine and drove after Aidan, trying to ignore the pain in her ankle. She'd prayed all evening that it wouldn't come to this. But fires nowadays ran so fierce and hot that anything could happen. This wasn't a fire anymore. It was a firestorm.

CHAPTER TEN

AIDAN JOGGED AROUND the corner of the barn and skidded to a halt. Everything was burning. The hillside between his house and the barn was on fire. The area around the solar panels and battery shed was burning. Hopefully the space they'd cleared around it was helping to keep the electrical system safe. On the right side of the driveway, the ancient live oak tree was on fire, orange flames shooting up to blend with the orange sky.

The fire was showing its true face now, and it was horrifying and mesmerizing all at once. It filled the foreground and the horizon. It blurred ground and sky. The wind was swirling every which way, and embers were blowing in random directions, igniting spot fires everywhere. It seemed, from where he stood, that they couldn't possibly hold their own against this monster. Especially when he looked toward the irrigated pasture. Everything between here and there was burning. Plan B was out of the question.

Time to make another plan. But, no matter what, they'd need the animals.

Aidan sprinted into the barn and ran to the back stall where he kept Chip's crate. He grabbed it and ran to get his dog, slowing to enter the stall carefully. If Chip got out now, Aidan knew he'd never see him again. Chip was cowering in the corner. The roar of the approaching fire must have him spooked. It sure had Aidan spooked. It rang in his ears and pulsed in his veins; he wanted to be rid of it, but it was everywhere.

"Chip, get in your crate."

Relief flooded him when his good dog obeyed, limping reluctantly into the crate. Aidan latched the door and picked up the unwieldy plastic box. This wasn't the easiest way to carry his dog, but now that he'd seen the sky and felt the wind he was pretty sure Jade would say that it was time for plan C. The pond. It was probably their only hope. And Chip would be better protected in his crate than if he was out in the open.

He left Chip's carrier near the barn door and slipped carefully through the tack room door in search of Elliott. Luckily for both of them, the poor cat was still huddled in the back of his carrier. It probably felt like the safest place to be. Aidan closed the carrier door and lifted the crate. Jade had the truck idling in front of the barn. He put Elliott's carrier in the back of the truck, heaved Chip's crate in, too, and grabbed the blankets Jade had requested. He threw one over the animal's crates, tucking the edges underneath in hopes that it wouldn't blow away. Then he jumped into the cab next to the box of kittens.

Jade started driving right away. "We can't get to the pasture."

"I noticed." Aidan gaped at the alien fiery world that had once been his ranch. His heart was a jackhammer, his blood keeping time in his throat and in his temples. "This doesn't look good."

"Time for plan C. Can we still get to the pond?"

"I think so. We'd better try."

"Don't I go left to get there?"

How was she still so calm? Aidan tried to force his own tone to match hers. "Yes. The lane is just past the barn." It would be easy to get lost on his own ranch. The smoke had turned everything that wasn't on fire an impenetrable black. Wild flocks of embers whirled past, and flames flared up everywhere. There went his wooden fences that lined the driveway. There went the tree that the cattle liked to shelter under on hot days. Aidan peered over the dashboard trying to help Jade navigate, but the landscape was foreign now. A burning shed loomed in front of them. "Back up," Aidan said. "You went too far to the left."

Jade's jaw was carved into a tense line as she looked behind her to reverse the car. "There's an awful lot of fire back there," she said. It was the first time he'd heard her sound frightened. The wind hit the truck and shook it.

Aidan could see fire in the side mirror. Poor Chip. Poor Elliott. "Just go back a few more feet. Okay, now veer right." The wind swirled the smoke, giving them a quick glimpse of the lane in the headlights. "You've got it. Go straight, twenty, maybe thirty yards and we'll be there."

"I need to leave my truck somewhere far away from us. In case the tank explodes."

Aidan thought for a moment. "The field below the pond is actually kind of a swamp. The water seeps through the ground down there. I leave it as a wetland for wildlife, but if we drive the truck right into the mud, it might actually save it."

"Okay, guide me."

They were a little farther from the fire now, and the smoke and embers weren't quite so thick. Aidan had Jade drive around the edge of the pond. There was no road here, so they bumped along through grass and brush until their wheels sank into mud. "This is it," Aidan said.

"I'll need a winch to get back out of here."

"I've got a winch," he told her. The wind pushed at the truck again. "Come on, let's get ourselves organized. The fire is right behind us."

She nodded and cut the engine.

He opened the door and stepped out into the windy night. Small fires were starting along the track they'd just followed. He ran around the front of the truck, his boots squishing into the soft ground, and opened Jade's door. When she hopped out, he scooped her up in his arms.

"What are you doing?" Her voice came out in a surprised shriek. "Put me down. I can hop."

"I know you can hop," he told her, trudging through the swampy field. She was so light in his arms. Easier to carry than Chip in his crate. If they weren't about to ride out an inferno in an icy pond, he might enjoy holding her like this. "We don't have time for you to illustrate your independence yet again. Okay?"

She glanced up at him, her arms around his neck. "What do you mean *yet again*?"

"I mean that you have a chip on your shoulder. You need everyone to know that you're a tough firefighter. That you've got everything handled. And mostly, you do. But, right now, you have to accept some help." When they reached the pond, he clambered up the raised bank and set her down on the ground. "I'll go get the animals. And then you can tell me what the heck we're going to do with them."

"There's rope in the truck. In the toolbox in the back. Will you grab it?" Jade's voice sounded more subdued than usual. She was probably in more pain then she was letting on. Whether she liked it or not, he had to be strong for them both right now.

He stumbled back over the swampy ground to the truck. He took Chip's crate first. No offense to the cats, but if that boiling sky rolled overhead sooner rather than later, he'd rather have his dog. Chip was restless in his crate, making it hard to carry, but somehow Aidan got him up the bank and set him alongside Jade. "I'll be right back." It only took a few minutes to get the two crates of cats, and the blankets and rope. And there they were, all lined up on the bank next to Jade. They could have been one big happy family, watching fireworks swirl in the sky above, if those fireworks didn't come from a wildfire hell-bent on destruction.

Jade had pulled out her flashlight and was shining it around the edge of the pond. She stopped as the light caught on something on the opposite shore. "Is that what I think it is?"

Aidan had forgotten all about it. Let the weeds grow over it. Sheila had wanted it along the edge of the pond for nautical decor. "It's a boat. I don't know if it still floats." He started around the edge of the pond. He and

Sheila had sat in the boat once or twice, way back when. They'd floated around the small pond, laughing. Then they'd had Colby and been too busy parenting to have time for such silliness. And then everything had been over.

He jogged along the muddy shore until he got to where it lay. Blackberry brambles crawled over it like a thorny net, and he had to pull and tear at them to free the small, fiberglass dinghy.

"I've got it," he called to Jade, and carried it to the water. There was a short rope tied to the front, so he held onto it and pushed the boat farther out in the pond. "I think it's floating." He jogged back along the bank, pulling the dinghy awkwardly behind him until he reached Jade.

"We can put the crates in here," he panted. It was hard to take a full breath with the smoke so heavy around them. "We'll cover them with wet blankets."

Jade tried to stand up, but sat back down hard. "You'll need to use the extra rope to tie the blankets down somehow, because the wind is going to get fierce if this fire goes right over us."

"Okay." Aidan picked up Chip's crate and sloshed into the chilly water, setting it on the flat bottom of the boat. He made his way back to Jade and handed her the rope attached to the bow. "Hold this. Don't let him float away." Chip whined plaintively as Aidan went to get the cats. He put Elliott's crate next to Chip's. He had to angle the kittens' crate a bit to fit them in, too. They were young. They'd been living on the sloping carport roof. Hopefully they could handle a sloping crate, too.

When Aidan turned around, Jade was standing on one foot at the edge of the pond, still clutching the rope. "You just don't give up, do you?"

"Nope." She hopped to where he'd left the blankets and scooped them up. "We only have a minute or two. Let's get these blankets wet."

"Sit down. Rest your ankle." He took them from her, and knelt at the edge of the pond, soaking the wool. Then he stood and tried to wring it out, twisting it to no avail.

"Let me help." Jade stood again, using only one leg, something Aidan filed away to be impressed by later. She hopped over to him and took one end of the soggy blanket. "Twist left."

They both started twisting, stepping closer as the blanket coiled, until water poured from the center. Then they laid the damp blanket carefully over the crates. They gave the second blanket the same treatment and put it on top of the first. From underneath the wool came the mewing of kittens, the yowling of Elliott and the whimpering of Chip. "I feel awful," Jade said. "But I don't know how else to keep them safe."

The wind was getting stronger, threatening to blow the blankets off. Fire was snaking through the fields toward them, and overhead the sky was glowing orange. Aidan grabbed the rope and dunked it in the pond to make sure it wouldn't burn. Then he lay it across the crates. He used his headlamp to examine the boat. "There are oarlocks we can use to tie the blankets down." He quickly attached the rope and sloshed around the boat to the other side to pull the rope tight through the other oarlock. Then he wrapped the rope around the crates until the animals were trussed under the blankets like a row of poorly wrapped Christmas presents.

"Hurry," Jade yelled, as he tied the final knot. The wind was high and wild now, blowing flames across the grass so they devoured the wooden lean-to near the pond. The smoke was hot in Aidan's lungs, making him cough. "That takes care of them," he gasped. "What about us?"

The wind pushed harder, engulfing the pasture around them in crackling fire as the dry grass burned like kindling. Jade hopped in to join him by the boat. "How deep is the water?"

"It'll get up to my chest pretty fast." Aidan held out his hand. "Get ready, it's freezing."

"It's better than roasting." Jade took his hand and clutched it tight, using him to keep her upright as she hopped and stumbled into the pond. "That's cold," she gasped as the water reached her hips.

"Hold on to my belt," Aidan told her. "We're going to head to the middle of the pond, okay?" He tugged the boat full of animals around. "Here we go." The air was stifling and the sky was glowing brighter, lighting his way into deeper water but raising the hairs on the back of his neck. This was it. Plan C. His sodden jeans and boots weighed him down, making each step even harder. Jade stumbled, and he felt her hands grip tighter on his belt as she righted herself.

"Are you okay back there?" He had to shout the words. They could be inside a jet engine, the fire was that loud.

"I'm okay," Jade yelled back. "This water is making my ankle feel better."

He almost yelled back *that's good news*, as if they were having a regular conversation, but he stopped himself. They were in the middle of the pond in the middle of a firestorm. There wasn't really much good news to be had. The water was only past his abdomen, but when he turned to face Jade it was up around her chest. She was holding a small, rectangular bundle over her head to keep it out of the water.

"Take this,' she gasped.

"What is it?" He put an arm around her upper back to hold her steady and took the bundle from her.

"My fire shelter. Let's put it over our heads, just in case."

A fire shelter. Aidan knew that firefighters only used them as a last resort. All through this long afternoon and evening he'd wondered if there would be one defining moment. A point where they would have to face the idea that they might not come out of this alive. Now that moment was here, and Aidan felt more calm than he'd imagined. But he also felt a fury grip him, and shake him to the core. *Not Jade.* If he died, so be it. But she was too precious and too important to die here.

"Just tell me exactly what you need me to do," he told her. "And I'll do it."

"It's kind of like a sleeping bag. One side is open. We're going to put it over our heads. If the flames get really high around this pond, we'll need to sink most of our bodies down into the water and still hold the shelter over us."

"You're already mostly in the water."

"No short jokes." She helped him open the bundle and unfurl the tarp-like bag.

The wind was picking up and tugging at the shelter, trying to pluck their means of survival right out of their hands. Aidan tightened his grip. The fire was all around them now, the air so hot it made Aidan wish he could just stop breathing.

"This is it. Sink down so just your head is out of the water," Jade commanded, tugging her side of the shelter over her head.

Aidan followed her example and pulled the sack-like shelter over his head. He gasped as he knelt, the icy water stealing what breath he had left. It was hard to keep hold of the shelter while trying to keep a grip on the rope that held the boat. Jade's head was a shadow barely above the dark water as they faced each other under the shelter. The wind shrieked over them and tried to wrestle fabric away from their grip.

"Are you okay?" Aidan yelled above the roaring.

"Yes. Just don't let go," Jade shouted back.

Suddenly the whole shelter lit up inside with brilliant orange light.

"Get down as low as you can," Jade said. "This is it."

Aidan sank deeper into the pond, the water closing around his neck, his blood blasting through his veins with cold, fear and adrenaline.

"If we lose the shelter, duck under the

water with only your nose and mouth out so you can breathe." It sounded like Jade's teeth were chattering. She was smaller than him. The cold must be terrible for her.

The icy water numbed Aidan's limbs, while the hot air pressed on him from above. He thought of the animals enduring the heat and prayed the wet blankets were enough. The smoke was so thick that each breath felt almost useless, like the fire was stealing all the oxygen.

Jade must have heard him gasp. "Slow shallow breaths," she said. "It shouldn't be too much longer."

He could feel her shivers ripple the water between them. "Do you need to hold on to me?"

He could swear he felt her glare at him. "I'm fine."

Trust her to demand her independence even when things were this dire. It would make him laugh if he wasn't so terrified. "I'm here if you need me," he told her. The wind shrieked and yanked at the shelter. Aidan clutched his fistfuls of fabric, refusing to let go. "How long do you think this will last?"

"I don't know," Jade said. "Don't panic. Try to think about something else."

Aidan cast about for something, anything, to think of besides what was happening right now. "Why are you a firefighter?" he yelled over the fire's chaos.

"Runs in my family," she shouted back. "My father was fire chief for years and years. My older brother Travis became a firefighter. Dean is a sheriff. And my other brother Ash works as a game warden. I guess we all got the public service gene."

Talking, even if they had to shout, kept Aidan from worrying too much about why the orange light in their shelter had suddenly gone red. "Did you ever want to be anything else?"

"No." As if to test Jade's answer, the wind tugged their shelter, lifting it up enough that Aidan could see flames roaring around the edge of the pond. "Pull it down!" Jade shouted, and they worked together to fight the wind, to keep their shelter, to save their lives.

"I hope the animals are okay." It killed him to know that Chip and the cats were alone in their crates, terrified.

"Those wool blankets should protect them," Jade said. "And they have a boat, so they're probably a whole lot more comfortable than we are."

That was for sure. Aidan couldn't feel much anymore. His body had gone numb. "What else did you want to be, besides a firefighter?"

"Nothing," she answered. "I wanted to follow in my dad's footsteps. I'm sure a shrink would say that I was trying to get his approval. He never wanted a girl. I'm sort of this constant thorn in his side."

"That's crazy. How could he not want a daughter like you?"

"He prefers sons."

Aidan tried to imagine it. When Sheila had been pregnant, he hadn't cared if she was having a boy or girl. He just wanted the baby to be healthy. "Your dad is lucky to have four kids. Maybe he doesn't realize that."

The red, flickering light outside their shelter seemed to go on and on, but the noise was fading, as if the jet plane that had passed over them was heading away now. Aidan had to keep talking, keep his focus

on something other than the claustrophobia
of being trapped in this fire. "I had a kid,"
he blurted out.

There was a pause before Jade said, "Can
I ask what happened?"

After years of not wanting to talk about
it, the words came pouring out. "His name
was Colby. He was the sweetest boy. Just
three years old." How bizarre that he could
talk about it calmly. Maybe the chaos around
them somehow eased the chaos inside. "He
got sick. The doctors couldn't save him."

"I'm sorry. That's so terribly sad." Jade
moved closer to him in the water, so their
knees were touching. It was a sweet gesture.
The most comfort she could offer since they
couldn't let go of the shelter.

Aidan could feel her shivering. "You're
cold."

She gave a weak laugh. "This isn't exactly
bath water."

How could he help her? The wind was
still tugging on the shelter, the fire was roaring around them. "Can you come closer to
me?"

"I don't think it will help. Let's just keep
talking."

"What do you want to talk about? Because my life doesn't make for good conversation." Having touched on Colby, he wanted to move on. He could only say a little before it hurt too much.

"No. Aidan, I'm glad you told me. It breaks my heart, but I'm glad I know. But if you want a lighter topic, what's your favorite color?"

That was easy. "Green. Like the fields in spring out here. What about you?"

"Blue. It's soothing. And it's my uniform color, so I guess I'm used to it."

He tried to think of something else to ask. He was so rusty at conversation. "Do you have a favorite book?"

"I like mysteries. Thrillers. Adventure. Stuff like that. You?"

"Science fiction," he confessed. "I'm a nerd at heart."

"I wouldn't have guessed that about you. I'd have figured you were reading some kind of Western, or maybe a thriller. You're this big tough rancher."

He rarely told anyone anything. But somehow he wanted to tell everything to her. "I was born on a ranch. But I didn't think I wanted to be a rancher. I majored in computer science in college. Got involved in a Silicon Valley start-up. I was in that world for several years before I realized I hated it. That's when I bought this ranch."

"I had no idea." She sounded a little stunned.

"It's not something I usually share. What would my fellow ranchers think of me if they knew I was a closet computer geek?"

"I'm sure they'd never speak to you again," she teased.

"Though my inner nerd still comes out. I have—" he paused, then corrected himself "—I *had*, all kinds of technology on my ranch. I've been obsessed with trying to deter predators like mountain lions in humane ways. I developed motion sensitive lighting on my property, and alarms. I mixed my cattle and sheep together into groups I call flerds."

"Flerds?"

"A flock and a herd mixed together. A flerd."

Jade gave a shaky laugh, and Aidan weighed his options. Was she getting hypothermia? This water was really chilly. The light inside their shelter had gone from red back to orange. Things seemed to be less intense. It was still getting quieter. Hopefully that meant the fire was passing and they could get out of this water before she got much colder. He had to keep her talking. Keep her engaged. "What's your favorite food?"

"Out of all the food out there?" She paused. "I love food. Don't make me pick a favorite. Even picking a favorite fruit is hard. I mean there are apples, which are such a good steady fruit to have around, but then there are all the summer fruits like nectarines, which are absolutely delicious. And cherries. I love cherries..." Her voice trailed off, and she laughed. "Please don't make me pick a favorite food."

"I can see that it's hard for you. How about this? Favorite candy bar."

"Snickers. My turn. Favorite cookie?"

"Oatmeal chocolate chip," he answered. "My mom makes the best oatmeal chocolate chip cookies. Yours?"

"Plain old chocolate chip," she said. "What about comfort food? What meal do you crave when you just want something you know will make you feel better?"

"Roast chicken and potatoes." It sounded so good, his stomach growled. "What I'd give to be sitting down to a big plate of that right now. Or spaghetti and meatballs."

"That's mine," Jade said. "Spaghetti and meatballs are the absolute best comfort food."

"With garlic bread," Aidan added.

"And a crispy salad. With that store-bought Italian dressing they serve at diners and places like that."

He didn't know how, but he could taste that exact dressing. "Agreed."

"And apple pie for dessert. No ice cream. Just nice warm pie."

"That sounds perfect." The orange light had faded to gray. The smoke was still thick, but Aidan was pretty sure the worst of the fire had passed. The wind had died down and it was no longer tugging at the shelter. "I think we can get out of here. What do you think?"

"Let's just peek out and see."

Aidan cautiously lifted up the edge of the shelter. It was dark and smoky, and a few flames flickered out in the field. But the storms of embers were gone and the big flames were gone. "I think it's safe."

Cautiously, they lifted the shelter and stood.

"It passed us. It's gone," Jade said, her voice hushed. "Look."

To the southwest of them, the flames were still burning strong. But around them it was mostly dark. Small dying flames glimmered in the field around the pond. "We made it." Aidan stared around him in wonder. He was still breathing. Still talking. They'd survived. Taking the shelter from Jade, he crumpled it into a ball and put it in the boat. He pulled at the blankets. They were warm and his stomach soured with dread. "Chip?"

A sharp bark had them both jumping in surprise. "He's okay," Jade said. "Oh my gosh, he's okay."

Aidan realized how worried she'd been, and how good she was at hiding it. "Cats? Elliott?" He poked at Elliott's crate through the blankets. An annoyed rustling shook the crate, and then the big cat let out a hiss. "Elliott is in the house," Aidan declared, relief making him silly. The kittens' indignant meows let them know they'd survived, too.

"I can't believe it." Jade flung her arms around Aidan's middle and held on. "They survived. We survived. Aidan, we made it!"

Joy swamped him as he clutched Jade close. Despite the thick smoke and the freezing water, he felt newborn. "We did it." Awe shook his voice. "Jade, we did it!"

"I'm so relieved." She held on tight around his waist, her cheek pressed to his chest, shaking and shivering against him. "We're alive. The fire is gone."

Aidan held her tight, supporting most of her weight. Tears slicked down his cheeks as he looked out at the retreating fire. Every breath felt new and holding Jade like this, knowing she was going to be okay, was the most precious thing of all.

"And now maybe we can get out of this pond?" It was the first time he'd heard Jade sound truly weak.

Aidan knelt down. "Put your arms around my neck."

"No, I'm fine. My ankle is totally numb. I can probably walk."

She was precious, but she still had the ability to frustrate him to know end. "Just let me help you? Before you freeze to death?"

"Fine. Just this once." Jade wrapped her arms around his neck, and Aidan lifted her and carried her to shore. He set her down on the muddy bank. Something along the shore caught his eye.

"Jade, shine your light across the pond." When her light flickered on, they could see two mule deer standing knee deep in the water, their antlers branching out, so graceful and beautiful in all the devastation. "We're not the only ones who had this idea," Aidan said.

"They're gorgeous." He could hear her teeth chattering as she spoke. Moving slowly, trying not to startle the deer, Aidan went to get their boat. "I feel like Noah, with his ark," he told her as he pulled the dinghy to shore. "Only we mainly saved cats."

"Of course we did. We're firefighters."

He didn't think. Just knelt down next to her, wrapped his arms around her and held her close. She hugged him to her and buried her face in his neck. After a long moment, he forced himself to release her, to put space back between them. "Thank you," he told her as he pulled away. "Thank you for keeping us safe."

"You're the one who had to carry me out to this pond. You found the boat. Thank *you* for saving our lives." Then she put an icy hand on Aidan's arm. "How are we going to get back to the barn? If there is a barn. My truck is stuck in the mud."

"I'll go get my truck. Assuming I still have a truck." Aidan stood and hauled the boat onshore. No way was he going back into that cold water again. He untied the ropes and carefully lifted the blankets. "Everyone all right in there?"

Chip shoved his nose through the gaps in the door of his crate and nuzzled Aidan's arm. Aidan's heart swelled with relief. "Hey, buddy. You're a trouper." He took the wet blankets and put them on Jade, who was shivering violently. "They're wool so they may help even if they're wet. We have got to get you warm."

"Maybe you can build me a fire." She giggled at her own joke and he grinned in sheer, stupid relief.

"I suspect I can find you some fire around here somewhere." He turned to scan the bank. "Stay here under the blankets. Is there a first aid kit in your truck?"

"Under the front seat."

"I'll be right back." He took the flashlight she'd left on the muddy bank. He flashed it to where the deer had been, but they were gone. He silently wished them luck. It would be difficult for them to find food in this charred landscape.

Following the flashlight's beam through the smoky night, Aidan made his way to her truck, dreading the burned-out shell he might find. But it was fine. The waterlogged meadow it sat in had saved it. Shining his light on the sunken wheels made it clear that he wasn't getting it out of here without a winch.

He opened the door of the cab and grabbed the first aid kit, relieved to find an emergency blanket inside. They'd survived a wildfire. No way was he going to lose Jade to hypothermia now.

Back at the pond, he wrapped the foil blanket around Jade's head and shoulders, then draped the wool blankets on top. "Stay here," he told her. "I'm going to walk back to the barn and see if I can get my truck."

She peeked out of her bundle of blankets.

"Everything is backward. I'm supposed to be rescuing you from this fire."

He knelt in front of her so they were eye-to-eye. "You did rescue me. Now I'm returning the favor." He set the flashlight by her side and turned on his headlamp. "I'll be back soon."

CHAPTER ELEVEN

JOGGING THROUGH HIS burnt ranch had to be the most surreal experience in a surreal night. In the light of Aidan's headlamp, everything smoldered. Smoke rose from the ground all around him, forcing him to follow one faint tire track in the lane running to the pond. Disoriented, he didn't realize he was at his barn until the wooden wall loomed up in the light of his lamp.

He stopped and stared, flooded with new relief. They'd done it. The fire had gone around, and spared the barn. It was another miracle in a miraculous night. They'd survived the fire. And somehow his barn had, too.

Aidan ran to the back of the barn and there was his truck, perfectly fine, along with all the other vehicles parked in the carport. Shivering, he got in the cab and started the engine, amazed when it purred to life.

Cranking up the heat, Aidan drove back toward the pond. It was much easier to see his way now. The heaviest smoke had lifted and soon he was close to the shore where he'd left Jade. He jumped out of the cab and ran to her, scooping her up, blankets and all, and carrying her to the heated cab of the pickup. "You smell like wet sheep," he told her as he set her on the seat.

"You must adore me then," she shot back, making him laugh.

"I'll get the animals."

Soon he had the crates loaded in the truck and he, Jade, Chip, Elliott and the two kittens were rumbling back to the barn. "We should have all just stayed in here," Jade said when she saw it standing tall. "We would have been a whole lot more comfortable."

"That's twenty-twenty hindsight," Aidan said. "We could have been trapped in here." He helped her out of the cab and they went into the barn. He immediately went to his duffel bag and pulled out some sweatpants and a sweatshirt. "Change into these."

For once she didn't protest or say she was fine. She just walked into a stall and came out a few minutes later, drowning in his clothing. But at least she was dry. He handed her a pair of clean wool socks, and she slid them on, laughing at all the extra fabric in the toes. But even with the added bulk, she managed to get her feet back into her sodden boots.

Aidan changed into dry clothing, as well, relieved to get out of his freezing, soaked clothes. When he left the stall where he'd changed, Jade was wrapped in one of his coats. It fit her like a dress, but she looked adorable in it. She busied herself getting water for the kittens and putting Elliott back in the tack room.

Aidan put a horse blanket on a bed of straw in Chip's stall. After a long drink of water and a bite of granola bar, the exhausted dog flopped down on the blanket. Aidan trained his headlamp onto his paws, trying again to see the extent of the dog's injuries. But Jade's voice, sounding a bit panicked, cut through his concentration.

"Aidan, get out here. There's something in the barn with us."

"What?" He rose and let himself out of the stall. He spotted Jade in the back corner, shining her light at the feed bags he'd stacked there.

"It's an animal," she said quietly as he approached her. "It must have come in here way back when we left the door open, to get away from the fire."

"Please tell me it's not a skunk."

He could see the faint flash of a smile on her lips. "It's bigger than that. A raccoon maybe?"

"What do you need me to do?"

"I think it's injured. I heard sort of a whining, wheezing sound. That's why I came over here."

Aidan hoped fervently that whatever it was, it wasn't too bad off. He had a rifle in a locked case in his tack room. If he had to, he could put the poor animal out of its misery, but he didn't want that job. "Why don't I grab one of the big crates I use for Thor and Odin? If it's not hurt too badly, we can try to get it in there."

"It's a wild animal," Jade said. "It's not going to just walk on into a crate. We need something to steer it in. Want to grab a couple of brooms?"

Aidan fetched two of the brooms he always had leaning against the wall and then got one of the big dog crates out of the stall. He put some straw in the bottom of it to provide some comfort to the animal, whatever it was.

He heaved the large crate into his arms and staggered with it to the back wall of the barn. He set it down carefully, so the open door was very close to the feed bags. He peered over the sacks of grain and angled his headlamp. Two green eyes looked up at him. Two pointed ears. A round head with fuzz on the sides. Aidan backed carefully away until he was standing beside Jade again. "You're not going to believe this," he said quietly. "It's a bobcat."

"A bobcat?" she gasped. Then she grinned up at him. "What is it with all the cats needing rescue today?"

"You're a walking firefighter cliché," he teased her. "What do you think we should do? I can't tell if it's hurt but I suspect its paws will be burnt. Look what happened to Chip, and he was only out in the fire for a few moments."

"We should trap it," Jade said. "Maybe

once it's in the crate we can see if it's injured. If it's not, we can let it go."

"Do you have a plan for this scenario?"

She laughed softly. "Several plans, of course. Plan A is that I'm going to sneak up and rattle the grain bags behind it. Hopefully that will make it run forward to the crate. You stand by with that big broom, and use it to make sure it doesn't bolt toward the front of the barn." She glanced at him. "Are you ready?"

"Ready as I can be when there's a wildcat in my barn."

She smiled. "You're tough. You can handle it. After tonight, we can handle anything." Jade limped over to the grain bags and used the handle of her broom to poke at them. Nothing happened. She poked again. Nothing. Then she knocked the broom hard against the wall behind the bags. Suddenly a blur of furry motion exploded from behind the bags. It darted toward Aidan but he blocked it with his wide broom, pushing it back toward the crate. It was a bobcat for sure, in full fearful fury, hissing, yowling and clawing at the broom.

Aidan gently steered the frightened cat

back against the wall with the broom. It was pretty big, at least twice the size of Elliott, he'd guess. Its coat was mottled brown and gray, and there were tufts of fur poking out of its ears. Jade joined him and together they managed to herd the bobcat through the door of the big dog carrier. Jade slammed the door shut and held it in place with her broom. "Got him." She stared down at the crate with a bemused expression on her face. "Of course, now we have to latch this door, and it's going to rip the skin off our hands if we try."

"Let me grab some gloves." Aidan jogged to where he'd left his leather gloves by the rest of his wet, discarded clothes and slipped them on. Back at the crate, he knelt down and warily lifted his hand toward the latch. A paw immediately slashed forward, and that's when Aidan's stomach churned. The bobcat's paw pads were raw, bleeding burns. His horror was enough to make Aidan forget his fear. He latched the crate, even though the cat slashed at his gloves, and then stepped back to meet Jade's questioning gaze. "It's burnt really bad. There's fur missing. There's blood where its paw pads should be."

Jade set her broom against the wall and ran a hand over her eyes. It was the first time that Aidan had seen a look of total defeat on her face. "Would it be more merciful just to shoot it?"

That had been his original idea, but now he couldn't face it. "No. Look, it's almost dawn. We can probably get it to a vet sometime tomorrow. It's still got a ton of energy and life in it. It's a fighter. We have to give it a chance to keep fighting."

A low growl came from the crate, as if the bobcat agreed with him. "See? It's not giving up, so we can't give up on it."

"Okay, you're right." Jade shook her head. "Sorry, I lost my nerve for a moment there. It's the hardest part of wildfires for me— all the innocent animals that get hurt and killed. None of this is their fault. I'll bet my next paycheck that this fire was started by some human being, or some flawed human technology somewhere." She put a hand to her mouth for a moment, as if to physically make herself stop. "Enough. I'll stop preaching now."

"I agree with you," Aidan said quietly. "I know I mentioned it earlier, but one of the reasons I love this ranch so much is I turned it into an example of how to coexist with wildlife. Yet, here we are with this poor bobcat. So preach all you want. Or, come with me to check on the rest of the animals. Maybe we can even put out some hot spots together. That should cheer you up."

Jade smiled, and Aidan could see the tension go out of her. "You really know how to show a girl a good time."

"I know you love to fight fire."

"Even I might be a little tired of firefighting tonight. But you're right. We should go check on the rest of the ranch. Though it's still too dark to see much."

"But my truck has a good heater. So there's that."

"You had me at heater." She took him by the gloved hand and started limping toward the front of the barn.

Her sense of humor eased the tension inside him, always. Laughing, he let her pull him through the barn, out into the, smoky air and into the nice warm truck.

THE SHEEP WERE fine. Aidan's horse, Payday, was fine. Jade wandered the fence line, her flashlight trained on the animals inside, trying to absorb this next miracle. Aidan's plan had worked. The sheep seemed to have come through unscathed. They grazed peacefully beneath the sprinklers as if there'd never been a fire. Payday came to the fence and nuzzled Aidan's hands. The beautiful horse seemed nervous, but he looked fine.

"I'll have to check them over again in the morning when it's light," Aidan said. "But this looks promising. I can see Thor and Odin out there wandering among them, and they look great, too."

Jade turned to shine her light on the dark pastures behind them. Smoke was still rising from the earth and there were glowing embers here and there. But nothing burned with any vitality. There wasn't anything left to burn.

She ran a hand over her tired eyes, trying to take it all in. They'd made it. For a few moments in the pond, she'd worried that they'd failed. That the fire was going to overtake them, burn their lungs, end their lives.

But somehow, working together, they'd

survived. And the animals had, too. It was more than she'd dared hope for, ever since she'd gotten stuck out here on Aidan's ranch.

Holding on to Aidan in the pond, after they'd emerged from their shelter, she'd felt more alive than she'd ever been. Each breath meant something now. His arms around her were not just supporting her, they were reminding her that she was still here, that she'd done her job, that she'd kept them safe. They'd kept each other safe.

Aidan walked over to her. "Want to head back to the barn? I've got granola bars. And apples."

"That sounds perfect." Jade climbed into the truck. Her ankle was much better. Its long soak in the icy pond must have taken the swelling down.

When Aidan turned on the engine, the heat blasted and it felt like heaven. She wasn't quite thawed out. It was hard to believe she'd been so hot, just a couple hours before. But being cold, or feeling anything, meant she was still alive, so she was okay with it. Back in the pond, under the fire shelter, she hadn't known if they'd make it. Thank goodness for Aidan, his calm voice and attempts at conversation. He'd gotten her through.

Back in the barn, Aidan laid several horse blankets on a dry portion of the barn floor. He handed Jade his sleeping bag and she climbed into it right away, too tired to eat anything. She just wanted to sleep. He sat next to her in the dark in his big parka, a blanket wrapped around him.

She looked up at him. "Aren't you going to sleep?"

"Eventually. I want to keep an eye on things a little longer."

Reaching sleepily through the dark, she put a hand on his leg. "The fire is out now. We're safe."

"You were so chilled in the pond. I thought I might lose you in there."

"I'm still chilled," she murmured. "I don't know if I'll ever be warm again."

"Do you want me to lie down with you?"

Suddenly it was all she wanted. His strength and warmth, next to her. "Yes, please."

She heard rustling in the dark as he stood, took a few steps and lay down on his side, facing her. "How can I help?"

She reached for his hands. "We're alive. We made it."

"It still feels so surreal," he confessed. "I wasn't sure what would happen."

"Kiss me?" She hadn't known she was going to ask for that. But suddenly she wanted that closeness more than anything. That vital proof that they were okay.

He raised himself up on one elbow, leaned over and brought his mouth to hers. It was a slow, tentative kiss. The kiss of two people who hadn't kissed anyone in a long time. But his mouth on hers was warm and soothing. Jade put her hands to his cheeks and kissed him with all the fear and desperation she'd felt in the pond. His heat and breath were the affirmation and comfort she needed.

Finally, slowly, they pulled apart. "Lie on my shoulder," Aidan whispered. "Lie close to me. I'll help you get warm, and you can rest."

Jade put her head on his shoulder and was asleep in an instant.

CHAPTER TWELVE

"JADE?"

A man's voice pulled Jade out of exhausted sleep. She was pretty sure she heard her eyelids creak as she forced them open. Her eyes were irritated and gummy, and she blinked, bewildered, into the sunlight. She pushed herself up to sitting, her bones and muscles stiff, and caught sight of the wooden beams overhead. She was here on Aidan's ranch. In his barn. They'd survived the fire. And the sunlight came through the barn door. They must have left it partially open.

Was Aidan calling her? Or had that been a dream?

She glanced down and there was Aidan, a restless lump under the faded blue horse blanket he'd pulled over himself last night. He sat up suddenly, as if sensing her scrutiny, and shoved a hand through his thick hair. It stood on end, gray-streaked with soot. For a moment he looked as out of focus as Jade felt, but his expression cleared when he looked at her. "Hey," he said softly, and Jade saw a warmth in his eyes that hadn't been there yesterday. "We made it."

"We did." It seemed almost impossible. "At least, I think we did. Unless this is what heaven looks like."

Aidan huffed a laugh. "I don't think heaven is this smoky. And hopefully neither of us went to the alternative."

Jade grinned, giddy in the realization that they were here and they were alive. "I don't smell any brimstone."

He put an arm around her shoulders and pulled her close, planting a kiss in her hair. "It's incredible to see you smile."

Jade leaned into him, relishing how solid he felt. "It's incredible to be alive." *And here, with him.* She shoved that thought away. He was basically a stranger. Yes, they'd kissed sometime around dawn, but that was nothing but gratitude. Sheer joy that they'd managed to survive and save the sheep and other animals. Though she'd never had a kiss like that before. She turned to look up at Aidan, wondering what it would be like to kiss him again.

"Hi," he said softly, meeting her gaze with an intensity that told her he was wondering the very same thing.

"Jade?"

She started, and pulled away from Aidan. That voice was definitely not a dream and it was a little louder now. It sounded like Mitch.

"Over here!" She slipped out from under Aidan's arm and stood, testing her weight on her ankle. It was sore, but so much better than last night. "In the barn," she called. She glanced back at Aidan. "I think it's my boss." Limping, she stepped out into the smoky morning and peered through the brown, hazy air. "Mitch, is that you?"

Boots crunched heavily on the gravel and two firefighters came into view through the lingering smoke. "Jade!" Mitch ran forward and took Jade by the shoulders. She could see relief in his eyes, and there was a watery quality to his gaze that might even be tears. "You gave us quite a scare."

"Tell me about it." Jade peered beyond

Mitch to greet the other firefighter. "Hey, Bill."

Bill Laslow shoved back his helmet, revealing a soot-streaked face and red eyes that spoke of a sleepless night on the fire lines. "We thought you were toast, girl."

Mitch pulled her in for a hug, a gesture so uncharacteristic that Jade stiffened, then gave him an awkward pat on the back as he released her. "I'm glad you came through."

"Jade's tough. What did I tell you?" Bill grinned and held up a hand for a high five.

Jade smacked his palm and returned his smile. "Takes more than a little old wildfire to kill me."

A third man came running down the driveway, sending gravel spewing from under his heavy boots. Jade recognized the thick dark hair, so much like her own. "Travis!"

Her brother scooped her up in his arms. His momentum swept her off her feet and swung her around in a circle. He didn't say anything, just held her close long after they stopped spinning. When he finally pulled back, Jade ignored the tears on his face, wiping her own instead. "Good to see you," she told him, putting her palms to his cheeks. She'd wondered last night if she'd ever see him, or the rest of her family, again.

"Good to see you, too, sis. That was a long night."

Jade's family wasn't good at sharing their emotions, but she could read the deep feeling beneath her brother's simple words. He'd been scared for her. Though maybe not as scared as she'd been when the fire roared through. She stepped back, swallowing hard. "It sure was. How are Dean and Ash? Are Mom and Dad freaking out?"

Travis grinned. "Maybe a little, yeah. I told them you were tough and you'd make it through, but we'd better call them once we can find some cell reception. Last I heard, Deputy Dean is evacuating folks ahead of the flames, and Ash is off on some mission in the Sierras. The one you asked him about last week, and he wouldn't tell you much."

Jade's shoulders tensed, like they did whenever she thought of the risks Ash took as a game warden. "Probably because he knows it's way too dangerous."

"Danger comes with the territory in this family, apparently." Travis reached out and tugged gently on Jade's tangled hair. "Seriously. I'm glad you're okay."

Aidan walked out of the barn, running his hands over his eyes as if he were still trying to wake up. He looked from Jade to the three men. "Good morning."

Travis stuck out his hand and Aidan came forward to shake it. "I'm Aidan Bell."

"Travis Carson. Jade's brother."

Aidan turned to Jade. "Should you be standing right now?"

Travis looked at her sharply. "What's wrong?"

"Just twisted my ankle last night." She glanced at Aidan and couldn't help smiling. She felt almost giddy with relief. "Someone had me soak it in the pond."

Travis understood her little joke. "Is that how you guys made it through?"

Jade nodded. "It worked. Even the dog and three cats made it. And a couple of deer, as well." She realized her words had wiped the smile off her brother's face. "It's okay, Travis. I'm fine."

"I shouldn't have let you drive out here all alone." Mitch shook his head. "I should have had someone else go with you."

"Then you would have had two of us stuck out here. And I had Aidan to help me out," Jade reassured him. "Turns out he's pretty good at firefighting."

Bill looked Aidan up and down. "You ever consider a career change? We can use more folks in these parts."

Aidan shook his head. "Nope. Definitely not."

"Aidan loves ranching." Jade nudged the big rancher gently with her elbow, trying to lighten the moment. "Especially his sheep."

He grinned down at her then, and she wanted more of the warmth and connection she saw in his eyes. He looked like a different person than she'd met yesterday.

"It's a nice ranch," Travis said. "Sorry about your house, though."

Aidan shrugged. "Houses can be rebuilt."

Jade wondered at Aidan's casual tone. But maybe letting the house burn was his way forward. She just hoped it would help. She couldn't imagine trying to live with the loss of a child.

She studied him as he looked around at the remains of his ranch, the smoldering ashes of all he'd built. His expression was hard to read. But she thought she detected a lightness about him, as if the fire had brought him some relief. Maybe, like her, he was just grateful to be alive.

"Let us help you get any hot spots put out," Travis said to Aidan. "We'll make sure there's nothing around that can reignite." He pointed out to the sheep, still grazing under the mist of the sprinklers. "You did a good thing there."

"And the metal roof on your barn." Mitch pointed toward the eaves. "That was a smart move."

Aidan's gaze met Jade's for a brief moment. "It was touch and go, but Jade helped me keep it from burning. I'm grateful for her help."

Warmth stole over Jade's chest, not pride, really, but a sense that her being with Aidan during the wildfire had made a difference for him in more ways than one. She may have gone into this career to prove to herself that she could keep up with her brothers, but she'd stayed in it because she wanted to help others. And last night, she had.

Though that wasn't all of it. What they'd shared last night, their feelings, that kiss, falling asleep in his arms, it had changed her, too. She'd never let herself lean on anyone like that. And now that she'd started leaning, it was a little lonely to be standing on her own two feet again.

AIDAN DROPPED THE coiled hose on the ground and screwed the end into the spigot that stuck up from the ground near what used to his house. Mitch had instructed him to hose off the smoking pile to ensure it was well and truly out.

Ever since they'd woken up, Aidan had been trying to decide how he felt about his house being gone. Last night, facing the choice of what to save, choosing the barn had been a no-brainer. But now he felt the loss of the old farmhouse. Even though the floor sloped on the disintegrating foundation, the windows let in the cold and the termites had been munching on the place for a century, he and Sheila had fallen in love with it. It had been their home, until Colby had died and Sheila left. Then it had become something else. A monument to loss. A collection of memories.

Aidan sprayed the hose onto the tangle

of charred timbers and melted appliances, watching the steam rise from the ruin with a morose satisfaction. He'd been right to let it burn. Cultures all around the world used fire to release a soul to heaven. He was releasing the soul of this house, the wan ghost of all his old hopes. Maybe in these ashes he could find something new to live for.

He moved slowly around the pile, searching for sadness or regret amongst the wreckage and finding none. Just a quiet acceptance. Toward the back of the house, he stopped in his tracks, stunned by what he saw.

A California poppy had survived in Colby's flower bed. Aidan dropped the hose and knelt in the ashes to marvel at the delicate veined petals, glowing orange in the soot-tinged air.

"Hi." Jade's voice startled him out of his reverie.

He turned his head to look at her and she caught sight of the flower. "What? How is that even possible?"

"I don't know." His voice went gruff and he cleared his throat.

She dropped to her knees next to him and brushed the edge of one vivid petal carefully with the tip of her finger. "It's amazing how fire sometimes skips just one small thing."

His eyes stung and it wasn't the smoke. He tried to blink back the tears that rose.

"This garden is special to you, isn't it?" Jade put a gentle hand on his arm.

"It was Colby's sandbox." Aidan brought the heel of his hand up to shove the tears back in his eyes. "I made it into a garden, as a way to remember him."

"Oh, Aidan." The sympathy in her voice didn't help him get his own emotion under control. "I'm so sorry for all you've been through."

He stared at the poppy, breathing in the strange relief this one simple flower offered. The poppy seemed to look back at him, proud, bright and defiant. "I'm sorry, too," he finally said. "But maybe it's time I started to be more than sorry."

"This poppy—" her voice was so quiet, it was almost a whisper "—it feels like a sign. And I don't really believe in that kind of stuff."

He felt it, too. An easing in his chest. Forgiveness, maybe, from Colby, from God, or from himself—he couldn't know which. "I hope so," he said. "I could use a sign."

She rose to her feet and so did he, brushing the ash and mud off his crusted jeans. She looked up at him with a softness in her deep brown eyes. "Mitch, Travis and Bill are getting restless. We put out any hot spots we could find, so I think your part of this fire is officially out."

That was great to hear. When he looked south, he could see that the smoke was still thick there, the fire was still going strong. But he was out of danger now. "I can't believe we did it."

Her smile was almost shy. "I can't believe we did either. We got lucky, you know."

He couldn't let her go without trying to tell her how he felt. "You were my luck. I wouldn't have known what to do without you."

She put a hand on his forearm. "We did it together." They looked at each other for a long moment and Aidan felt that pull again, the bone-deep need to hold her in his arms. Soot-stained and weary, she was still the most beautiful person he'd ever seen.

"I have to leave."

"Where will you go?" He hadn't thought about her leaving. He had been dazed all morning, trying to take in all the loss and gratitude, and it had kept him firmly in the present moment.

"Back to our base in Ukiah to get changed. We'll get that poor bobcat to the emergency vet there, too. Do you want me to take Chip, as well?"

"I'll take him down to Willits. He knows the vet there, so he'll be more comfortable."

"That vet may have evacuated."

He hadn't thought of that. How the whole map of his little world out here on the north coast was altered, at least temporarily. "Then I'll get him to Ukiah. I don't want to send him off alone, though I appreciate the offer."

"Sounds like a plan." She looked at him, then over at the smoke in the southern distance. "After Ukiah, we'll head out to the fire line. We've got to keep fighting. It's heading toward my town now. Though no way are we going to let it get as far as Shelter Creek."

"I appreciate that. My cattle are sheltering there." He wanted to say more. About how much he admired her strength, confidence and skill. About how it had felt, holding her in his arms. But how could he say those things? He'd known her less than a day. Yet they'd shared more with each other in that day than he'd shared with anyone in years.

Which just meant he was a hermit, not that they had some special connection. He couldn't let his years of isolation fool him into reading too much into one embrace, or a kiss that had been more about sheer relief than anything else.

"I'll walk you back to the truck." He took one last look at the miraculous poppy and fell into step beside her, conscious of her small stature next to him, her lithe athletic build reminding him of how she'd fit so perfectly in his arms as they'd slept.

"What are you going to do now?" Jade bumped his arm gently with her shoulder as they walked down the hill toward the barn.

"Walk around my property a little. Assure myself that there really is no more fire. Then head into town to get Chip help and grab a meal, a shower and some sleep."

"And after that?"

Aidan shrugged, not sure how to look so far ahead. "Rebuild, I guess."

"You still want to stay out here? On your own?"

"I can't imagine leaving this place. I love this land. I did from the moment I came here. The first time I saw these rolling hills I knew this was where I was meant to be." The land was almost unrecognizable now in shades of black and gray, with smoke still dimming his view of the surrounding hills. He felt burned-out himself. Hollow after last night's emotions and fears.

They'd reached the barn now. Mitch, Travis and Bill were standing around their truck. Jade's truck was there, too. They must have used a winch to get it out of the mud. The crate with the bobcat in it was strapped in the back, a blanket covering it.

Jade turned to Aidan. "I said goodbye to Elliott. I felt really sad about leaving him. Can you believe it?" She held up her arms, still scratched from wrist to elbow.

Aidan smiled at her devotion to a cat who clearly hated her. "At least you have a souvenir of your dysfunctional relationship."

"Ha. Will you hang on to him until his owners get back? Or I'm sure there's a shelter in Ukiah that will take care of him, if that's easier."

"I'll figure out something. He'll probably be happier with me. Maybe he can come to the motel."

"That family seemed to love that cat. I'll bet they come back soon."

"I assume so. But no matter what, I'll take care of Elliott. You don't need to worry about him anymore. You've got a fire to stop." He hated the idea of her back out there, pitting herself against that wildfire yet again. But that was her work. Her life. Her choice.

She sighed. "Yeah. Thankfully, the wind has died way down. Can you feel that?" She raises a few fingers to test it.

She was right. With all the trees and bushes gone, Aidan hadn't noticed before, but the wind wasn't pulling at his clothes or tugging at his hair. The air was finally still.

Jade went on. "I think we have a chance at containing it in the next few days."

"If anyone can put it out, you can. I've seen your skills."

She smiled faintly. "I hope so." She glanced at her waiting crew, then back at him. "You take good care now."

He didn't want her to go. The knowledge hit him in the stomach and ached in his chest. It made no sense. Of course, she had to go. She was a firefighter caught here by chance. Not his friend. Not meant for him. "You, too, Jade. Thanks for everything."

She put her arms around his neck and he hugged her back, cherishing the feel of her close to him. "Maybe we'll make that dinner some time," she said quietly as she pulled away. "Spaghetti and meatballs."

"That would be great." Aidan manufactured a smile. He was sleep-deprived, adrenaline-crashed. He'd feel better once he got some food and rest. Plus, there was nothing to do but accept that she had to leave. "Good luck."

"If you're ever in Shelter Creek, stop by the fire station. If I'm not there, they'll know where to find me."

"Will do."

Jade started toward her truck and then paused. Turned. Ran back and gave Aidan another hug, pressing her head to his chest while he tried to memorize the feeling of her in his arms. Then she looked up at him with the calm gaze that had helped him keep his own fears in check last night. "I hope you can try to let go of the past a little now. You've been given another chance to live, Aidan. We both have. Let's make it count."

He pulled her close again and brushed his lips across the top of her head, then reluctantly let her slide out of his arms. He couldn't promise her that. Or anything. The future felt blank and foreign. He was still in shock that he was here at all. "Thanks, Jade, for everything."

He followed her to the trucks and shook hands with Mitch and Bill. Bill got into the cab but Mitch hesitated. "We've got the bobcat," he said. "We'll figure out a way to get your crate back to you once we get it to a vet."

"Take your time," Aidan told him. "I'm just glad it will get some help soon. I hope it makes it."

"Me, too." Mitch put a big hand on Aidan's shoulder. "You did a good thing rescuing it. And an even better thing, helping Jade get through this." He seemed to want to say more, but cleared his throat instead. He gave Aidan's shoulder a final squeeze and went to the truck.

Travis had been talking quietly to Jade,

but now he approached Aidan and shook his hand. "Thanks for looking out for my sister," he said.

Aidan smiled despite the way his heart hung heavy in his chest. "I think it was the other way around. She kept us safe. She's a heck of a firefighter."

Travis grinned. "It's in our blood. Take care, Aidan." He held out a hand to Jade. "Are you ready?"

"I guess so." She gave Aidan a brief wave. "Stay in touch. Let me know how you're doing."

"Likewise." He wanted to say more but there was no way to articulate the thoughts racing in his head. Especially when they all seemed to coalesce into two words. *Don't go.*

Jade followed Travis to her truck and Aidan watched in amusement as she tried to wrest the keys from her brother. Travis must have known the right words to defuse his sister's independent streak, because she hobbled around to the passenger's side, glaring at him while he laughed at her. Then Travis started the engine and they were off, bumping slowly up the lane, now a gray gravel strip in a black landscape.

Aidan peered into the back of Mitch's truck, where the bobcat was curled in a ragged ball in the corner of the big crate. "Good luck," he whispered. "Heal well. Be safe." Then Mitch started the engine, and with a final wave out the window, followed Travis and Jade away from the barn.

Aidan watched the trucks until they disappeared over the hill, heading for the road out, inexplicable loss heavy in his chest. The sound of their wheels faded out and the quiet that followed was as thick as fire smoke. Strange how it was even hard to breathe, now that Jade was gone.

He was just tired. He needed to get himself together. There was still plenty of work to do. Aidan headed for the barn, inhaling the comforting smell of horse and hay, proving to himself that he could breathe just fine. "Hey, Chip." He poked his head over the stall door where the cattle dog lay, head on his paws, so mad at Aidan for locking him in here again that he didn't even lift his head. He just rolled his eyes up and glared at him, as if he still couldn't believe his master's betrayal.

Aidan went into the stall and sat down next to the dog, keeping his body alongside Chip's so he wasn't forcing the dog to make contact. "Hey, buddy, I know you're mad at me. But the ground burned your paws last night. This was the safest place for you today, until things cooled down."

Chip pricked up his ears but kept his head down. Aidan rubbed Chip under the collar. "You're a great dog and I know you only wanted to help. But this fire was something you couldn't help with. It was bigger than anything you or I have ever experienced before."

The dog sat up, looked toward the stall door and whined.

"Oh, buddy." Aidan rubbed his dog's ears. "You want Jade, don't you? She's gone. She was only passing through." He sighed and brought his forehead to Chip's. "We're both going to miss her, aren't we?"

Chip raised a paw and put it on Aidan's arm, as if he understood the hollow feeling in Aidan's chest.

Aidan carefully took the paw and leaned

down to peer at the pad. It was hard to tell how badly it was burned. "The fire is all out now. Let's go wash these again and see what we're dealing with, okay?" He unhooked the chain from Chip's collar. Then he carried his dog out of the barn to tend to his paws.

CHAPTER THIRTEEN

AIDAN TRAINED THE hose on a clump of charred bushes that was smoldering suspiciously. He was uphill from the barn, making sure the fire was definitely out. They'd fought so hard to save this one structure, no way would he lose it now out of negligence. It was only late morning but it was hot and dry, and the wind had picked up again, tossing ash around like confetti. Wiping a gritty forearm across his eyes, Aidan looked out across his ranch.

Black, gray and green. The colors of his new reality. Black twisted trees, gray fields, the black-and-gray ash pile of his former home. The one green pasture was a small, defiant oasis of life. Even the sheep were gray, their wool covered in ash and soot. Most of them were lying down, chewing cud, resting from their stressful night. Aidan had checked on them again a while ago and, miraculously, none of them seemed injured. Payday had one small, singed patch on his hindquarter from an ember, but it seemed minor. When Aidan put salve on it, the big horse didn't even wince.

Jade and the other firefighters had been gone for a couple hours, but it felt longer. Aidan knew he should go to town, get a motel room, find some food and have a shower. But his land's survival and his own had tangled together during the fire. He'd only worry if he left now, before he was sure that every last spark was out.

Over the sound of splashing water, Aidan listened to the silence. No birds, no rustling of leaves or grass. No cattle, no horses, just the occasional bleat of a sheep. It was a silence of absence. Absence of life, of livestock, of wildlife…of Jade. Strange how she'd spent less than twenty-four hours on his ranch and yet with her gone, something essential was missing. A vitality and a meaning that ran deep. When her truck had disappeared down the driveway, he'd felt as charred and bleak as the landscape around him.

But he'd be okay. Maybe that's what this

fire had taught him. That even with absence, even with permanent, aching scars on his soul, life was still worth fighting for. Facing death, some part of him had awakened and fought hard to live. Like the land around him, he wasn't completely ruined. The ground would renew with the first rain. Grass would rise out of this scorched soil. He wouldn't rise from these ashes easily, but he could push himself up with sweat and hard work. He could come out of this crisis changed and ready, as Jade had mentioned, to live again.

It was the first time, since Colby died, that he'd felt anything like hope. That he'd thought of anything besides taking the next breath or putting one foot in front of him.

A noise on the driveway had him looking up. A truck was bumping down his driveway. It looked like Maya's, but without a trailer attached. Aidan brought the hose with him and clambered down the slope toward the barn, skidding through muddy ash to land in the gravel below. He turned off the water, and went to greet his visitors.

It was Maya and Caleb, with an older woman Aidan didn't recognize. Maya was first out of the truck, bounding toward him to throw her arms around him. "You made it!" She stepped back to look him up and down with wide eyes. Caleb came to join them and put a hand on Aidan's shoulder.

"You had us pretty worried, man." Caleb studied him. "You're a mess, but you're still here." He stepped forward and pulled him in for a quick hug. "Glad to see you."

"We ran into Jade in Ukiah," Maya told Aidan. "She talked the sheriff into letting us through the roadblock to check on you. We brought you a sandwich and some other food we grabbed at the market there. Aidan, we thought we might not see you again. Jade said she was out here with you?" Maya put her hands to her mouth. "I'm sorry I'm babbling. I'm just so relieved, but I'll stop talking."

The older woman approached with a paper grocery bag. She had silver hair cut short and a sweet smile. "I'm Lillian, Maya's grandmother. You need to sit down and eat something."

She reminded him of his neighbor, Nellie. And because he'd spent so much time with Nellie, he knew better than to argue. Plus, his stomach felt hollowed out with hunger. "Thank you, ma'am. It's nice to meet you. I appreciate you coming out here to see me."

Lillian glanced around at the burned grass, fencing and bushes along the driveway. "You were hit pretty hard."

"It's incredible that you saved the barn," Caleb added.

"We saved the sheep shed, too," Aidan said. "Mainly because it's metal, but still. I can keep my business going out here."

"But, Aidan, your house." Maya glanced up the hill. "It broke my heart to drive in here and see it gone."

"We couldn't save everything." It was hard to think about the house. It was such a mess of regret and relief to have it gone. "I can camp out in the barn until I get something set up." Aidan gestured for them to come inside. "Pull up a hay bale."

They all sat down and Aidan reached into the bag, almost crying with gratitude at the sight of the big sandwich wrapped in deli paper. They were all quiet, watching him eat. It wasn't until he'd wolfed down the sandwich that he told them what had happened, and how he and Jade had worked together to survive.

"It must have been terrifying," Maya said when he finished.

"I'm not gonna lie, it wasn't the easiest night. But Jade kept setting new plans, and backup plans, and I just followed them. Whenever they stopped working, she came up with something new for us to try."

"Jade's a strong person," Maya said. "She was a few years behind me in high school, but everyone knew how athletic and tough she was, even back then."

Thinking of a younger Jade, giving everyone a run for their money in whatever sport she chose, brought a smile to Aidan's face. "She's something else," he said quietly.

Caleb reached into the grocery bag and pulled out a sports drink. He handed it to Aidan. "You know you're welcome to stay with us. The firefighters seem pretty sure they'll contain the fire before it gets anywhere near Shelter Creek. We can haul your sheep down to our ranch if you want to take a little downtime. You might want to regroup for a while."

Aidan shook his head. "Thanks but no.

I've got to start rebuilding up here. The sooner I get going, the better."

Caleb's lips pressed together as if he wasn't happy with Aidan's answer. "Do you have any help?"

"I'm good on my own," Aidan assured him. "I can always hire someone for the big projects."

"Aidan's a loner, remember?" Maya's expression was gently teasing.

She knew nothing of his past. He'd never told her. And though a few days ago her words would have rung true, now they didn't. He didn't want a lot of hired hands around right now, but he liked that Maya and her family had come to check on him. And he missed Jade with an ache that didn't seem like it would go away anytime soon. So he couldn't be a total loner. Not anymore.

Lillian had been quietly listening, but now she spoke. "I have a friend who has a trailer on her ranch that they aren't using. Maybe we could haul it up here for you to live in, until you rebuild? I hate to think of you camping out in this barn."

The generosity of these people might shake him up even more than the fire had.

Aidan barely knew them. He only knew Maya because of her job as a wildlife biologist. A couple years ago, she'd brought Caleb to visit and learn about humane predator management. And she'd brought a few other ranchers to visit since then. Yet here her grandmother was, offering him a trailer. "You're very kind. If it's not too much trouble, I'd appreciate a roof over my head."

Another pickup rattled down the driveway. Aidan stood and craned his neck, wondering who it could be. A tall, blonde woman got out, slung a black duffel bag over her shoulder, and started toward them.

Maya went to the door of the barn and waved the woman over. "Aidan, this is Emily, our vet from Shelter Creek. I asked if she'd come up here and take a look at your animals. I was afraid some might be injured. Of course I didn't realize that you and Jade were going to pull off some kind of miracle and bring your ranch through in such good shape."

Aidan had no idea how he'd ever repay Maya for her generosity, getting a vet out here so quickly.

Emily shook Aidan's hand. "I'm so glad

you're okay. Maya told me a lot about you."
Emily looked at Maya. "Wow. It's a wild
drive out here, with everything still smoking."

"I know. It's heartbreaking. Aidan, did
you see any wildlife come through last
night? Emily volunteers her free time as
our vet at the Shelter Creek Wildlife Center. She might be able to help out any wild
animals, as well."

"It's been quiet today," Aidan told them.
"No birds, nothing. But last night we saw
rabbits on the run, and a couple of deer
waited out the worst of the fire in the pond
with us. And we caught a bobcat with
burned paws. The firefighters took it down
to the emergency vet in Ukiah."

"A bobcat?" Emily's eyes were wide. "Impressive. How did you catch it?"

"It took refuge in the barn. We cornered it
and then used brooms to poke it into a crate.
It was hissing and spitting and pretty upset,
but we got it in there."

"Well done," Maya said. "It's not easy to
catch those, but you've just given it a chance.
It couldn't get far with burned paws." She

glanced at Emily. "Maybe it can recuperate at the wildlife center?"

"I'll stop in Ukiah and check with the vet when I leave here," Emily said. "I'm sure they'll be glad for us to take it once it's ready for rehabilitation."

It was a relief to know that the bobcat would have Maya and Emily to help it get well. But Aidan had another animal that needed looking after. "Speaking of which, my dog, Chip, got out during the fire and burnt his paws, too. But they don't look too bad to me. I washed them pretty well and put him in a stall. I was just about to run him down to the vet."

Chip must have heard his name, because a low woof came from his stall.

"I have him locked up there to protect his paws. He's not happy."

"That's smart," Emily said. "Let me take a look at him now."

Caleb put a hand to Aidan's arm. "How about I see how your sheep are doing? And you've got your horse out there, too, right?"

"I'd appreciate that, Caleb. I looked them over this morning, but the smoke was still pretty thick and we were still putting out some hot spots. You might be able to find any problems that I missed. Just be mindful of the dogs. You've met them before. Thor and Odin."

Caleb grinned. "I love those dogs. I have a couple of their cousins working on my ranch now." He headed for the pasture, his big strides covering the distance easily.

Aidan led Maya, Emily and Lillian toward the barn.

"After I take a look at Chip and your other animals," Emily said, "maybe Maya and I can take a walk around and make sure there's no other wildlife out there suffering." Emily looked downhill from the barn where the blackened hills rolled out for miles. "It looks so bleak, but I know that wild animals have many survival strategies."

"A lot of them will make it," Maya assured her. "They'll outrun it or find shelter. Aidan, the birds will probably be back here soon, feasting on all the bugs that are going to come out of hiding."

"Good to know." Aidan couldn't help but smile. Maya loved science and all living beings so much that it might not occur to her that more bugs wasn't good news for everyone.

He turned to Emily. "I don't know if you can help me with this, but I've got a couple feral kittens, too, who we managed to catch right before the fire got to them. Do you know anyone in Shelter Creek who might want to try domesticating them?"

Emily glanced at Lillian, who had her hand pressed to her heart. "I think I do. Lillian, want to give it a try?"

"I'll take them," Maya's grandmother said. "I've been wanting to get some cats. And I'm sure if they are too wild for me, I can find someone who will give them a good home."

"I appreciate that," Aidan told her. "Their parents were barn cats, who had a pretty good life out here with the mice and all. But now, the way things are..." he trailed off, waving an arm at the moonscape surrounding them.

"It will be my pleasure," Lillian assured him.

Aidan led the way into the stall where Chip lay on his side. The cattle dog rolled onto his stomach, but Aidan noticed he didn't get up. His paws must be hurting him a little more, now that Aidan had cleaned off the debris. Emily examined the dog all over. Then she applied some salve and wrapped his front paws with gauze and tape. As she worked, Aidan leaned back against the wooden partition and blew out a long slow breath. It would take hundreds of little steps just like this one to recover from this fire. But with people like Emily helping him out, he'd get things put to rights around here, eventually. And for the second time in the past twenty-four hours, he was glad he wasn't alone.

"I DON'T THINK fried chicken has ever tasted this good." Jade looked down the table to where her mother sat next to Dean. "Thanks for making a feast, Mom."

"We're just glad that fire is out and we get to have you all back home." Her mom looked pretty tonight, a flowered headband holding back her shoulder-length brown hair. She had a streak of gray at her forehead now. She smiled at her husband at the head of the table. "I guess that's just the way my life was meant to be. Waiting on you, Stan, when you were a firefighter, and now waiting on my kids."

"Well, Jade's poor choice last week gave us the most worrisome wait we've ever had." Jade's dad fixed her with a stern look from beneath thick, gray brows. Stan Carson hadn't tolerated mistakes from his firefighters when he was chief, and he definitely didn't like to see his children make any either.

"Dad." Travis put a hand on his father's arm. "It wasn't Jade's fault that a tree fell across the road."

"But she said herself that she probably wouldn't have gotten stuck out there at all if she hadn't gone back to try to save that fool rancher." Her father twisted the pepper mill as if he were wringing the neck of a small animal.

"He's not a fool." The words came out louder than Jade had intended and everyone turned to look at her. Thank goodness Mom had insisted on a nice dim candlelight dinner, or everyone would be able to see Jade's face turn beet red under their scrutiny. "He'd promised his elderly neighbor he'd save her prized sheep. He was determined to keep his word."

Her father's expression hardened. He

never backed down in an argument. "If you hadn't gone back for him a second time, you wouldn't have put your life at risk."

Jade wished she hadn't told that part of the story to anyone. But it was too late now.

Dean came to her defense. "Jade was trying to do her job and save the guy's life. Which, by the way, she did."

"People who refuse to evacuate get what they get."

Jade knew her father wasn't really as heartless as he seemed. Every soul lost in a fire he'd fought weighed heavily on his mind, especially now that he was older and retired. Not that it made his harsh words feel any better. "Look, Dad, I'm sorry I gave you guys a scare. Maybe you're right that I shouldn't have tried to go back for him. But think about it this way. If I hadn't gone back to his ranch a second time, that tree might have fallen right on top of me."

"Oh my goodness, can we change the subject please?" Mom paled and put her head in her hands.

"Great idea," Jade said. "Let's criticize someone else now. How about Ash, since he's not here to defend himself?"

Travis and Dean burst out laughing, and Jade laughed along with them, but she didn't actually find it funny. These post-mortems her father liked to perform on her life choices were a tradition she didn't appreciate—especially because he never seemed to do the same for her brothers.

She interrupted the laughter without thought, without a plan. "Dad, you know what? I'm twenty-eight years old and I'm still sitting here wondering if you wish I'd been born a boy."

Her family's answering silence was solid as a wall. But Jade couldn't stay quiet any-more. Maybe it was surviving the fire and being given a second chance. The words just wouldn't stay inside. "I'm so tired of com-ing up short in your eyes, Dad. When I was young, I did every sport you wanted, and I got great grades in school. But you were never satisfied."

"Jade, that isn't true," her mom intervened.

"It feels true to me," Jade told her. She looked back at her father who'd crossed his arms over his chest and was glaring at her. Probably wishing she was still a kid so he could send her to her room.

Jade's heart was banging in her chest at the unfamiliar feeling of speaking her mind to him. "I graduated top of my class from the fire academy and I've taken on more and more responsibility at work. I'm apprenticing so I can qualify for the captain's exam. And now I've survived a wildfire out in the middle of nowhere and all you can do is criticize?"

Jade stood and pushed down the tears that were rising. She didn't cry. Wouldn't cry. Not in front of her brothers and a father who'd resisted any show of emotion. Who'd pushed her to be tough. Well, now he could see just how tough she'd become. "I'm sorry I wasn't born with the right anatomy for you, Dad. If I were a man, you might respect me the way you respect my brothers. But as it is, I don't think there's anything I could ever do that would make you proud. So I'm done trying." She turned to her mother. "Thank you, Mom, for making us such a good dinner. I'm sorry to leave early, but I think I've had all I can take."

Jade went to the hall for her coat. In the dining room, her family still sat in stunned silence. She felt guilty for ruining her mom's dinner but strangely, she didn't feel terrible about what she'd said. Just relieved that she'd finally said it.

CHAPTER FOURTEEN

PEOPLE FROM SHELTER CREEK were generous to an extreme. Aidan looked around the barn in wonder. In the week since the fire, they'd done everything from give him the refrigerator he'd just plugged into the wall, to delivering the pile of donated wood at his feet that he'd use to replace the fencing along his driveway.

Then there was the trailer, on loan from a woman named Annie Brooks, who was a friend of Maya's grandmother. She'd recently gotten married and she and her husband had dropped it off the day after the fire. The trailer was huge, and so comfortable that Aidan was wondering if he even needed to rebuild at all. Maybe he could just buy it from Annie and be all set.

Except there was something about being a guy in the middle of nowhere, living alone in a trailer, that was a little too hermit-like, even for him. He should build a real house, eventually. It was hard to imagine it right now. He'd been living a day at a time, focused on cleaning up, repairing and looking after his livestock. It should have kept him too busy to think about the fire, and Jade. But she came back to him every night in his sleep, in dreams where flames roared high and he was trying to pull her away from them, but she insisted on staying and beating at them with a towel.

And then there were the dreams where she lay close and peaceful in his arms.

Aidan tossed the hay bale he was holding into the wheelbarrow and hung the hay hooks on the wall. He grabbed the handles so hard he almost tipped the wheelbarrow over. He had to get a grip. Dreams were called dreams for a reason. They weren't real, and there was no point in thinking about them once the night was over.

Aidan took the hay over to the pasture where the sheep were grazing and divided it into portions that he tossed over the fence. There wasn't much grass left with so many sheep on this one small piece of land. Aidan climbed through the fence to say hi to Thor and Odin. The dogs had finally settled down after the fire and seemed content to lie in the sun with the sheep they guarded.

Saying goodbye to the dogs, Aidan retrieved Chip from the stall where he had to wait when Thor and Odin were near the barn and the pasture.

Keeping Chip close, Aidan headed up the hill to where his house used to be, to check in with Maya, Annie and Lillian. The women had driven up from Shelter Creek early this morning with their cars packed with donations. As Aidan approached the trailer, Maya's old three-legged dog, Einstein, heaved himself up and shambled over to greet them. He and Chip got along well and after a moment of tail wagging, the two dogs flopped down in the sun for a companionable nap. Chip's paws were healing well, but he still required a lot of rest.

The women had brought donated bed linens, towels and other supplies with them. "Let me get that," Aidan said to Lillian, who was wrestling a box of pots and pans out of the trunk of her car.

"Only because you're at least twice my size. Not because I'm old." She shook a finger at him, but it was accompanied by her sweet smile.

They both looked up at the sound of wheels on the gravel of Aidan's driveway. He recognized the truck immediately. "Nellie!" He set the box back in Lillian's trunk and jogged to meet his neighbor, opening the door for her when she shut off the engine.

Nellie jumped down, spry as ever, and gave him a big hug. "I'm so glad you're okay, Aidan." She looked rested and surprisingly happy, considering she'd just lost everything in a fire.

"How have you been? I haven't been able to call since our cell tower is still out, but I've been hoping you were okay."

"I've been fine. I'm staying with my sister in Healdsburg. She owns a yarn shop there and she caught a cold, so I ran the shop for her the last several days. I'd called the sheriff's office after the fire, though, so I knew that everything had burned." A troubled look clouded Nellie's usually cheerful expression. "Truth was, maybe I just wasn't ready to come look at it. It took me a few extra days to gather my courage."

"That's understandable," Aidan said. "I'm just glad you're all right."

"Thanks to you, Aidan. You got me out of here just in time. I was so worried about you that night. But then I saw the news reports about how you made it through the fire."

"Oh yeah. My five seconds of fame." The news outlets had gotten wind of his story and sent reporters up to interview him. Since he was pretty much cut off from the world here without cell reception, he hadn't seen any of the coverage.

Tears welled in Nellie's eyes. "I'm so sorry if you got stuck here because of me and my sheep."

"I was stuck out here because I'm stubborn." He pulled his friend in for another hug. "Don't be upset, Nellie. We're both still here. That's what matters."

He was still here, thanks to Jade. Just the thought of her, her name, her courage, created a new kind of lonely in Aidan's heart. All this time he'd longed for Colby who was out of his reach. It was different to miss someone who was just a couple hour's drive away. In theory he could go to her and see how she was doing. But they weren't friends. Just people connected because of circumstance.

Aidan brought his attention back to Nellie. "I'm sorry about your property. I drove up there the day after the fire to see if I could salvage anything."

Nellie nodded. "I just came from there. Not much left to salvage is there?"

It was an understatement. The fire had taken everything. Nellie's house, barns and outbuildings had all been historic, weathered wood. Now they were ash. "It's a real loss."

Nellie shrugged. "What you went through a couple years ago with your family is a real loss, Aidan. A few buildings don't matter much in comparison."

As always, she'd said exactly what was in her heart and, while some people might think her blunt, he'd always appreciated her candor. "Where are your mules and llamas?"

"At my cousin's property out on the coast near Bodega Bay. They seem pretty happy there. He's offered to keep them as long as I want."

"Good to hear it. Would you like to visit your sheep while you're here?"

Nellie's face brightened. "I'd love to. And

you need to let me know what I owe you for their room and board."

"Nothing, Nellie. It's been an honor to keep them for you. They've settled in really well."

"Nonsense. You have to let me pay you."

Aidan shook his head. "I'm the one who owes you. Remember how you fed me and kept me going after I lost Colby? I don't think I'd be here without you. Let me take care of your sheep, for as long as you need me to."

He led her to the trailer, where Lillian, Maya and Annie had gathered out front, giving them space for their reunion. "Ladies, this is my neighbor and good friend Nellie. Nellie, this is Maya Burton and her grandmother Lillian, and Annie Brooks."

"Nice to meet you," Nellie said. "But Annie and I don't need any introduction. Our sheep have been competing with each other at the county fair for decades."

Annie stepped forward and took Nellie's hands in her own. "I didn't realize you were the neighbor Aidan told me about. I should have realized it when I saw the good-looking sheep he's been babysitting. I'm so sorry about your property."

"Thanks, Annie. It's a big loss. But we're blessed to be alive, aren't we? Would you all want to walk with us? Aidan is taking me to visit my sheep."

"I think Maya and I will stay here and keep working on Aidan's trailer." Lillian smiled at Annie. "But you should go. We all know you'd rather be with sheep than with us."

Annie grinned and shrugged. "You know me too well." She took Nellie's arm and linked it with hers. "Shall we?"

Aidan listened to the two women talk about the fire as they picked their way through the blackened grass to the pasture. He still had all the sheep in the one irrigated field, though it was grazed all the way down now and he was supplementing their diet with hay. He'd need to move them out of here soon, before the remaining grass was trampled into dust. He'd been fixing fences and using sprinklers to get another field ready, though the poor sheep would be living amongst ashes for a long time to come.

They all stopped at the fence and watched

the sheep. Most were gathered around the piles of alfalfa hay Aidan had left for them, but several were lying down in a group with Thor and Odin, enjoying the morning sunshine and chewing their cud.

"They look downright peaceful," Nellie said, turning to Aidan in amazement. "They've come through this fire just fine."

Aidan smiled down at his old friend. He loved her wide-eyed wonder at the world. "They don't have to worry about insurance companies and rebuilding, like we do."

Nellie's smile faded and she looked uncertain all of a sudden. "That's what I wanted to talk to you about. I don't think I'm going to rebuild."

Aidan felt her words in his stomach. It had never occurred to him that she wouldn't come back here. That they wouldn't eventually resume their Sunday night dinners, and their habit of checking on each other a few times a week. "Why not?"

"I'm getting older, much as I hate to admit it. When I think about what I want to do with the years I have left, rebuilding a ranch on my own just doesn't seem that inviting."

"What are you thinking of doing?" Aidan

could hear the shock in Annie's voice. She would probably run her ranch forever. In the time they'd spent together since the fire, Aidan had learned a lot from the veteran rancher. In every conversation it was clear that she still loved her work.

"My sister asked me to move in with her and teach knitting classes at the shop. It will be nice to spend more time with her and have some free time, for the first time in my life."

Aidan tried to take in what Nellie was saying. It made sense, but selfishly he didn't want her to leave. "What about your sheep? And your land?"

"I'll put them up for sale. I need to make sure the sheep go to a good home. Are either of you interested in buying them?"

Aidan hesitated. Nellie's sheep were prized for their wool, but that would take his business in a different direction. Did he have room on his plate, what with all the building and repairs he'd need to do in the next couple years?

"If Aidan doesn't want them, I'd certainly consider taking them," Annie said. "I still enjoy raising sheep, the shearing, the whole bit. And your sheep give top-quality wool, Nellie. I know it well, from all the years I came in second to you at the fair."

Nellie's smile was full of relief. "I'd be so happy if you wanted to buy them, Annie. I know they'd have a great home with you. And don't you go feeling sorry for yourself about the fair. There were plenty of years that I came in second to you."

Annie grinned. "And now it won't be any fun to go, because without you there, I'll be bound to win."

"I'll come cheer you on, anyway."

Aidan watched the sheep eat and listened to the two women reminisce. Nellie was always so active and youthful, he often forgot she was in her seventies. Of course she'd want to slow down and live in town and have some fun. The dull ache in his chest that had been there since the fire seemed to get a little bigger, a little heavier. He was going to miss her a lot.

As they walked back to the trailer, Aidan managed to pretend he was enthusiastic about Nellie's decision. She made him promise to visit her in Healdsburg at least once a month and she offered him first dibs on her land if he wanted to expand his ranch. He listened to it all with a smile that hid his desolation at her decision. Without her here, he'd be truly alone up on this ridge. Is that what he wanted?

It was definitely what he'd wanted after Colby's death. Just him, the land and his grief. But now that idea seemed lonelier and kind of depressing. Maybe it was just the bleak, monochromatic landscape. He was living in a black-and-white photo now. Once the rains came and the grass and bushes started to grow back, he'd probably feel better.

When Nellie left, Annie and Lillian went back into the trailer to continue organizing Aidan's temporary home. Maya stayed with Aidan, watching Nellie's truck disappear down the driveway. "I have good news," she told him. "That bobcat you caught is going to be okay. We've moved it down to the Shelter Creek Wildlife Center. It can live there until it's well enough to be released up here on your ranch again."

"That's great news," Aidan said, but his voice came out stiff and toneless. Nellie was gone. He hadn't realized how much he'd come to rely on her friendship.

"Are you okay?" Maya put a hand on Aidan's arm. "It must be sad to learn that your friend is moving away."

"I'm fine." Aidan straightened his shoulders. Of course he was fine. He and Nellie hadn't even spent that much time together, really. He'd be okay without their Sunday dinners.

"Maybe it's none of my business," Maya said. "But I have to say something that's been on my mind." She looked around at the ranch. "It's beautiful here. And you turned this place into such an exemplary, sustainable ranch that has educated so many people about how to live in harmony with wildlife. But this fire offers a chance for a change. Have you ever thought about moving closer to a town? I know a couple of really nice properties for sale near Shelter Creek."

A memory flashed in front of Aidan's eyes, of Colby toddling across the grass near the barn, laughing as the sun glinted in his blond hair. All his memories of his son were here. "No." He said it too abruptly and quickly tried to soften his tone. "I love this place. I don't see myself leaving."

Maya was silent for a moment. He liked that about her. The way she really seemed to listen and think before she answered. "I understand what it's like to want to hide out from the world," she said softly. "I did it for many years. I don't know what happened to you, Aidan, but I've always noticed that you seem a little sad. Just remember that you don't have to go through life alone, no matter what burden you carry. That's what I learned when I moved back home to Shelter Creek."

Aidan usually tried not to pry. Tried to stay out of other people's business. But something in her words and tone made him suspect that she'd been through something big. That she understood what it meant to carry pain on your shoulders every single moment of every day. "Why were you hiding?"

"A car accident," she said quietly. "I was driving. Caleb's sister was in the back seat without a seat belt and she was killed. My friend Trisha was in the front with me and she injured her leg badly. She still limps to this day."

"I had no idea." Aidan tried to put her story together with his image of her. She'd always seemed so confident and strong. Someone who took on the world and changed it for the better.

A rueful smile tugged at the corner of her mouth. "It's not something I advertise. It's the hardest thing in my life. I live with a lot of regret and guilt. But I've learned that I still deserve a full life, with friends and family and love."

If she'd hit him over the head with one of the pots she and Lillian had delivered, his ears wouldn't be ringing any harder than they were now. "I feel like you've looked inside me. Are you sure you don't have X-ray vision in addition to your biology skills?" His voice came out shaky with emotion.

"Do you want to talk about it?"

Did he? He'd kept the story inside for over two years. Until the fire. And Jade. But if anyone could share this burden with him, it was Maya, who carried so much grief of her own. He pried open his heart and told her what he'd only shared with Nellie and Jade.

About Colby, about Sheila, the blame and the guilt. "I guess, like you said, I've been hiding out ever since."

Maya took his hand in both of hers. "It's okay to hide out. Some wounds need a lot of time before they're not totally raw anymore. But don't hide forever, okay? Come see us in Shelter Creek. As soon as that cell tower gets fixed, I'm calling and inviting you. And you'd better say yes." She brightened and let go of his hand. "We can invite Jade and all have a meal or something. I'd like to get to know her—" She stopped suddenly and regarded him with a shrewd expression. "You just got the loneliest look on your face. You miss her, don't you?"

This woman was way too observant. Must be all the time she spent watching animals. "I barely know her. But I felt something." He shrugged. "It's probably just that we survived this fire together, and then she was gone."

"Go see her," Maya said. "Go down to Shelter Creek and pay her a visit."

"She'd probably think it was strange. She was just doing her job." Except that kiss, falling asleep with her in his arms, it hadn't felt like she was just a firefighter then. She'd felt like an angel and a dream and so much more.

"Of course she'll want to see you. Like you said, you survived together. That's a bond that doesn't go away." Maya clasped her hands together. "Visit her this weekend. Grandma Lillian and I can stay up here Saturday night and keep an eye on your sheep if you want."

Her enthusiasm was kind of funny. "Are you the local matchmaker?"

Maya laughed. "Usually my grandma and her friends take care of the matchmaking. But maybe they've rubbed off on me a little." Her smile faded. "Honestly, I just know how healing Caleb has been for me. If there's a chance there's something between you and Jade, you owe it to yourself to go find out."

She was offering him a chance to do exactly what he'd wanted to do in the week since the fire. She was giving him the courage to try. But still, what would someone as special as Jade want from him? He was a broken man carrying way too much trouble in his heart.

"Just try, Aidan. If it doesn't work, at least you'll know, and you can let it go."

He blew out a long, stress-filled breath. "Saturday? As in day after tomorrow?"

"That's the one. We'll take care of Chip and the sheep and everything. We can try out this fancy trailer of Annie's. You can crash at my house. Caleb will be happy to have you stay the night."

"Are you sure?" She was like Chip when he was herding the sheep. Totally single-minded and nipping at his heels.

"Someone he can talk to about wild-life management and sustainable ranching methods?" Maya rolled her eyes. "He'll be in heaven."

He and Caleb did have that in common. Maya wasn't allowing him any more reasons to say no. And a plan was forming, in a small, hopeful corner of his mind. "And you'll find out if she's working Saturday night?"

"Sure. But if I can't call you, I'll have to tell you when we get here on Saturday."

"That will be fine."

She beamed a satisfied smile at him.

"Shall we go in and finish setting up your new digs?"

"Yes. And thank you, Maya. For everything."

"Hey, I've made it partway up the hill. I'm happy to help someone hanging out near the bottom."

He had been at the bottom. Wallowing in grief and helpless to move forward. But he wasn't there now. Jade had pulled him partway up the hill, he realized. She'd changed him. And now with Maya extending a hand, he just might make it a little further up.

CHAPTER FIFTEEN

JADE WAS PUTTING away her equipment when she heard Danny Thompson talking to someone outside the open door of the garage. Probably just a local, stopping by to say hello. She hung her coat and stretched her arms up in the air, feeling muscles and bones ease into place. Her back was still a little sore. She'd slipped on a hillside while fighting the fire last week, after she'd left Aidan's ranch, and landed right on a rock. The bruise below her ribs was impressive, and the aches and pains were hanging on days later.

"Jade?" Danny stuck his head around the door of the garage. "There's someone here to see you."

Jade walked across the garage. Hopefully this wasn't another reporter. Ever since word had gotten out about how she and Aidan had survived the wildfire, news agencies had been coming by to try to talk to her. She'd hoped the interest had died down along with the flames.

She stepped out into the sunlight and there was Aidan, standing in her driveway with a bag of groceries on the ground on either side of him. Her heart jumped in her chest and she put a hand to her sternum to calm it. "Aidan?" He was as tall, and striking as she'd remembered, wearing faded jeans, a pair of clean, tan work boots and a light blue T-shirt. "What are you doing here?"

His smile was a little tentative. "I was thinking maybe we could make that meal."

The meal they'd planned as fire raged over them. As they'd tried to keep themselves calm. What a sweet gesture. It was so good to see him, Jade wanted to rush into his arms. Which was ridiculous. They barely knew each other. But he was the only person who knew what it was like, who'd been through the fire with her, who understood how precious every day had seemed ever since. "You show up at a fire station and offer to cook, you're going to get a definite yes."

Aidan laughed. "You haven't tasted my cooking yet. Don't get too excited."

It was good to see him smile. Bizarre to see him here on the station driveway, when for the last week he'd seemed like part of a surreal dream.

"Danny, this is Aidan. Aidan, Danny." Jade glanced at her watch. "Five-thirty. Perfect timing for dinner." She went to take a bag of groceries for him, then hesitated. Should she hug him? He didn't hold out his arms, so she picked up a bag and gave him a smile instead. "It's really nice to see you again."

He picked up the other bag and fell into step beside her. "I hope I'm not intruding, just showing up like this. I would have called, but there's still no phone service up at my ranch."

She'd wondered how he was, up there. She'd even thought about manufacturing a reason to go check on him, but she'd been working so much. And it had seemed odd, how connected she felt to him. She met people, and helped people, all the time in this job, and didn't feel a need to find out how they were later on.

She led the way through the garage and up the stairs to the firehouse. There were just a few staff here today. Over half their crew was still out mopping up the fire that had destroyed Aidan's ranch. A few others were on much-deserved days off.

Kayla was on one of the couches in the living room, watching the news and mending the pants she'd ripped on their call today. "Kayla, this is Aidan. He's the guy I made it through the fire with and he's making us dinner tonight."

"No way." Kayla jumped up and came to greet them. She took the bag of groceries out of Aidan's hands and put them on the wide counter that separated the kitchen from the living room. "We should be making you dinner," she said, and held out a hand to shake his vigorously. "Jade told us what a pro you were in the fire."

Jade put her bag on the counter next to the other one and waved a hand around. "So this is our fire station. Kitchen, dining area and living room. The bathroom's over there down the hall." She gestured toward it. "Please make yourself at home."

"I will." Aidan went around the counter

into the kitchen and began unpacking groceries.

"What are we eating?" Kayla pulled out a stool at the counter and plunked down.

"Spaghetti and meatballs," Aidan answered with a wink at Jade. "Green salad with Italian dressing, garlic bread and hot apple pie for dessert."

"That's awesome. Total comfort food." Kayla gave Jade a shrewd look. "Jade, I'm still trying to find that patch kit you mentioned for my jacket. Can you show me where you put it?"

Jade stared at her friend. "What?" And then realized what was going on. There was no patch kit. Just Kayla, motioning subtly toward the bedroom.

"Sure, I'll show you." Jade followed Kayla into the bedroom and shut the door behind them. "What are you doing?"

Kayla put her hands to her cheeks. "You didn't mention that your rancher was gorgeous!"

"Kayla, come on. It didn't matter what he looked like. We were just trying to make it out of there alive."

"Well, you did, and he's here and he's

handsome. He looks like some kind of warrior or something. All rugged with that thick blond hair."

"He's a nice guy. When the fire was really bad and we were in the pond, we kept ourselves calm by talking about food. We described our perfect, most comforting meal. Tonight he came to make it as a thank you. That's all."

"We help a lot of people, and they don't show up to cook us dinner, Jade. Clearly he's interested in you."

"Well, if he is, I guess I'll find that out eventually. We don't have to make a big deal out of it right now, okay? Let's just treat this like any other dinner on a work night."

"But you like him, right? I mean, how could you not?"

Irritation was building beneath Jade's skin. She'd never been much for this kind of girl talk. And Aidan was so much more than a good-looking guy. It felt uncomfortable to have him reduced to something that one-dimensional. She'd shared so much more with him that night in the dark, with fire all around. "I'm not looking for a relationship right now. I need to keep my focus on work. Please can we just go out there and make dinner and act normal?"

"Sure, hon. You keep telling yourself that. But I hope you give the guy a chance. Work isn't everything."

Jade thought of her father and his dismissal of all she'd accomplished. She hadn't heard from him since she'd stormed out of her parents' house a few nights ago. Ever since, she'd been working even harder, studying for her exam, feeling like she had more to prove than ever. "Work means a lot to me." She opened the door to go back to the kitchen. "Thanks for trying to look out for me, though."

"Anytime. You go on out there and spend time with your *friend* the rancher. I'll give you guys some space."

Jade nodded and went out to the hall, and Kayla shut the door between them.

"Would you like an assistant chef?" Jade approached the counter and saw that Aidan had already found a cutting board and a knife, and was mincing onions and garlic. The giant pasta pot was on the stove. "Looks like you found what you need."

Aidan looked up from his chopping. "You guys have a well-stocked kitchen."

"Cooking is our main source of fun around here in the evenings. Unless there's a fire."

"You had any of those recently?"

"You mean since your fire? A bunch of our crew is still out cleaning up from that one. Today we had a car fire out on the highway. That was exciting."

"Dangerous this time of year," Aidan said. "Something like that could start a whole new blaze."

"It sparked a small fire at the side of the road but we got there in time to put it out." Jade reached into a cabinet, pulled out two water glasses and filled them. She set one down near Aidan. "No drinking on duty. I hope you're okay with water."

"I'm not much of a drinker," Aidan said. "A beer once in a while is enough for me."

"Likewise." This was awkward. During the fire they'd had a purpose, and plenty to figure out together. But small talk had never been her strong point. And if this was a date, which it wasn't, she had little experience with that either. Growing up with three older brothers, and the town's tough fire chief as a father, no boy had dared to ask her out even if they'd wanted to. And nowadays, when men found out she was a firefighter, they usually lost interest. She just wasn't feminine enough for most guys, apparently.

"Want me to make the salad?" At least it would give her something to do.

"That would be great." Aidan pulled a few heads of lettuce out of a grocery bag and handed them to her. "How have you been?"

"Busy." Jade dug in the cabinet next to the sink for the colander. "We stayed on the fire lines for several days and then I've been on duty here quite a bit. How's the ranch?"

"Burnt."

She burst out laughing. "I'm sorry," she said when he looked her way. "I'm not sure why I'm laughing so much. It's not funny."

He was smiling, though. "I know, but what more is there to say about it? It's burnt to a crisp. I'm starting from scratch. Living in a borrowed trailer, sleeping on borrowed sheets, putting a fence together from donated materials."

Jade ran water over the lettuce, cleaning

each leaf carefully. "That's nice that people have donated stuff."

"It's this town you live in. Shelter Creek. Everyone is so generous. Maya's grandmother and her friends keep bringing me things I didn't even realize I needed."

Jade shook water out of the lettuce. "Ah. The Book Biddies. They're in a book club together, but they're also really involved in this wildlife center we have in town."

"Well, now they've adopted me as another project. But I can't complain. I'd probably still be sleeping in the barn without them."

Jade focused hard on tearing up the lettuce, appreciating the cool feeling of it on her hands. Just the words *sleeping in the barn* brought back the comfort of being in his arms during their nap. She'd thought about it every time she crawled into bed since. It was fine sleeping alone, so why had she felt so much more complete in the few hours she'd slept next to him?

"How have you been since the fire?" Aidan stopped his food prep to take a sip of the water she'd given him.

"Good, I've been good." That was the easy answer, but there was something about him that didn't let her take the easy route. "Actually, I kind of had it out with my family. Well, with my dad, that is. He just can't seem to see any of my achievements. I finally told him that I'm tired of the way he criticizes me so much. And how he doesn't act that way with my brothers."

Aidan glanced at her, eyebrows raised. "How did that go?"

Jade sighed and reached for her own water glass. "About as well as you might expect. As in, he glared at me, I got upset and then I left. That was three days ago and I haven't heard from him since. I guess I have to decide if I want to pretend like it was all no big deal and let things go back to normal, or if I'm actually going to stand my ground about this."

"That's a tough call," Aidan said. "There's a reason I don't live in Wyoming, even though my family has a ranch there. My dad and I just don't see the world the same way. He's very old school. He hasn't changed the way he runs his ranch since I was a kid. We'd be arguing every day if I lived there."

"So you're suggesting that I move across the country?"

"Nah, I wouldn't want you so far away." Aidan froze, glass halfway to his lips, as if he regretted what he just said.

Jade looked away, trying to take it in. He was suggesting that she mattered to him in some way. Maybe that he felt some of the connection that she did. She could tell him anything, it seemed, because more words spilled out. "The thing is, ever since the fire, I just don't want to put up with the way he's treated me. Maybe working so hard to stay alive made me realize that I don't have time to waste on someone who doesn't see the good in me. But he's my dad, so now I feel awful."

"He must be blind, if he can't see how great you are." Aidan set his glass of water down. "Don't blame yourself if your father is too shortsighted to see what an incredible daughter he has in you."

"That might be the nicest thing anybody has said to me in a long time. I thought you were this grumpy rancher, but here you are cooking me a meal and giving me compliments."

His gaze met hers. She'd startled him. A flush rose from his neck and spread over his cheeks. She'd never been one to flirt but it was fun to realize that she could rattle this stoic man a little.

Despite any embarrassment, his blue eyes were steady on hers. "You deserve compliments," he said quietly.

Now her own cheeks were getting warm. Jade changed the subject. "Tell me what to do here. Shall we get going on the meatballs? I can heat up the oven."

He looked at her in surprise. "Oven? No, I cook my meatballs in a pan."

"A pan? How is that a good idea? They're going to be all tough on the outside and raw on the inside."

He laughed. "Are we ever going to be able to agree on how to do something?"

Jade couldn't help but smile back, realizing how easily she got sucked into their bickering. "You know what? You brought the food, you offered to cook, so you're the boss of this. Just tell me what to do."

"Can you say that again so I can record it on my phone?"

"Don't push it." Their banter reminded Jade of hanging out with Travis. Except when Travis smiled, she didn't get a sparkly feeling inside.

"As meatball boss, I decree that we're going to mix these sautéed onions and garlic into the meat, and roll ourselves small meatballs."

"Small, strange, pan-fried meatballs, coming up." Jade went to wash her hands, smiling to herself. She didn't usually enjoy cooking this much. Having Aidan here made the mundane task into something special.

"Wait until you taste them before you trash them."

"I suppose I can do that." Her cheeks hurt from smiling. It was fun to joke with him again.

While they cooked, Aidan told her how he was working on rebuilding the fences around one of the larger pastures so he could get his sheep out of the field they'd been in since the fire. And how Thor and Odin seemed to be getting restless in the small pasture near the barn. They were used to living half-wild far from any people and preferred it that way.

Jade was happy to learn that Chip's paws were healing under the careful care of Emily

Fielding. And that Elliott the cat had been picked up by his grateful family.

"They called you a hero," Aidan said, stirring the tomato sauce. "They are so grateful that you got them to evacuate, and then risked your own safety to rescue Elliott."

"Aw, shucks. Well, you know I have a special cat connection."

Aidan grinned. "You rescued Elliott, two kittens and a bobcat in one night. That's a strong connection for sure."

"And Elliott's family?" Jade asked. "They have another house, right?"

"Yes, lucky for them the house near my ranch was a weekend vacation home. He's some big tech company executive so they still have their family home in San Francisco to live in."

Jade took a sip of her water and tried to imagine Aidan living that life. "Do you ever miss it? When you see a guy like that who can have multiple homes, who is obviously doing very well financially? You could go back to work in the Silicon Valley and be set for life."

"I don't miss it," Aidan said. "I don't think there's enough money in the world to make it worth doing something that made me feel dead inside. There are people who love working in that industry. They are so fired up to make a new app, or improve a piece of software. I just don't get excited about it. I could do the work and be successful at it, but I was so restless."

"Hey, what's cooking?" Bill stomped up the stairs, stopping short when he saw Aidan wielding a pair of tongs to set the meatballs into the frying pan. "We have a new chef." He took a closer look at Aidan. "I remember you. You're Jade's rancher."

"Not *mine*," Jade said. "But we're lucky to have him here cooking us dinner."

"I wanted to say thank you for all that you did to save my ranch." Aidan set down the tongs, and he and Bill shook hands. "I hope you like spaghetti and meatballs."

Bill patted his ample stomach. "I love it. But I have to go light on the pasta."

"There's garlic bread, too," Jade chimed in with an extra sweet note in her voice.

"Don't torture me." Bill crossed his arms across his chest and fixed Jade with a mock glare.

"It's a special night," Jade explained.

"Aidan and I planned this meal while the fire was running right over us. Can you make an exception on your diet? I will personally make you oatmeal for breakfast. Sugar-free and everything."

Bill let his hands drop to his side. "When you put it that way, I'm in."

"Then help me set the table. We're going to be ready to eat soon. Where's Danny?"

"Here." Danny came around the corner from the stairwell. "It smells incredible in here. What can I do?"

"Go find Kayla," Jade said. "She's in her room."

Jade and Bill got silverware and plates from the cupboard, and Bill set the table while Jade checked the garlic bread in the oven. The loaf was wrapped in foil, so it was hard to tell if it was ready. She reached out and touched the foil with her fingers. "Ouch!" She pulled them back and stuck them in her mouth.

Aidan was there in an instant. "What did you do?" He pulled her over to the sink and ran cold water over her fingers.

"I was testing the bread, to see if it was ready."

He burst out laughing, looking down on her with an incredulous smile. "You made it through a wildfire on my ranch with barely a scratch, but you can't make garlic bread in the kitchen without burning yourself?"

They were shoulder to shoulder at the sink, Aidan's hand firm over her own. It felt good to be next to him, to laugh this way, to know that he was here, ready to help her when she needed it. How many years had it been since someone wanted to look after her like this?

Bill must have overheard. "Jade's not known for her cooking skills. We're lucky if we don't have to send out for takeout when it's her night to cook. But her kitchen disasters do keep our firefighting skills sharp, so there's that."

Jade turned to look at him in open-mouthed outrage. "I have never let the kitchen catch on fire, just to be clear."

"Maybe not on fire," Bill said. "But there was the night of the homemade pizza when the smoke alarm got going. We had to evacuate, it was so smoky in here." He turned to Aidan. "All the neighbors came by to see why in the world a smoke alarm would be going off in the fire station. They got such a kick out of it, they were all offering to help put out the fire for us."

"Which was *not* a fire," Jade reiterated. Her cheeks might be on fire, though. "It was just a whole lot of smoke and some very sad pizza."

Aidan turned off the water and grabbed a dishtowel to dry Jade's hands as if she were a little kid. "So when we were in the pond, talking about our favorite meals, you didn't mean this was your favorite meal to cook?"

His grin was infectious and got Jade laughing. "You never specified that it had to be a meal we could cook. I thought we were talking about our favorite comfort food to eat. My mother makes great spaghetti and meatballs. So does the Italian restaurant in town."

"Okay, then. I must have inhaled too much smoke. I thought we were talking about food we liked to cook." Aidan took Jade gently by the shoulders and steered her around the counter and out of the kitchen. "Why don't you sit here and watch? That might be safer for all of us."

"Good call." Bill put his hand up and gave Aidan a high five.

"Fine. Do your male bonding thing." Jade plunked down on a stool, feeling a little silly, but also relieved not to be responsible for wrapping up the meal. She hated trying to figure out when meat was cooked enough, or if sauce tasted right. Maybe she was lacking some kind of cooking gene, because it all seemed like kind of a waste of time to her. You spent all this time cooking something nice and it was gone in minutes. And then you had all those pots and pans to wash. She'd rather eat a granola bar and use the time to go for a run. Still, she felt the need to defend herself after Bill and the pizza story. "I can cook a few things. The most important things. Toast, salad, coffee and scrambled eggs. What else does anyone really need anyway?"

"Spaghetti and meatballs, from what you told me that night during the fire." Aidan grinned, but his teasing held no hint of meanness. It seemed that he just wanted to make her smile, and it was working. Jade couldn't remember laughing this much in a long time. Certainly not in the past week, when her mind had been preoccupied with the fire, and then with her conflict with her father.

Danny and Kayla appeared and took a seat around the table. "Are we ready to eat?" Kayla asked. "It smells amazing."

"I think we are," Aidan said. "Let me just plate up the food. Bill, do you want to take these plates to the table?"

"I'm perfectly capable of doing that," Jade protested, standing up from her stool.

"You're the guest of honor," Aidan told her. "Go pick your favorite seat and get ready to be waited on."

Jade flushed, but did as she was told. She kicked Bill in the ankle after he delivered her plate, but he just laughed and gave her a squeeze on the shoulder. "It's okay. We all still love you, even if your meals threaten our health and safety on a regular basis."

Aidan was the last to be seated. They'd left him the head of the table, and Jade was seated to his right. He raised his water glass. "I'd like to propose a toast. To all of you, who risk so much to keep the rest of us safe. And to Jade, who saved me and my ranch and my livestock, when I thought all hope was lost."

The mood around the table sobered for a moment as they all raised their glasses in Jade's direction. She wasn't used to being honored. Didn't know what to feel. "Come on then," she told them, setting her glass down. "Let's eat this amazing meal."

When they'd finished eating, Jade and Aidan brought their plates into the kitchen, but Danny and Kayla shooed them out, insisting that they'd wash up.

"That was the easiest cooking night I ever had." Jade looked up at Aidan feeling suddenly awkward. This evening had been so fun, so easy. They'd all talked and joked while eating Aidan's delicious food. Jade was amazed at how well Aidan, who'd lived so alone for so long, fit in with the crew. But now what to do? It was getting late in the evening. They all tended to crash early in case they were woken up by a call during the night.

"I should head out," Aidan said. "I'm staying at Caleb's tonight and he invited another friend, a guy named Jace, over to play some cards."

"That sounds like fun," Jade was relieved that she didn't have to figure out what to do next.

"Nice to meet you all," Aidan called out. The fire crew crowded around, thanking him for dinner.

"I'll walk you out," Jade said, when Aidan was finally free of the backslaps and handshakes. She led the way down the stairs and out a side door, and they walked side by side to Aidan's truck. The night was crisp and clear, and the stars hung bright overhead. Jade drew in a deep breath, grateful for the fresh air after such a big meal. "What a nice night."

"I had a lot of fun." Aidan stopped by his truck. "I hope it was okay that I just showed up."

"It was fine. But why don't we get each other's phone numbers? That way, once your cell tower gets fixed, you can give me a call if you're coming this way." Jade pulled her phone out of her pocket and opened the contacts section. "Put your number in here?"

Aidan typed it in and handed it back.

"Here, I'll call you now, then you'll have

my number." She pushed the call icon and his pocket buzzed. "There it is."

"It's been a long time since I got a woman's phone number," Aidan said. "I'd like to call it and ask you out on a real date. Would you answer if I did?"

Oh wow. She hadn't been expecting this. The word *date* was ricocheting around her brain, crashing into things, creating chaos. Dating wasn't in her plan. And he lived a couple hours away. When would she even have time?

"I'll always answer when you call," she told him. "I'd like us to be friends. But I don't know if I can date anyone right now."

He was stoic as always, but in the light of the streetlamp Jade could see the way the muscles in his jaw tightened. He'd lost his kid. His wife had left him. This was probably the first time he'd reached out for any connection like this.

But what would they do if they dated? She didn't want to hang out on his burnt ranch, full of tragic memories. But if he came to Shelter Creek, everyone would know they were dating and she'd always avoided that. Making her way in such a macho profession meant she had to work extra hard to be taken seriously. If she was seen out and about in this small town with a boyfriend, her colleagues would see her as more feminine. Less serious.

Guilt and regret squirmed in her stomach. "You seem like such a good guy. And I know going through the fire has given us a special bond. But I'm really focused on my work right now. I want to become a captain and I've almost got the qualifications." She stumbled to a halt, running up against the real reason she couldn't date, and hadn't dated for a few years now. Dating meant trying to meet someone's expectations. She'd never been good at that—her father had made that clear. She didn't want to try to live up to anyone else's standards. Didn't want to fail anyone, anymore.

"I get it. I do. You've got a lot going on." Aidan gave her a sheepish smile and Jade realized that tonight, at dinner, the usual sadness had been gone from his eyes. He'd been smiling and laughing and…present. Now that shadow was back, and her chest ached to see it. "Give me a call if you ever want to hang out. Just as friends."

"Sure." The fun night had morphed from happy and celebratory into something awkward. Not having dated much, Jade wasn't sure what to say or how to navigate this. Not when there was this ache building in her throat at the realization that this was goodbye. That she might not see him again. And she wanted to. She swallowed hard. "Thank you again, Aidan. Good luck with rebuilding."

He nodded. "Good luck with work and everything." He unlocked his truck, got in and drove away. Jade watched until his taillights disappeared around the corner. A hollow feeling started near her heart and seemed to grow with each breath. It was almost as if he'd taken a piece of her with him into the night.

CHAPTER SIXTEEN

MAIN STREET WAS crowded as people searched for the perfect spot to set up their chairs for the Shelter Creek Founders' Day parade. It was one of those fall days that started out frosty in the morning but would get hot by the afternoon. Jade wove her way along the sidewalk, smiling at people she knew as she clutched a cardboard tray that held four steaming cups of coffee. She was on duty today, though because the parade went right in front of the fire station she'd get a chance to cheer it on. As long as no emergencies presented themselves.

A woman was walking toward her with platinum-blond hair flowing from beneath a large sun hat. She looked familiar but it still took Jade a moment to place her. The woman stopped and said, "Jade, honey, how are you?"

Of course. It was Monique, owner of Monique's Miracles—the local beauty salon where Jade had her long hair trimmed to slightly-less-long a few times a year. Only, the last time Jade had seen her, Monique's hair had been a fiery red. The stylist's color tended to change with the seasons.

"Hi, Monique, good to see you. I'm doing fine. And you?"

"Looking forward to a gorgeous day." She nodded toward the coffee tray. "Don't tell me those hunky firefighters you work for have you picking up their coffee?"

The warmth Jade had felt upon recognizing Monique faded away. "No, of course not. I had a break and a craving. I offered to pick up a few extra."

"Well, that's good to hear. Don't let them make you fetch and carry for them. Or cook. You're as tough as all of them put together, and don't you forget it."

"I won't, Monique. Thanks for the pep talk. I'd better get back to the station, though. My break is almost over."

"See you soon, I hope. And put some deep conditioner on those dry ends."

"Absolutely." Jade manufactured a smile and kept walking, but Monique's words had her troubled in a way the friendly hairdresser might never understand. Jade loved fighting fires, but as Monique had so blithely pointed out, every choice she made was fraught. If she offered to get the others coffee on her break, was she caving to a stereotype? But she'd really wanted a latte. And yes, the ends of her hair probably were pretty dry. Fighting a wildfire up close and personal had that effect. But no one suggested to her colleagues that it was time for a deep condition.

It was frustrating. And lonely. For a brief moment she thought of Aidan. How he'd cooked her that amazing meal and made her feel perfect, just the way she was. How much fun she'd had getting to know him that night.

She wished she could stop picturing his smile, almost shy when he'd asked if they could spend some time together. She wished she could have said yes. She wished she could shut off the sense of longing that flowed like an unruly current in her veins. As if some part deep inside of her had become connected to Aidan during that fire, and needed him close to be okay.

Which made her want to twist off that

feeling, like she might turn off a leaky faucet. Since when had she ever needed anyone? She was a strong, independent woman. The last thing she needed was a man to make her whole. Isn't that why she'd just stood up to her dad after so many years? To stand on her own and not be defined by her relationship to a man? Walking away from her family that night had been painful, but she'd felt stronger ever since.

Jade shifted her grip on the coffee tray. This thing was a little awkward to carry for such a distance. It was only one more block to the fire station, but she stepped into the green grass of the town square and made her way to a bench to set the coffees down. Shaking out her hands, she felt the blood flow back into them with relief.

Jade looked around the square and recognized a few people lounging on the steps of the gazebo, not too far from her. Maya and Caleb were drinking coffee and talking to a man in a denim jacket and cowboy hat, who had his back to her. Jade glanced at her watch. She had almost ten more minutes before she had to be back. Enough time to say a quick hello. Picking up the coffee tray, she approached the group, waving her greeting.

"Jade!" Maya stood and came down the steps toward her, Einstein hopping at her heels. "Great to see you. How have you been?" She glanced down at the tray. "Are you bringing us refills?"

Jade reached for Einstein's floppy ears. The dog was so cute. "Sadly, no. They're for the folks at the station today." She returned Maya's offered embrace with her free arm, the other keeping the hot coffee away from her friend. "Good to see you. Are you going to watch the parade?"

"We thought we'd check it out. Shelter Creek's official centennial seems like something to celebrate. We're waiting here for a few friends to arrive. Can you sit with us for a moment?"

"For a minute, thanks." Jade waved to Caleb as Maya climbed back up the steps to sit by her husband. "Hi there."

Caleb tipped the brim of the dark, felt cowboy hat he wore. "Hey, Jade."

And then their companion turned, and Jade realized who it was under that coat and cowboy hat. "Aidan. Hi."

"Hi, Jade. Good to see you again." If she hadn't known him so well, she would have missed the way his smile curled down at the corners just a little. That curve of his lips told her that this meeting was as bittersweet for him as it was for her.

Suddenly shy, Jade sank slowly onto the step and faced him, casting around for something to say. She came up with "What are you doing here?" which didn't sound very polite.

But he kept it polite, with a coolness that turned his pale blue eyes a little icy. Jade instantly missed the warmth she'd seen there the last time they met. "Maya and Caleb kindly invited me down for the day. Honestly, it's nice to get away from the ashes for a few hours."

"I bet. How is the ranch? How are the sheep and the dogs?" It was awkward making small talk when all Jade wanted was to ask the big questions. *How are you feeling? Are you sad? Are you lonely? Are you angry?*

"They're all good. Chip's paws have healed up well. Those kittens you saved are living the high life here in town with Maya's grandmother. The sheep are probably wishing there was a little more grass around, but they're doing all right with hay for now."

"Good. I'm glad to hear it." Had it really been less than two weeks since he'd brought dinner to the fire station? That didn't seem like enough time to have created this awkward chasm between them.

Thankfully, a child's squeal had them all turning to see a laughing toddler approaching, running toward Einstein with a wide-legged wobbly stance that could melt anyone's heart. A man in a straw cowboy hat and a blonde woman jogged up behind the little boy. Jade realized the woman was Trisha Gilbert, who worked at the vet's office and the wildlife center. The man was her new husband, who Jade had seen around town but had never actually met.

"Hang on, Henry," Trisha called, but she was too late. Henry crossed from the grass to the paved path, lost his balance on the new footing and sat down hard. "Henry fall," he announced calmly.

"You sure did, buddy." The man scooped Henry up and raised him in the air before bringing him down to kiss his tummy. Then he settled the toddler comfortably in his arms. "Hey, folks," he said. "Henry sure knows how to make an entrance."

"Glad he's okay," Maya said.

"At this age it seems like he falls every few minutes." Trisha put her hands to her heart in mock despair. "I'm trying to get used to it." She smiled at Jade. "Good to see you."

"Nice to see you, too, Trisha." Jade watched as Henry grabbed at his daddy's hat. "Henry gets cuter every time I run into you two."

Trisha knelt to greet Einstein. "Have you met my husband, Liam?"

Jade shook her head. "I haven't, though I've seen you around town. Hi, Liam. Welcome to Shelter Creek, about a year late."

Liam grinned at her, a wide smile that would make anyone, even a stressed-out firefighter like herself, smile back. "I appreciate that. And all that you do to keep our town safe."

It was the perfect opening to go, and Jade wanted to leave. How was it possible to feel someone near you? Aidan was seated at the other end of the wide steps. There had to be at least two yards between them. Yet somehow Jade felt his presence there, as energy and warmth that seemed to radiate from him to her. It made her want to take his hand, to walk this town square arm in arm, and talk about anything, everything, like they had in that fire. "Speaking of keeping the town safe, my break is going to be up soon so I'd better get going." She stood and waved to Aidan, Caleb and Maya. "Thanks for letting me hang out with you all for a few minutes. Enjoy the parade."

Aidan stood when she did. "Nice to see you again." His voice was that deep, calm rumble she'd come to rely on during the fire.

"Nice to see you, too." Nodding to Trisha and Liam, Jade started back across the grass, but Maya caught up with her after a few paces.

"Can I walk with you? And talk with you about something?"

"Of course." Maybe Maya and Caleb needed some help with fire precautions. Certainly after witnessing how quickly Aidan's ranch had been cut off in the fires, they must have some questions about their own property.

"It's about Aidan," Maya said.

Oh. Jade just nodded, and resisted the urge to run. She'd never been a girl who wanted to gossip about men, compare notes or share feelings.

"I'm trying to get him to buy some property closer to Shelter Creek, and I wondered how you'd feel about that."

There was no way Jade was capable of explaining the rush of emotions that was flooding her chest, so she went with the cynicism that came easier. "Good luck with that. He's got some pretty strong emotional ties to his ranch."

Maya nodded, keeping pace with her as they left the town square and started down the sidewalk toward the fire station. "I know he does. I know his story…or at least some of it. It's not healthy for him to be out there by himself. His one neighbor, Nellie, is selling her land. He'll be all alone with his memories out on that ridge."

Jade shrugged, though the information hit like a blow. Nellie was his lifeline, his family. Aidan had risked his life for her sheep. But Aidan wasn't her business. She'd made that choice after their dinner that night at the fire station.

"I think it's nice that you want to help him, Maya. But what does this all have to do with me?"

Maya glanced her way with a shy smile. "Maybe I'm wrong, but I got the sense you two have some pretty strong feelings for each other. I guess I wanted to know if it would upset you to have him around here more."

Years of living with brothers had made Jade an expert at hiding her feelings. "Not at all. It's fine with me. The guy can live wherever he wants." Here in Shelter Creek? The thought fluttered through her stomach. What would it be like, running into him at the store, or at town events like this one? Knowing he was close by?

Maya slowed her steps, and remembering that her friend had to get back to the gazebo and her plans for the day, Jade slowed, too. "Thanks for asking me, though. And it's nice of you to try to help him out."

Maya shrugged. "I like Aidan. I want to see him happier and less alone. The fire seems like a chance for him to start again somewhere where he can have a community around him. But I don't know if I'll convince him. He's pretty stubborn."

Jade smiled, remembering how rocky their first several hours had been together. "He is that. But he's also a good man."

Maya stopped and took Jade's hand in hers. "I know what it's like to be in a job where you feel like you have to be tough all the time. Before I came back to Shelter Creek, I worried that if I had a lot of feelings, or if I got into a relationship, I'd lose some of the toughness I needed for my work. I worried that I wouldn't be respected."

Jade nodded slowly, amazed that Maya seemed to have lived her own struggles.

"But I promise you that moving back here, reconnecting with friends and family, and marrying Caleb, has all made me stronger. And a whole lot less lonely, too."

This was so far out of her comfort zone. An unsettling earthquake, cracking the barriers Jade had built around her heart.

"You'll be strong, Jade, no matter what you do. That's just who you are. You can be single or not, alone or not, and it won't make a difference in how tough you are. Except that, if you let love in, it might make you stronger in ways you never imagined."

All Jade wanted was to get away from Maya's words, and all their potential and their challenge. They were words to think about later, in private, to mull over and examine. There wasn't anything she could say now except "Thanks."

"Anytime." Maya grinned. "One thing that's changed about me? I've gone from trying to stay away from people, to getting all mixed up in their lives. Now I'm even dispensing totally unwanted advice. I blame my grandmother and her friends for that. They are a bad influence."

"I know you're trying to help," Jade managed. "But I better get back to the station. Good luck convincing Aidan to come down off that ridge of his."

"Thanks. I'll need it."

Jade turned toward the fire station, pondering Maya's words as she made her way up the sidewalk. Maya had always been cool-headed and tough. None of that had changed since she married Caleb. And she'd done great work since then, starting and running the wildlife center, working closely with the ranchers in the area to find ways to coexist with wildlife. She hadn't lost anyone's respect by letting Caleb into her heart.

Jade pictured Aidan lounging on the gazebo steps just now, so relaxed compared to the man she'd first met. The pang that radiated through her stomach might actually be jealousy. *She* wanted to be the person who helped him relax, who got him to leave his ranch for parades and fun events. But she didn't have time for all that. Or was that just her need to prove that she was strong? Maybe Maya had been trying to deliver some clarity, but Jade felt more muddled than ever.

Irritated, she stomped through the open garage door of the fire station and headed for Mitch, who was inventorying some of their medical supplies stored in the big cabinet in the back.

"I was just about to send a search party out for you," he said, taking the cup she offered with a smile. "Everything okay?"

For a moment Jade was tempted to tell him about Aidan, Maya, the whole thing, but what was she thinking? She was at work and she had to be professional, especially with her boss. "Just really crowded. Not a good day to go on a latte run."

He nodded. "Guess we should keep that in mind for the future."

"Where are Travis and Ian? I'm sure they're ready for their caffeine."

"Out back with a couple of the interns." Suddenly Mitch's eyes got a little wider and he set his coffee down. "I'll deliver those for you, Jade." He took the tray from her. "Looks like someone is here to see you."

Aidan. Jade's heart jolted into her throat and she turned around. But it wasn't Aidan. It was her father, standing at the entrance to the station, dressed in his old uniform, his hat in his hands.

"Whoa. Okay, hang on." Jade turned back to Mitch and grabbed her own coffee cup. She'd need caffeine for this. Mitch gave her dad a quick wave and disappeared out the back door. Jade took a big gulp of the warm, sweetened coffee and walked toward her father. "Hey, Dad."

Her father's mouth was compressed into his usual firm line but his white hair was different today, smoothed back with pomade. "I don't have much time," he said with his customary abruptness. "I have to go get on the float for the parade."

Jade's nod masked her relief. If he was going to give her a lecture, at least it would be short. "Yes, you can't be late. Are you ready to smile and wave to the crowd?"

"No. Not until I say something to you."

And so it began. The lecture on how she should never have stormed out of dinner. That she was emotional, ungrateful and so on. "Okay, shoot." She squared her shoulders, refusing to let him know how intimidated she'd always felt in his presence.

"I'm sorry."

There was no way she could have heard him correctly. "You're sorry?"

"I didn't realize you felt so criticized by me."

Jade opened her mouth, but couldn't find any words, so she shut it again. She'd never heard her father say anything like that before, not even to her brothers or her mom. She closed her eyes for a moment, but when she opened them he was still standing there, twisting his hat, looking supremely uncomfortable. She needed to say something. "Thank you for coming here to tell me that."

He swallowed audibly. "I guess I like to share my opinions more than I should."

Jade nodded. "You're a hard act to follow as it is, Dad. When you add in your take on my various shortcomings it can feel pretty overwhelming."

He nodded, averting his gaze for a moment. Jade studied him, noticing his thinning hair and the deep lines around his mouth and eyes. He'd always seemed so much larger-than-life to her, but for an instant she saw him differently. As a man who was desperately trying to communicate, but didn't know how. Suddenly she wondered about his own childhood. He'd never spoken of it much. Had his own father berated him for his faults?

When her father met her gaze, she was surprised to see unshed tears in his eyes. "You're my only daughter. And you tried so hard, your whole life, to follow in your brothers' footsteps. And to follow in mine. I have some idea how hard it can be for a woman to make it in this career that has always been dominated by men. I guess in my mind I was toughening you up. I was trying to make you strong, and ready to face all the flak that would come your way."

Jade thought about Maya's words earlier. "You definitely made me tough, so that part worked." Maybe it had worked too well. Now she couldn't let anyone in. Not even Aidan. Not even after they'd shared so much in the fire.

"I know you're angry at me. And disappointed that I haven't been the parent you needed. If you tell me what it is you want me to do, I'll try my hand at it."

It was a tough question. Jade had spent so much time thinking about what she didn't want when it came to her dad, it had never occurred to her to consider what she would prefer. She sipped her coffee to give herself a moment to think. "I guess I'd like you to notice when I succeed. Maybe even mention it now and again. And when I mess up, you have to understand that I don't need you to point it out. I'm perfectly capable of seeing my own shortcomings. I know, better than anyone, when I make mistakes."

He put a hand to her shoulder, not an embrace, more of a manly squeeze. "I'll keep that in mind." He glanced down at his watch. "I'd better go. Can't be late. Have a good shift."

"Will do." It had been the strangest shift of her life. First Monique's thought-provoking comments, then Aidan, then Maya's heart-to-heart and now this. "Enjoy the parade, Dad."

But he'd already turned away and was striding down the street toward the town square. She watched him until he turned right at the corner, toward the elementary school where the parade would start.

Jade walked back into the station, glad that her break was over. She was ready for chores, to clean and organize. She'd even cook if it would give her a break from the emotions spiraling and tumbling through her mind. Sparks in a wildfire that she had no idea how to control.

CHAPTER SEVENTEEN

AIDAN THREW ANOTHER log on the fire burning in the pit he'd dug several yards away from his trailer. "It still feels a little weird to *build* a fire."

Caleb's big laugh boomed into the quiet night. "Think of it this way, there's nothing left around here to burn. It should be the most carefree fire you've ever built."

Aidan glanced around at the three men seated on the sections of log he'd placed around the firepit. It wasn't luxury living, but it was great to have somewhere to entertain outside of the trailer.

"I wonder how long it will be before fire seems normal?" Jace took a sip from his beer. He was a friend of Caleb's, and he and Liam, the man Aidan had met at the parade the other day, had come up to Aidan's ranch with Caleb. The three of them had spent the day helping Aidan build a storage shed near the barn. Since most of his outbuildings had burned and the trailer was small, Aidan needed somewhere to keep supplies.

To thank them, Aidan had grilled some burgers, handed out beer and bottled water, and built this fire. It was about all he had to offer these days.

Liam had been a little quieter than the rest of them this evening. "Visiting your ranch today has made it all hit home," he said. "I'd read about the fires out here, back when I lived in Texas, but it's another thing entirely to see the damage a wildfire can do up close."

"Gotta be prepared," Caleb said. "You can ask one of the local firefighters to come by and inspect your ranch, Liam. They'll help you to get ready." He paused, and Aidan didn't miss the way his buddy glanced at him in apology before speaking again. "Ask Jade to do it. She's probably the best person for the job, since she went through the fire with Aidan up here."

Sometimes Aidan wished he hadn't needed Maya to take care of his livestock so he could go down to Shelter Creek to make dinner for Jade and the other firefighters. Because now she and Caleb knew he was sweet on her, and that she'd rejected him. They felt sorry for him, and he didn't want that. He'd been through so much. If Jade didn't return his feelings then so be it. It might hurt, but he could live with loss. He'd prefer to live without the pity, though.

Sensing his discomfort, Chip got up from the blanket he was lying on and shoved his nose into Aidan's hand. Ever since the fire, Chip had been a little uneasy, sticking close and lacking his usual confidence. Aidan couldn't blame him. He hadn't quite gotten his legs under him either.

"I'll ask her," Liam said. "I appreciate the advice."

"Hey, Aidan, finish telling us that story," Jace said. "What happened when you saw that mountain lion on your porch?"

Before he'd got up to fix the fire, Aidan had been telling them about a particularly bold mountain lion that had napped on his back porch one evening, staying there for a few hours.

"Chip here was going nuts, barking at it through the window. And that big old cat was just looking at him like, 'I dare you to come out here.'"

"Weren't you concerned for your livestock?" Liam leaned forward on his stump, his water bottle in hand. Neither he nor Caleb had wanted a beer when Aidan offered.

"They were pretty secure. I've left the horns on some of my cattle and they were with the sheep, pastured closer to the barn. I also had motion-sensitive lights around that area, so I figured they were safe."

"Are those cattle the same ones Caleb is babysitting for you right now?" Jace said. "Those are some cool-looking animals."

"They remind me of the longhorns we've got back home in Texas," Liam added.

Aidan nodded. "Caleb has all my cattle right now, which I appreciate. I've got some help coming starting next week, to get my fences repaired. Then I can take them back."

"But you'll have to buy hay," Caleb said. "Why not leave them at my place for a little longer? I've got plenty of pasture for them."

"I don't want to overstay my welcome," Aidan said.

"Chances are we'll have a fire around

Shelter Creek one of these days. Then you can take my cattle for me." Caleb was staring out into the night like he could see the fire on the horizon. He was an interesting guy. Generous and welcoming, but a little dark and brooding, too. Aidan wondered what his story was, then remembered what Maya had told him. Caleb's sister had been killed in the same crash Maya was in during high school. So the guy certainly knew what trouble felt like.

"The fires sure are getting bad," Jace said. "Vivian and I just had a big talk with our kids about what we'll do if we need to evacuate. It's our new reality, I guess."

"The trickiest part is getting the livestock out," Aidan told him. "I'm lucky that so many folks from Shelter Creek could get up here and haul out my cattle and horses. But I still had all those sheep, and the livestock haulers I called were completely booked. I'd suggest keeping at least one pasture well irrigated, with extra sprinklers ready in case you can't evacuate them." He paused, remembering that night, the way he and Jade had worked so hard to get ready before the fire got to them. They'd been lucky to have those few hours to prepare. "In a way, the fact that my ranch is so isolated was good, because when I'd thought about fire, in the past, I'd never counted on having any help to deal with it."

"You are out in the middle of nowhere," Caleb said. "Have you thought any more about moving a little closer to civilization? A new ranch has come on the market close to Shelter Creek. It's just southwest of town and it's a pretty big spread. I've known the owner my whole life. He runs sheep and cattle now. He's retiring, and none of his kids want to carry on the business."

Aidan wondered if Maya had put Caleb up to this. She was on a mission to bring him closer into town. He knew why. After the confidences they'd shared, she saw herself in him. She wanted the town to fix his loneliness, just like it had healed hers. But he didn't know if he could leave this land, no matter how lonely he got. "I appreciate the suggestion, but I've got a great piece of property here. I've worked hard to make it what it is." He corrected himself. "Was."

"I get that," Caleb persisted. "But you're a pretty good distance from town. Relocate and you can still ranch, but be close to friends."

"Like us." Jace grinned. "Our wives have a book club. We can have a beer club." Then he glanced at Caleb and Liam, both holding their water bottles. "Or a pool playing club. Or a hiking club. Or something."

"Team roping," Liam said. "I've been thinking about trying it. Any of you cowboys up for the challenge?"

"I might be." Jace grinned and looked at Aidan. "Did you know that I used to work on Liam's family's ranch? And we both had a pretty good run in bull riding in our day. Until I got the kids and Liam got a bull with a killer streak. In fact—" he skewered Liam with a shrewd glance "—have you mentioned your roping aspirations to your wife? With your leg held together by hardware, I doubt she's going to approve of your plans."

Liam's grin was completely unapologetic. "I haven't mentioned it, no. I'm just waiting for the right time to bring it up."

Jace busted out laughing. "I'll need you to come down and rope, Aidan. Caleb's got too many injuries from his combat days, and there's no way Trisha is going to let

Liam get in the arena." He leaned over and clapped Liam on the shoulder. "You can be our coach."

Aidan grinned at the banter between the two men. "I've never done any rodeo. But I grew up on a cattle ranch and I know how to rope."

"So it's settled," Jace said. "Check out that ranch Caleb mentioned. The rodeo is in July, so we've got time to practice."

It was tempting. Except leaving this ranch would mean leaving so much more. His memories. What he'd built from scratch. Plus, did he want to be closer to Jade? To see her around, a constant reminder of what he wanted but couldn't have? He was trying to accept her choice. To be grateful that they'd been there for each other during the fire. But it was a lot easier to be accepting when he didn't have to worry about running into her.

The truth was, her rejection had hurt like heck. He shown up to make her dinner that night with nothing to go on but the connection he'd felt to her during the fire. It was a strong connection, filled with feelings so deep they seemed impossible after just one night spent surviving together. But during dinner his confidence had grown. He and Jade had laughed together, teased each other, and it felt to him like they fit together in a way he couldn't remember fitting with anyone. Love had never been easy like that before.

Love? Where did that word come from? He was going way too far. Maybe he'd just been alone too long, to think that what he felt for her was love. But whatever he called the feeling, he couldn't shake it. That sense that he was incomplete without her at his side.

But at the same time, he wanted what was best for her. She wanted to focus on her career right now, and he wanted her to be happy. So he had to wait, and hope that whatever he was feeling, she'd start to feel it, too. And if she didn't? Well, he knew about heartache, and putting one foot in front of the other, even when it felt impossible. He'd been doing that for years now.

Aidan brought himself back to the question at hand. "The land I have, the ranch I built means a lot to me. I don't think I'll be leaving anytime soon."

Jace nodded. "We can get attached to our property pretty quick in this business. It's like the hills and valleys are an extension of ourselves."

"That's how I feel." Aidan swallowed the emotion that rose in his chest. Time for a new subject. "Hey, Jace, you got any rodeo stories you can share?"

The former bull rider grinned. "Maybe a few. How much time you got?"

Aidan settled back on his stump and took a sip of his beer, relieved to have moved on to a lighter topic. "I've got all night." He set his beer down and leaned back, looking up at the stars scattered overhead. Years ago, in school, he'd read a Native American legend that said the sky was like a big bolt of cloth. The stars were holes in that cloth, letting in light from a world beyond. He liked to think of Colby up there, playing in all that beautiful, glimmering light. Maybe he was poking holes in the fabric with a stick, so more light could get through to the people down below. Spreading light, just like he had here on earth. Tears welled up in Aidan's eyes, and he was glad he was in the shadows. He let go of the sadness, let go of any decisions he had to make and let Jace's words run over him like water. It was the most relaxed he'd felt in a long, long time.

"YOU'RE KICKING MY butt today." Travis stopped on the sidewalk and put his hands to his knees. "Whatever happened to starting a run at a reasonable pace?"

Jade jogged in place while her brother sucked in oxygen. "I didn't start fast. You've just been going out too often. Drinking way too much beer over at the Redwood Inn."

Travis straightened and started jogging again, and Jade slowed her pace to give him a break. He was her brother after all.

"We can't all live like nuns."

"What?" Jade socked her brother in the arm. "I'm not a nun."

"Really? When's the last time you had a date?"

"Don't try to change the subject," Jade scolded, leaving the sidewalk and cutting across the park. A trail started near downtown Shelter Creek, then ran along the creek for a couple miles or so. It was a nice break from running on pavement. "I know why you're going to the bar every night. It's to see Lena Morris. Are you two dating?"

"No." Travis glared at her. "And it's none of your business. How about you go and get a life of your own instead?"

"I have a life." Jade let Travis onto the trail, jumping over the raised root of a red-wood tree. "A busy life where I make time to work out every day, and I don't sit in a bar drinking every night, trying to get someone to notice me."

"First of all, I'm not there every night. I'm at the fire station most nights. And second, what happened with that rancher who came by the station? The one from the fire. Danny told me all about it."

"Nothing." Jade focused on the trail in front of her. It narrowed as it ran along the side of a steep hill. She'd been staying in the present this past week, trying not to think about Aidan. Or the way she'd wished she could talk with him when she saw him in the town square with Maya last weekend. The way she'd wished she belonged with him. She was a mess. All week he'd been on her mind, in her heart, distracting her from her work. All the more reason she shouldn't

date him. She didn't have time for this level
of distraction.

"Why not? He's a good-looking guy who
can hang in there under stress, right? And
he obviously likes you or he wouldn't have
shown up that night."

"He was there because he wanted to
thank everyone." It wasn't completely true,
of course, but if Travis wanted her to mind
her own business when it came to dating,
than he could do the same.

"Yeah right. Trust me, he wanted to see
you again."

"Whatever. I just want to focus on work
right now. I have so much to do. I want to
take that captain's test as soon as I can."

They pelted down a hill and the trail cut
through a flat valley full of dry grass and
the tall bleached skeletons of Queen Anne's
Lace. The path was wider here, and Travis
sped up so he was running alongside her.
"Why are you in such a hurry?"

"I need to get home and do errands," Jade
told him.

"Not on the run. With your career. Why
do you have to take that test as soon as pos-

sible? I haven't taken it yet and I've been fighting fires longer than you."

Jade shrugged. "Maybe I have more ambition than you."

"Or maybe you have more to prove." Travis glanced over at her. "Come on, Jade. This is all about Dad, isn't it? You figure if you make captain before me, he'll give you some kind of stamp of approval."

"That's not it!" Jade resisted the urge to shove her brother right off the trail. "I just want to get ahead. More responsibility. A better salary. Plus, Dad said he was sorry and that he's going to try to be nicer. This has nothing to do with him."

"Right." Travis's flat tone made it clear he didn't believe her.

She glanced at him over her shoulder. "What are you worried about? That I'll get promoted ahead of you?"

"I'm worried that you don't really have a life." They'd reached the spot where the trail met up with the highway just outside of town. Travis led the way onto the margin of the road so they could head back. "I'm also worried that, despite your big announcement at dinner a couple weeks ago, you're still letting Dad's opinions dictate your choices. You still want to prove yourself to him."

The margin they were running on widened into a turnout. Jade pulled up next to Travis. "Things are different. I've accepted that in Dad's eyes, I'll never be as good as my brothers. Hopefully he won't tell me that so often, but I doubt he's really changed inside. My goal is to let that all go, and live my life the way I want to."

"Really." Travis skewered her with a knowing glance. "So what you want is to work all the time, never have fun and give up the chance to get to know a guy who might just be a really good fit for you?"

"It's not that simple." Jade swiped at the sweat that was trickling down her forehead. Travis was warmed up now and setting a really fast pace. "He lost a child a couple years ago. I don't think he's relationship material. He's still very sad about it."

Travis shoved her on the shoulder, sending her staggering to the side.

"What was that for?" Jade glared at him in sisterly fury. "What are you, ten years old?"

"Are you?" He was laughing at her, totally unrepentant. "How is it that I, a dumb guy, can see what you can't? Of course the guy's sad, if he lost a kid. Who wouldn't be? But maybe he's ready to be more than sad. With you."

The turnout ended and they had a gravel margin to run on again. Jade took the lead. "Let's be done with this conversation."

"Don't be so scared, sis. The bottom line is, do you love him?"

She whirled to face him, jogging backward. "How can I love him? I spent an afternoon and a night with him, fighting a fire. I spent an evening with him eating dinner."

"Turn around before you run right off the road, you goof."

Jade glared at her brother, but turned around and fell into step beside him. They ran in silence for a moment, the word echoing in Jade's ears with every footfall. *Love. Love. Love.* Her heart beat in time to the word, her blood joined in, until her whole body was infused with peace and acceptance, until she confessed, in sullen tones, "Fine. I do love him. But that's crazy. How can I love him?"

When she glanced at Travis there was a

triumphant gleam in his eyes. "I thought so. I don't know how you can fall for someone so quickly. But here's the thing. We haven't exactly been encouraged to have emotions in our family. We were brought up to be tough. Stoic. Goal-oriented. So if you think you love this guy, then you do. We don't have those kinds of emotions often. So don't take them lightly."

"You sound like you know what you're talking about." Jade regarded her brother closely. He'd never revealed anything about his love life, but there had been someone a few years after high school...Laney somebody? Jade had been busy with sports and schoolwork then,. She hadn't really paid attention to what her big brother was up to.

"Call the guy," Travis said. "And stop overthinking everything. You've let Dad take up permanent residence in your head. Kick him out and start living your life."

Ugh, she hated it when her brother was right.

"I'll race you back," Jade called over her shoulder and started sprinting, pushing hard off the pavement, her arms pumping with the rhythm of her gait. She'd never admit it, but she was scared. Terrified, really. She loved Aidan. She was in love with the big, stubborn, sweet rancher who'd been through such hard times. Who had made her laugh and smile even as they fought to survive. The joy of it, and the fear of it, gave wings to Jade's feet, and soon she'd left her brother far behind.

CHAPTER EIGHTEEN

AIDAN SAT ON the edge of Colby's flower bed and rubbed Chip's ears. The cattle dog endured it for a moment, then flopped down on the charred grass and rolled to expose his belly. "Oh it's like that, is it?" Aidan scratched the dog's gray-and-black speckled tummy and looked at what used to be his house. If he closed his eyes, he could remember it. The way the sun used to stream in through the kitchen window in the morning. The way Colby loved to run down the long hallway that connected the kitchen and dining room with the living room.

So much had happened in that house, and now it was ashes. All he had was the photos, his computer, the random artifacts of his life that he'd collected in the few moments he had before the fire.

He looked down at the poppy, flourishing since the fire. It had sent out new stems and those stems had buds. There were four flowers on it, each one a pure, brilliant orange. Aidan traced a petal with his finger. "I miss you, son," he whispered.

The crunch of wheels on gravel had him looking up. An unfamiliar car stopped in front of the wreckage that had been his house. A silver SUV. Did he know anyone with a car like that?

He should go meet them, but he was unwilling to break the tenuous connection he felt with his son, sitting here on Colby's old sandbox, with the boy's favorite flower. A small person got out of the SUV, came around the front and started walking toward him. He'd recognize that purposeful gait anywhere. It was Jade, dressed in jeans, a fitted red T-shirt and hiking boots. He'd never seen her out of uniform. His heart thudded against the walls of his chest as if it was trying to get out and go to her. Rising to his feet, Aidan watched as Chip ran to her, greeting her with a friendly bark and a wildly wagging tail.

"Hey, buddy." She slowed to pet the dog's head. "Seems like you're feeling a lot better."

He should go to her, but somehow his feet

were stuck to the ground, as if the soles of his shoes had melted there.

"Hey, Aidan." She stopped in front of him, jiggling her keys in her hands. "How are you?"

"I'm good." The shock that had kept him still faded away and he smiled. "Better now that you're here." He gestured to the charred wood at the flower bed's edge. "Can I offer you a seat?"

She grinned. "Why, thank you." She sat a ways away from the flower, but gestured to it. "Your survivor here is doing better than ever."

"It really is." Aidan sat down and put his elbows on his thighs. "I'm glad you dropped by. How have you been?"

She shrugged. "Busy. Thinking a lot. How about you?"

He was stuck on that word *thinking* but kept his cool. "I'm okay. Thinking a lot, too, actually." Though it was hard to think with her so near. He wished things were different. That he could reach out and wrap his arms around her, and feel the way she fit, so small but just right, against him.

She drew her knees in and angled herself

to better face him. "Thinking about what?" He was tempted to say the weather or rebuilding or something mundane. But Jade brought out the truth in him. He couldn't hide under her direct gaze. "I guess I've been thinking a lot about the night Colby died."

Her lips pursed in a sympathetic expression. "I'm sorry. I didn't mean to pry. Do you want to talk about it?"

"I think I do, if that's okay." He wanted her to understand why he'd come to the decision that had surprised him so much.

"Okay, I'm here." She wrapped her arms around her knees, as if settling in to listen.

"I keep thinking about how fast Colby's fever spiked that night. He didn't even seem that sick, you know? Just a low fever, and he still wanted to play and be silly with me. Then all of a sudden he got so tired, and I felt his forehead and I knew something had gone really wrong."

He reached for Chip, who'd lain down between them, and ran a hand down the dog's back. "Sheila, my wife at the time, was down in San Francisco that night. She'd been spending more and more time there, doing research to start her own graphic design firm. I found out later that she'd been having an affair with a former colleague of ours. He's the guy she's married to now."

Jade reached for him then and put her small hand on his. "I'm so sorry."

Aidan shrugged. "I'd talked her into living up here. She hated it. I was oblivious to the fact that she was starting to hate me, too. But the result was that I was on my own that night, trying to get to the hospital. Colby was buckled into his car seat in the back and I just drove those miles as fast as I could, like I knew, on some level, that death was on our heels. When he got quiet, in the back, I assumed he'd fallen asleep."

He paused, trying to breathe as the old familiar panic closed in. "Later at the hospital they told me it was the flu. That his immune system had overreacted to it…" He trailed off, overwhelmed, yet again, by the horrible trick of nature that had caused his son's body to fight itself that way.

"Aidan, I've seen this happen. I've been on emergency calls when kids get sick like that. Even if you'd called paramedics to meet you on that road, I'm not sure there's much they could have done. They wouldn't have been able to diagnose what was wrong. They would have hydrated him a little, but what they have to offer in an ambulance..." Jade's voice trailed off, and she watched him carefully as if she were worried he might break.

"I wish I'd called anyway. I've been blaming myself ever since. I should have lived closer to a hospital. I should have pulled over and checked on him. I should have called 911. But sitting out here these past few weeks, on this empty land, I've realized that even if I am to blame, Colby wouldn't want me to spend my life feeling terrible. He was the most joyful kid. He'd want me to be happy, too."

Jade nodded, her hand still light and cool on his arm. "I didn't know him, but I agree. I can't imagine he'd want to see you suffer like you have."

Aidan nodded and looked down at the poppy. "I've decided to let this place go. I don't want to be in a prison of memories and regret anymore. I've loved this land, I always will. But I want to make a new start somewhere else."

Jade stared at him, her eyes wide. "Are you sure?"

"Yeah." He was. The certainty had settled bone-deep. Maybe it was spending time with her at the firehouse. Or the evening he'd spent hanging out with Caleb, Liam and Jace. Or because all he had left here was a barn and a sheep shed. Whatever the reason, he was ready to come down from this ridge and join the world again.

"Where are you going to go?" Jade smiled gently. "I'm sure wherever it is, it has to accommodate a whole lot of sheep."

"You know I love my sheep," Aidan grinned back. "Caleb and Maya keep telling me about this ranch just south of Shelter Creek. But I don't want to crowd you."

Her smile grew wider, but her eyes went shy. "I'd like it if you were closer to me. I came here to tell you—well, to ask you—if you'd still like to go on that date some time."

He gaped at her, unable to contain the enthusiasm in his voice. "Are you sure?"

"I'm more than sure. I feel something with you. And I keep feeling it, even now. Like we're connected." She put her palms to her cheeks, which were turning an adorable shade of pink. "Ugh, I'm no good at this. I always say too much. Or not enough."

"That makes two of us." He reached for her hands and gently pulled them from her face, gratified when she wrapped her fingers around his. "I feel it, too. I want to be around you, Jade. As much as possible."

"Me, too."

They both fell silent. She was looking at their clasped hands, so Aidan looked, too. It was strange how things as fragile as skin and bone and muscle could feel so alive with connection. Just sitting her with her, his whole body seemed to wake up with new energy and hope.

"What do we do now?" Her voice was tentative, and he remembered that her confidence was mostly reserved for work.

"Want to take a walk? I don't have much to offer here beyond ashes and a borrowed trailer, but I still have a nice view."

"And sheep."

He laughed. "And sheep. Want to visit them?"

"I'd like that."

He stood and pulled her up along with him, and kept pulling so she stepped right into his arms. He sighed as she slipped her strong arms around his waist. He wrapped his arms around her shoulders and inhaled the scent of her hair. Funny how he still associated her with the smell of smoke, but now she smelled different. Floral. He took another breath and realized it was lavender. How perfect for her, to use a calming scent like that. She'd settled all his old pain, so he could finally feel like himself again. He kissed the top of her head. Her hair, bound in a ponytail, was silky under his lips. "I could stand like this for a long time," he murmured.

She tipped her head back to look up at him. "Then stand here," she said.

Her warm smile was an invitation he couldn't resist. He brought his mouth to hers, relishing the way she kissed him back, the way all the broken pieces of his soul bonded together with her touch. Her lips were soft and forgiving, and he lingered there, brushing kisses lightly over her mouth, feeling her precious breath, her heat and her light.

Her brown eyes held layers of kindness and compassion, and she blinked with dark, full lashes when their gazes met. "I love you," she said quietly. "I'm sure it's too soon to tell you that but—"

"I love you," Aidan cut her off before she could dilute the beauty of those three words. "I've known it for a while now. So I don't think it's too soon." His smile hurt, it was so big. Relief and hope thrumming through his body, waking up every last part of him that that had died along with his son that night.

Her smile was pure sunlight and clear air and life. "I'm glad." She hugged him tightly. "So glad."

They stood together in silence, except it wasn't silent. A bird called, somewhere farther down the ranch. Another answered. Maya had been right. First the bugs emerged, then the birds returned. Life returned. Aidan closed his eyes as a wave of gratitude almost knocked the wind out of him.

Jade, ever restless, stirred in his arms. "We've got love,' she murmured. "Now what do we do?"

"Let's take that walk." He stepped back and offered his hand, and they wandered down the driveway toward the barn with Chip at their heels.

"It's a beautiful ranch," she said, gazing

out over the hills that rolled out toward the Pacific. The afternoon light cast a golden hue over the charred earth.

"It is," Aidan said. "I'll never forget it."

"We'll always honor him," Jade said quietly. "Wherever we are. I promise."

Aidan squeezed her hand gently, willing back the tears that rose behind his eyes. "I'd like that," he said. "I was so scared to move on from this place. It felt like if I left here, I was abandoning Colby. Failing him one more time. But now I know that I'll carry my son in my heart, wherever I go."

"Shelter Creek is a good place to heal." Jade looked up at him hopefully. "If that's what you want."

"I'll go look at that ranch for sale tomorrow," he assured her. "I could use some healing."

"I think we all could." Jade glanced up at him with a quirk of humor in her smile. "Race you to the barn?"

"You think you can beat me there?" He let go of her hand and took off running, his heavy work boots pounding in the gravel.

"Not fair!" It didn't take her long to race right past him calling, "You forget, I've had to keep up with three brothers my whole life!"

Chip tore after her joyfully, barking and jumping in doggy bliss.

Aidan charged after them both, pelting down the hill like a kid, feeling the hard years lifting off his shoulders and floating away into the clear blue sky. It had been so long since he'd felt like this. Whole. Happy. Alive.

EPILOGUE

One Year Later...

JADE PULLED UP to Aidan's ranch house and grabbed the bag of sandwiches off the passenger seat of her car. As she approached the front door, Chip rose from his favorite sleeping spot on the porch that ran the length of the building and bounded down the steps to greet her. "Hey, buddy." Jade rubbed the dog's head and accepted a kiss on the hand. "Where's that owner of yours?"

The front door opened and Aidan stepped out, arms open to greet her. "How's the newest fire captain in Shelter Creek?"

Jade ran up the steps and threw her arms around his waist. "Can you believe I passed the test?"

"I can absolutely believe it." Aidan held her close and kissed the top of her head. "I've seen you in action, remember?"

He stepped back and gently tipped her chin up to kiss her. By the time he was done, Jade's legs felt a little shaky. "Come on," he said. "I've got something to show you." He led her around the side of the house to the big flagstone patio that served as his backyard. Making the area around his house inflammable was the first thing he'd done when he moved to his new ranch. From here they had a view across the valley, with the whole of Shelter Creek nestled below. It was only a ten-minute drive into town, but up here they were in their own world.

Aidan gestured to a table Jade had never seen before. A fancy wooden table with matching chairs that he'd set in just the right spot to take in the glorious view. The table was set with two place settings, and even a bouquet of flowers.

"This is your new patio furniture?" Jade sat down in one of the comfortable padded chairs. "It's luxurious. I love it."

"It got here just in time to celebrate." He poured her a glass of water from the pitcher on the table. "What did your dad say about you passing the test?"

Jade still hadn't processed her dad's reaction. "He just said congratulations. And that he was very proud of me. That was it. No critiquing my score, or asking me what goal I'll achieve next. Nothing."

"He's trying. He really is." Aidan smiled at her and she saw the pride in his blue eyes. "I'm glad you gave him another chance."

"You're just saying that because he likes you. He's always talking about what a good man you are, and how well you run your ranch, as if he knows anything about that. I could swear, lately, that he has a man crush on you."

"He just knows how much I love his daughter."

Jade stared at him in surprise. "Did you tell him that?"

"Not in so many words. But I asked his permission to marry you."

"Permission?" Jade stood up, she was so indignant. "You don't have to ask him…" Then Aidan's words sank in. "You want to marry me?"

He came around the table to take her hand. He led her a few steps closer to his beautiful view and went down on one knee.

Jade's heart leaped in her chest and she

put her palms to her cheeks, barely able to comprehend what was happening.

Aidan looked up at her with his icy-blue eyes and a nervous smile on his face that reminded her that underneath his tough exterior was the most warm and sensitive person. "Jade Carson, I love you more than I can even explain. You rescued me, you rescued my heart, you turned my entire life around. You're the only person on this planet who can make me laugh in the middle of a wildfire. You're the person I want to go through life with. Even the hardest parts of life. Will you marry me?"

She'd never thought of herself as the marrying kind, but the past year of loving Aidan had shown her a different side of herself. A side that wanted to give him everything, and to make sure he knew happiness every day. "Of course I'll marry you." She knelt, too, and threw her arms around him, hugging him tight. "I love you. And I'm so glad to have this life with you." Those were words they said often, to remind each other of all that they had, and the night it all could have ended in a wildfire.

Aidan folded her into his arms and held

her close. "I'm so grateful for our life, too."
He kissed her hair and Jade relished the gentle gesture. "Thanks again for the rescue."

"Right back at cha," she whispered.

* * * * *

*Be sure to look for the next book in
Claire McEwen's
Heroes of Shelter Creek series,
available soon!*

THE WESTERN HEARTS COLLECTION!

19 FREE BOOKS in all!

COWBOYS. RANCHERS. RODEO REBELS.
Here are their charming love stories in one prized Collection:
51 emotional and heart-filled romances that capture the majesty
and rugged beauty of the American West!

YES! Please send me **The Western Hearts Collection** in Larger Print. This collection begins with 3 FREE books and 2 FREE gifts in the first shipment. Along with my 3 free books, I'll also get the next 4 books from The Western Hearts Collection, in LARGER PRINT, which I may either return and owe nothing, or keep for the low price of $5.45 U.S./$6.23 CDN each plus $2.99 U.S./$7.49 CDN for shipping and handling per shipment*. If I decide to continue, about once a month for 8 months I will get 6 or 7 more books but will only need to pay for 4. That means 2 or 3 books in every shipment will be FREE! If I decide to keep the entire collection, I'll have paid for only 32 books because 19 books are FREE! I understand that accepting the 3 free books and gifts places me under no obligation to buy anything. I can always return a shipment and cancel at any time. My free books and gifts are mine to keep no matter what I decide.

☐ 270 HCN 5354   ☐ 470 HCN 5354

Name (please print)

Address   Apt. #

City   State/Province   Zip/Postal Code

Mail to the **Reader Service:**
IN U.S.A.: P.O. Box 1341, Buffalo, N.Y. 14240-8531
IN CANADA: P.O. Box 603, Fort Erie, Ontario L2A 5X3

Visit
ReaderService.com
Today!

**As a valued member of the
Harlequin Reader Service,
you'll find these benefits and more at
ReaderService.com:**

- Try 2 free books from any series
- Access risk-free special offers
- View your account history & manage payments
- Browse the latest Bonus Bucks catalog

Don't miss out!

If you want to stay up-to-date on the latest at the Harlequin Reader Service and enjoy more content, make sure you've signed up for our monthly News & Notes email newsletter. Sign up online at ReaderService.com or by calling Customer Service at 1-800-873-8635.